W9-BWO-385

PRAISE FOR KYLIE SCOTT

"Pure rocker perfection in every single way. . . . *Play* is a splendid marriage of romance and comedy, a possibly even better book than its stellar prequel, and I would recommend it to anyone who likes their love stories with a side of giggles." —*Natasha is a Book Junkie*

"Kylie Scott is quickly becoming one of my favorite authors at combining funny with sexy, and I can't wait to read more from her. *Play* is a definite must-read book!" —*The Smut Book Club*

"*Lick* is a breath of fresh air with a unique story line; think *Hangover* meets contemporary romance." —*The Rock Stars of Romance*

"*Mal* is taking us all by storm. . . . Go buy this book. Seriously. You won't regret it." —*Fiction Vixen Book Reviews*

"Engaging, quite humorous, and at times a heartbreaking picture of first love . . . A swoon-worthy romance." —*Smexy Books*

"*Play* does not disappoint! It's sexy, naughty, and hilarious with a side note of serious that makes it all so real. I'm an affirmed Stage Dive groupie and I'm ready to follow those men on tour wherever they go! Rock on!!" —*Up All Night Book Blog*

"I'm now officially addicted to Stage Dive. I highly recommend it to readers out there who enjoy rock-star romance books and the New Adult/Contemporary Romance genre." —*Book Lovin' Mamas*

"With each book in this series, I become more attached to the characters and more enamored with author Kylie Scott." —*Guilty Pleasure Book Reviews*

"The stuff my rock-star dreams are made of. A thrill ride. I felt every stomach dip in the process. And I want to turn right around and ride it again. [For] every girl who's ever had a rock-star crush, this would be the ultimate fantasy."   —*Maryse's Book Blog*

"This book rocked my world!! *Lick* is an addictive blend of heartwarming passion and lighthearted fun. It's a story you can lose yourself in. The perfect rock-star romance!" —*Aestas Book Blog*

"An engrossing, sexy, and emotional read."   —*Dear Author*

"Scrumptious and delicious. Firmly in my top ten best books this year!"   —*The Book Pushers*

"Fun with great characters, a rocker story line, good angst, and plenty of sexy times. I would strongly recommend this book to anyone looking for something sexy and heartwarming."
—*Fiction Vixen*

"A nice start to a rock-and-roll series. Very much looking forward to the next one."   —*Smexy Books*

ALSO BY KYLIE SCOTT

Lick
Play
Lead
Deep
Dirty
Twist

3 1526 05136045 8

WITHDRAWN

Chaser

Kylie Scott

ST. MARTIN'S GRIFFIN ☙ NEW YORK

This is a work of fiction. All of the characters, organizations, and events portrayed in this novel are either products of the author's imagination or are used fictitiously.

CHASER. Copyright © 2018 by Kylie Scott. All rights reserved. Printed in the United States of America. For information, address St. Martin's Press, 175 Fifth Avenue, New York, N.Y. 10010.

www.stmartins.com

Designed by Steven Seighman

The Library of Congress Cataloging-in-Publication Data is available upon request.

ISBN 978-1-250-08323-4 (trade paperback)
ISBN 978-1-250-08329-6 (ebook)

Our books may be purchased in bulk for promotional, educational, or business use. Please contact your local bookseller or the Macmillan Corporate and Premium Sales Department at 1-800-221-7945, extension 5442, or by email at MacmillanSpecialMarkets@macmillan.com.

First Edition: April 2018

10 9 8 7 6 5 4 3 2 1

*To my readers, thank you for sticking with me and
I hope you enjoy it.*

ACKNOWLEDGMENTS

With thanks to my agent, Amy Tannenbaum, Eileen Rothschild, and everyone at St. Martin's Press, Pan Macmillan Australia, and Pan Macmillan UK.

Thank you to Danielle and KP at Ink Slinger PR. Special thanks to all the book bloggers and reviewers out there who work so hard to share their love of books with the world.

To the Groupies, you rock! Thanks for making every day that little bit better.

And to my readers, thank you so much for picking up my books. I hope they make you smile.

Chaser

CHAPTER ONE

"Face it, Eric. You're a fuckboy."

I turned away from the shapely ass I'd been checking out, and frowned. "Jesus, Nell. That's a bit harsh, don't you think?"

"No, not really," she said, smoothing a loving hand over her small baby belly.

I fixed my gaze on her face, ignoring everything and anything to do with her midsection. I did *not* want to know anything about her pregnancy. Not that I wasn't happy for her and her husband. We'd all gone to school together and been friends a long time, after all. But for lots of really good reasons, me and babies didn't mix. Every time I saw Nell's bump, it worried me. I said a little prayer to please let her and the baby be okay this time, and then did my best not to think about it again. Not to remember the baby we'd lost last year. There were things much more happiness-inducing going on in the bar area than falling into grief and regrets again.

". . . I don't even need to look to see. That's how predictable you are. I can tell when a hot woman walks into the bar just by seeing your eyes light up like a cat that's spied a mouse." She paused, then ranted, "Eric? Eric!"

"Yeah?"

She cocked her head. "You're not even listening to me, are you?"

"Of course I am." Mostly. I was sort of torn between outrage at Nell's insinuation, and an itching desire to follow the perfect behind. Didn't make Nell right, however.

"This is what I'm talking about," she said. "Your attention span makes a gnat look gargantuan."

"Calm down. I said I was listening to you."

"So what did I just say?"

"Well, basically you said that I'm a douche," I said. "Which hurts."

Nell crossed her arms. "Oh, really? Now you're pretending you have feelings?"

"Of course I have feelings."

"Sure you do. And why do I think you're a douche?"

"Ah . . ." I stared off over her shoulder, catching sight once more of the back of the particularly lovely looking female being shown to her table by Lydia. Lydia was the third owner of the Dive Bar, along with me and Nell. But back to the far more important babe: long brown hair hung down to her shoulder blades and a shapely ass swayed with every step. Goddamn. Summertime with all the skin on display was pretty great. But then again, winter with its tight jeans and sweaters, like my new about-to-be-best-female-friend-with-benefits had on, was also pretty fucking awesome. Too bad I could only spy on her from behind. I wonder what her rack was like. Not that I was fussy. Full, generous, slim, pert, soft, firm; it was all good. It's like I always say: life is like taking off a girl's bra. You never know exactly what you're gonna get, but however it turns out, it's basically awesome.

"Eric?" Nell picked up a knife, immediately dragging me out of my daydreams. She started tapping it against a cutting board all impatient like. "I'm waiting."

"Women and stuff," I said, the obvious answer. Generally, it was always one or the other. "You think I'm a douche because of women and stuff."

Her eyes narrowed. " 'And stuff'?"

"Am I wrong?"

"No."

Phew. "Okay then."

"Seriously, Eric. One day you're going to wish there was more to your life than the next piece of ass." She stopped cutting to gesticulate with her hands, one of which was still alarmingly wielding the knife. "I mean, the closest you've ever come to a long-term relationship was with Alex, and that was only because Joe stole your online identity to woo her!"

"Ha. Ha." I bet Nell had planned that line a week ago, and was just waiting for a chance to wheel it out. "Can I get back to work now?"

"Whatever." She slapped the knife down. "You're a lost cause. I give up on you."

Thank God for that.

Baby hormones made Nell even scarier than usual. Just the other day, she'd ripped me a new one for breathing too loudly. Now she was calling me a manwhore. Talk about unfair. Sure, I'd slept with a number of women. I liked women—a lot. But there was more to me than just my sex life. It kind of did hurt that one of my oldest friends, who I'd been through some serious shit with, didn't share that opinion.

Anyway, forget Nell and her bad mood. There were more pleasant duties to attend to on the restaurant floor. Being that it was mid-afternoon, things were pretty quiet. No one was waiting for me to fix them a drink at the bar. Taka, the waiter on duty, stood behind the counter, busy folding napkins and cleaning cutlery and shit. I was good to go.

"I've got this, Lydia. You should take a break," I said. "Get off your feet for a while."

She gave me a knowing smile before smacking me hard in the chest with the menu. All that stuff about women being soft and sweet was such bullshit.

"Sure, Eric," she said. "Just don't scare her away."

"When have I ever scared a customer away? Hell, my personal magnetism is the only thing that keeps this bar afloat."

No answer. Instead, after a long look, Lydia turn on her heel and headed out back. Probably off to discuss my inadequacies with Nell. Where to bury my body in the woods and things like that. This was the problem with co-owning a business with two women. Being the only one with a dick, I got blamed for everything. A stock delivery arrived late—my fault. The register acted up—also my fault. Someone broke a nail or some shit—me again. All this attitude thrown my way, despite me faithfully keeping my word and not sleeping with any more of our waitresses. Yes, employees were off-limits. Fine with me. Things tended to get awkward when it was time to move on. Didn't matter that I was always up front with things being about a good time, not a long time.

So no messing around with the staff. Female customers, however, were another matter entirely.

"Hey there," I said to the curvy brunette.

The woman gave a slight smile, not even meeting my eyes. Her features were strong yet stunning, a long straight nose and a heavy jaw. Not pretty, exactly. But striking, despite the shadows under her hazel eyes. Probably midtwenties.

"I'm Eric." I handed over the menu with an easy smile. "Welcome to the Dive Bar."

"Hi," she murmured, immediately checking out the menu while I continued to check out her. No wedding ring. Lots of curves. A blue sweater stretched beautifully across her tits. Definitely more than a handful there, thank you God.

"Let me guess." I braced my hands on the back of the empty seat opposite her.

"Let you guess what?" she asked without looking up, disinterested.

"Your drink."

"What makes you think I'm drinking?"

"Why else would you be in a bar?" I countered, waiting for her, pleading with her to look at me. It was hard to dazzle her with my winning smile if she wouldn't even face me.

"Well, you also serve food and I happen to be hungry."

"Good point. So you'd just like some ice water or something?"

Finally, her gaze shifted from the menu to me and stuck. Blue eyes took me in, looking over every inch with interest. The faintest trace of color lit her cheeks. Excellent.

"All right, go for it," she eventually invited. "What's my drink?"

"Well . . . you've got an understated kind of style," I said, flexing the muscles in my arms just enough to catch her attention. It was pretty much the main reason I rolled back my button-down shirt's sleeves. A subtle, yet important part of the show. "So first off, I'm thinking you're into the classics. A martini or an old-fashioned, maybe?"

"No."

"No?" I let my gaze wander over her, trying to take in every detail and not get stuck staring at her breasts. It wasn't easy, but fortunately I'm big into self-discipline. Eyes up. "Maybe you're more of a straight down the line kind of girl. How about a beer?"

A hint of a smile crossed her lips. "I don't mind beer. But that's not what I was going to order."

"Mm, a challenge. I like a challenge."

"God. I'm really not a challenge." She exhaled. "I take it this is your trick, guessing what people drink?"

"Usually I'm pretty good at it."

"Sorry to ruin your winning streak."

"Nah, that's okay." I grinned. "Mom always said I needed to be put in my place pretty often or my ego got out of hand."

Something strange passed across her face. "Sounds like a good mom."

"She's a great mom. But let's get back to talking about you," I said, following my script. Women usually ate this smooth shit right up. Yet something in her gaze made me hesitate. "If you'd rather I just took your ord—"

"Absolutely not." She gave me a teasing smile. "You promised me a magic trick, now you need to deliver. What did you say your name was?"

"Eric Collins."

"Eric. Hi."

"I'm the owner here." It was only partly a lie and it made me look good. Successful.

"You are?" Her brows arched in surprise and she gave the place a looking over, taking it all in. I waited patiently. We'd worked damn hard to turn the dump into the cool bar and restaurant it was today. Raw brick walls and shining dark wood. Mirrors lined the wall behind the bar along with neat rows of bottles. Big windows to let in the light and some metal industrial touches.

"It's a great place," she said. "You must be very proud."

"That I am." I offered my hand and she slipped her slender, warm fingers into my palm. "Nice to meet you . . ."

"Jean Antal."

"Jean. What a lovely name."

Still holding onto my hand, she shrugged. "My mom was a David Bowie fan."

"Can't beat Bowie."

"No, you can't."

"Guess that makes you the Jean Genie."

"Ha. Yeah." She gave another of those ball-tightening chuckles. I could happily listen to her do that all day long. Except suddenly the happy fell from her face. "It was her favorite song."

Shit. Damn. I softened my tone. "Your mom passed?"

She blinked. "No."

"No?"

"Sorry." She shook her head, looking flustered. "Both of my parents are alive and well. I just meant it was her favorite song when I was young. That's all. Nothing else."

"Well, that's good."

"Hmm." Her gaze fell to our still embracing hands and at roughly the speed of light the slight pressure of her grip and the warmth of her skin were gone. "Crap. I didn't mean to paw at you."

"Pawing is altogether encouraged."

Startled laughter burst out of her. "Look at you with the long hair and that face and everything. You're a hell of a flirt, Eric."

"Thank you very much. You're rather easy on the eyes yourself." I smirked. "And I still owe you a trick."

"Right, my drink," she said, shoulders slouching as she relaxed. "Guess away."

"Okay." I squinted at her, searching for inspiration and trying not to get too distracted wondering what she'd look like naked and lying on my bed. It wasn't easy. But like I said, self-discipline. "I'm going to say a black widow."

She blinked. "A what widow?"

"A black widow. Blackberries, silver tequila, lime juice, and sugar syrup," I said. "I think that's what you should order."

"And why should I order that?"

"It's sweet but with a kick." I gave her my best grin. "I think you'd like it."

"So this has nothing to do with you suspecting me of murdering any husbands?"

"No, of course not." I laughed. Then stopped. "Oh, man. You're not married, are you? I mean, you are single, right?"

Her mouth opened, but nothing came out.

Shit, shit, shit.

"Relax, Eric." Jean tucked in her chin, looking over the menu again with a faint frown. "I'm single."

"Good." I exhaled, smiling once more. "That's good. Otherwise, asking you to dinner tonight would have been all sorts of awkward."

She said nothing.

No matter. We could get back to that later. "I've never seen you in here before. Are you a local or just passing through?"

"Actually, I just moved to the area," she said. "Today, in fact."

"That's great!"

As much fun as a one-nighter could be, I'd been thinking lately about perhaps getting more serious with someone. Maybe. Just to try it out, at least. It was entirely my idea; it had nothing to do with Nell's daily lecturing.

The truth was that I was getting close to thirty. And a lot of heavy shit had gone down last year. It had been hardest on Nell most of all. But she'd bounced back, happily pregnant and with the right guy this time, Pat. It didn't really make sense that I would be still struggling with it all.

Probably what was getting to me was just the fact that Joe was settling down with his new girlfriend. Joe, my brother. My *younger* brother. Who had never even been popular with the ladies, for fuck's sake. Ever since Alex had come to town, however, he'd been walking around smiling like he'd won the jackpot.

Anyway, whatever the cause, I'd been feeling a little . . . I don't know. Not lost. Just the thought had been hanging around in the back of my head. It didn't seem as bad an idea as it would have a few years ago. Actually, this could be perfect. I drank in Jean's stunning face and gorgeous curves. We could hang out together, catch some movies, do couple shit. Hold hands even. It would definitely show Nell I wasn't some shallow fuckbot.

But I was getting ahead of myself.

"Where are you from originally?" I asked, getting back into the conversation.

"Jacksonville, Florida."

"Yeah? You ever go to the Night Garden or Emory's?"

Delight lit her face. "I love Emory's, best club in town."

"Passed through there a few years back on my way to Miami," I said. With that energy and edge, I figured she might be from the party crowd. "Good atmosphere and the DJ was something else."

"My friends and I used to go dancing there every Saturday night." She stared off at nothing. "Those were the days."

"Hey, just 'cause you moved to Coeur d'Alene doesn't mean your life's over. This town is awesome, plus now you can come hang out here. We have live music most weekends," I said. "You'd be very welcome."

No response for a moment. Then she quietly said, "I'll be around."

Taka seated some customers at a table nearby, pausing to give me an amused look. Typical. They'd all have to wipe those smirks off their faces once they realized I was boyfriend material. Taka, Nell, Lydia, the whole lot of them.

"So, Jean." I braced my hands on the back of the chair opposite her, leaning in a little, trying to get her attention. It worked, her gaze snapping back to me. "Can I make you a black widow? On the house, of course."

"Is that how you make money?"

"No. That's how I make friends."

She snorted. "I'd love a black widow. But can you make it virgin, please?"

"You want it without the tequila?" I asked, surprised. Being anti-alcohol seemed like the kind of thing she might have mentioned earlier, given the topic of our conversation.

She didn't get a chance to respond.

"Jean." Andre wandered up to the table. Giving me a slap on the back before giving her a friendly smile. Too friendly. And how did he know her name? Warning bells went off inside my head. Because despite Andre being over a decade older than me, women loved the guy. "How are you doing? I'm free now if you're ready?"

"Ready for what?" I asked, irritation edging into my voice.

"I'm moving into one of the apartments upstairs," Jean said, fingers clasped together on the table.

"You are?" My brows rose.

"That's right," said Andre. "You two are going to be neighbors."

"Huh." I tried to keep my face blank as my brain scrambled to catch up. *Hell no* being my first and foremost reaction. Next door was a little too close. I'd only just tuned in to the idea of having a girlfriend, let alone the thought of having her right there next to me.

"Now there'll be me, you, Jean, Joe, and Lydia all up there." Andre rubbed his hands together, all happy like. Fair enough. He owned the building and turning the upstairs into apartments last year hadn't been cheap. "That's all of the apartments rented."

"Great," I mumbled.

Jean just nodded, going back to looking over the menu.

"You said you were hungry. What can I get for you?" I asked, shaking off my suddenly sour mood.

"Everything here is good," said Andre. "Especially the pizza.

I haven't had lunch yet, mind if I join you? I can show you around and help you unload your stuff after, if you like."

"That'd be good," said Jean. "I definitely need food."

"I can help too." I stepped back, unhappily making room for the man. "Probably Boyd or Taka as well. We're not that busy."

"Thanks," she said.

Dammit. Andre might have been one of my oldest friends, but this was not part of the plan. Cock-blocker. First they'd be all chatty and shit, sharing a meal. Then bam . . . they'd be having sex. This was not okay. I wanted to have sex with Jean. And be the one to listen to her talk and get to eat with her, etcetera (insert boring boyfriend stuff here).

"I'll have the potato, caramelized onion, and bacon pizza, please," she said.

"Vegetarian for me," added Andre. "And a beer, thanks."

"Sure thing." I slightly narrowed my eyes at the bastard. Not that he noticed.

"Black widow? Virgin?" Her eyes sparkled, the lines of her face softening again.

It should be noted that the softening only happened when she looked at me. Maybe I wouldn't drop Andre's beer on him after all. We'd see.

"You got it," I said, writing up the order. "Be right back with the drinks."

I handed the food order over to the kitchen and headed for my bar. In an hour or two, Vaughan would be in for the busier night session. For now, however, the space was mine, all mine.

When we first came up with the idea to open the Dive Bar, everyone involved knew exactly what they wanted. Nell would rule the kitchen, Pat would help put up the money but otherwise stick to his tattoo parlor next door, and I'd be in charge of the bar. Of course, running the place had been a hell of a lot more work than any of us anticipated. Lydia bought out Pat and took over running the restaurant floor. A great move. But Nell still loved the kitchen, and I stuck with the bar.

It was my thing. What I was good at and where I felt I belonged.

The original long wooden surface still had the names and crap carved into it from back when the place really had been a dive bar. I grabbed a cloth and gave it a quick polish. Forget Jean and her pretty rack for a minute, time to get the bar all cleaned up before the night began. Neat lines of shining bottles, gleaming taps, and racks of glasses. Probably didn't say much about me, now that this bar felt like home. But I loved it anyway.

Over at their table, Andre and Jean maintained a steady stream of conversation. I kept a close eye on them. On a scale of one to ten, I'd give the smile on her face a six. Seven at most. It was polite, friendly. Nowhere near as warm and inviting as the ones she'd given me. Tens all the way. Thank fuck for that.

With ease, I threw Jean's cocktail together. Muddling the black-berries and squeezing the lime. Measuring the sugar syrup. It kind of killed me not to add the tequila. It was like asking Vincent van Gogh to hold off on the color blue the next time he painted the stars. To tell John Bonham to go easy on the skins next time he played "Moby Dick." Though yeah they were dead. But you know what I mean . . . just wrong. I gritted my teeth and added some soda water and an extra splash of lime to try and balance the tequila's absence.

As I poured Andre's beer, I let my mind wander back to Jean. Maybe we would date. Seriously. She was hot, nice, no obvious signs of crazy. Except maybe that crack about murdering her ex-husbands. Most importantly, I was pretty damn sure the woman was into me. Come to think of it, having her living close by could be a good thing. I worked weird hours sometimes. It'd definitely save me from having to do any extra driving. I wondered what Mom would think of Jean. I'd never taken a girl home to meet Mom, but maybe with her I would. In your face, Nell.

Drinks ready, I stepped out from behind the bar. Only weirdly enough, Nell was suddenly rushing out of the kitchen.

"Jean, is that you?" she called. "My god! Why didn't you tell me you'd arrived?"

I froze. How the hell did they know each other? This was not good.

"You looked busy, I figured I'd wait." Jean glowed, happy as anything. Her smile dial had just hit eleven.

Nell waited in front of the table as my-still-maybe-but-perhaps-now-possibly-not future girlfriend got to her feet. Next came lots of hugging and happy feminine squealing noises. Damn. Wonder if Nell told her anything about me? Maybe this situation could still be salvaged.

"I'm so glad you moved to town," said Nell. "This is going to be great."

"I hope so." Jean sighed.

"It will be. You'll see. A whole fresh new start."

Then the two women separated, giving me a perfect profile of Nell's baby bump. But way worse was Jean's matching one. The woman was pregnant. Very much so. The martini glass slipped from my numb fingers, smashing when it hit the hard floor.

"Holy shit," I mumbled to no one.

CHAPTER TWO

I'd been tricked. Betrayed.

After Andre and Jean ate their lunch, we headed outside to deal with her stuff. The cold wind suited my mood to perfection. Talk about disappointed.

"Don't lift that, it looks heavy," I snapped.

Jean blinked. "It's a pillow."

"The world's largest pillow ever. You can't be too careful." My gaze roamed over her swollen middle. "You're . . ."

"Pregnant?" she asked with a voice dripping poison and sugar. "Are you having trouble with the concept?"

"Absolutely not. I was just going to say huge, that's all."

She blew out an exasperated breath. "Thanks, Eric. That makes me feel so much better."

"I just . . ."

"Don't bother." The woman turned back to her sensible, medium-sized SUV and got busy riffling through the contents. I was surprised she'd been able to squeeze into the driver's seat. Boxes and stuff took up almost every inch inside the vehicle. Each and every box seemed to have been neatly labeled with the contents. The woman took her organization seriously.

She looked over her shoulder. "You know, I can't help noticing that Eric-the-smooth-moving-flirt has been suddenly replaced by Eric-the-awkward-jerk."

"Well, you said you were single." I folded my arms defensively across my chest.

"I am."

And then there was an awkward silence.

"Yeah, but . . . I mean, in your condition . . ." I fumbled to a halt.

She turned, face all scrunched up. Like I was the one with the problem.

"Just hop out of the way so I can grab some boxes," I said, voice gruff.

Still nothing from her.

"It's a second-story walk-up and you have a lot of stuff to get up there. You should be taking it easy." Hands on hips, I tapped my black leather boot against the sidewalk, waiting her out. "Jean, I'm not trying to insult you. It's the truth."

She swore quietly, going back to fussing with the contents in the vehicle. I don't think any woman has ever given me the silent treatment quite this quickly. Usually I'm good for at least a couple of hours after seeing them naked.

Man, I still couldn't believe this was happening.

God hated me or something. Pregnant women and me were enema. Anathema. Whatever. Now that I'd seen her out in the autumn light, however, she looked younger than I'd first guessed. Despite her tired eyes, her skin was smooth, soft looking. She was likely closer to her early twenties than mid.

"How old are you?" I asked.

"Why do you care?"

I shrugged one shoulder. "Just curious."

"How old are *you*?"

"Nearly thirty."

She sniffed. "I'm twenty-two."

Young, like I'd thought. She was probably too immature for me, anyway. "Come on, Jean. Let me get some of the boxes."

Boyd ambled out of the Dive Bar, turning his head this way and that, looking up and down the street. I raised my hand and he started over in our direction. The big cook would make short work out of moving all this stuff. Behind us, Andre and Nell came out of the tenants' entrance to the Bird Building. The place was a big brick building about a hundred years old. Just past the door was an entryway with stairs leading up to the second floor, followed by two empty shops, their windows covered in flyers about local events. Concerts and parades and shit. They'd been vacant for a while, unfortunately. Andre's Guitar Den came next, then Pat's tattoo parlor Inkaho, and the Dive Bar on the corner.

"Everything's good to go. Alex and I gave it a cleaning last week just to be sure," said Nell, smacking a kiss on Jean's cheek. "You'll meet Alex later. She's probably busy working or something now. She's sort of a shut-in."

"You two didn't have to do that," said Jean. "Thank you."

"Anytime."

Andre leaned against the SUV. "Your furniture got delivered yesterday too, so it's all good to go."

"Excellent," said Jean. "I can't wait to sleep in a decent bed again. Road trips when you're seven months' pregnant kind of suck."

"I bet."

"Who's minding the kitchen?" I asked.

"Lydia will text Boyd if they need something," said Nell. "We're only going to be a few feet away from the place."

I frowned.

"I own the kitchen, Eric. Not you," she said. "You're in charge of the bar, that's all."

One of Jean's eyebrows inched up slightly.

So I might have implied that I was the sole owner. Shit happened. I crossed my arms. "Fine. No need to bite my head off."

"My best online friend just moved to town. We've been texting and skyping for months. She's been an absolute rock for me through all the nerves of being pregnant again," said Nell. "Stop messing with my happy."

And then there was an awkward silence. Great. If only there was some way to get out of helping without looking like a raging asshole. The possibility of anything happening between me and Jean had been buried six feet deep, never to be spoken of again.

After rubbing his hands together enthusiastically, Andre took a step forward. "Let's get you moved in."

"Right." Jean stepped back without further argument. "Okay."

Boyd managed a shy smile. Then he grabbed about half the contents of the vehicle in one swoop and headed inside. With her pillow, a green retro-style handbag, and one small box, Jean followed. I'd wanted to take the box, which looked heavy, but couldn't think of a way to say so without inviting further wrath. Pregnant women were fragile. Nell knew that more than anyone. She should have been backing me up on this.

Andre and I loaded up next while Nell watched, making useful suggestions. Not. Her husband, Pat, must have been busy doing a tattoo, or no doubt he'd have been corralled into helping too.

The apartment Jean rented was the largest, situated directly above the Dive Bar. My brother, Joe, had been the builder in charge of the project, turning all of these old office spaces into apartments. The others were studio style. But this one had a main bedroom on the right by the door, and a separate office-type space to the left, along with the bathroom. Guess the office space would be perfect for a nursery. Down the end of the short hallway was the open kitchen/dining/living area. Joe had done a terrific job; the place looked like it belonged in a magazine.

And there stood Jean in the middle of it all, crying her god-damn eyes out, sobbing like her heart had been broken. Without thinking, I just snapped.

"What'd you do?" I yelled at a wide-eyed Boyd.

The big man cringed, gaze darting from Jean to me and back again.

"Did you say something?" Given Boyd was an elective mute, it was highly unlikely. But you never knew.

"Eric, it's all right," said Jean, wiping her face with the palms of her hands. "He didn't do anything. I just . . ."

I set my boxes on the ground, face tight. "You just what?"

"This place," she said.

"Hey now," I said, my voice becoming a little sterner. "It might not be exactly what you had in mind, but my brother Joe built this place and I think he did a terrific—"

"It's just perfect." She looked around the room with a quivering smile. "I love it."

"Oh-kay."

Obviously sensing that the attention was off of him, Boyd made his escape. Fair enough.

"Don't you think it's amazing?" she asked.

"Ah, yeah. Sure." My brother did good work and it was a damn nice apartment. But it wasn't the Sistine Chapel or anything. "Amazing."

"Yes," she gushed, spreading her arms wide open as if she could embrace the apartment. "It already feels like home."

"That's good . . . I guess."

"It's great," amended Nell, who entered behind me just in time to offer a constructive correction. She wrapped her arm around

Jean's shoulders and gave her a squeeze, while shooting me some sort of weird look. What it meant, I had no fucking clue. What, was I supposed to be a mind reader?

Andre set his load of crap down next to mine. Then he saw Jean's red eyes and his forehead wrinkled. "Something wrong?"

"No, nothing," I said. "She loves the place."

He nodded as if in understanding. Show-off.

"How embarrassing," said Jean. She fished a Kleenex out of her jeans pocket and blew her nose. Cheeks pink, she studied the hardwood floor, not meeting any of our eyes.

"Baby hormones," said Nell. "Best fun ever."

"I cried yesterday because a grocery store was out of chocolate milk."

Nell cocked her head. "That, however, might be taking it a little too far."

"Jean's allowed to feel whatever the hell she wants to feel," I said, a little pissed. Nell should be more careful. The last thing we needed was for Jean to start crying again. I stood tall, body rigid. "And chocolate milk is pretty great. You know, if you're into that sort of thing."

Jean just kind of gave me a blank look. But at least she wasn't crying. Absolute silence followed. Nobody said anything, though Nell was gazing at me all weird again.

Eventually, Andre coughed into his fist.

"I was joking, Eric," said Nell slowly.

"Oh." I swallowed. "How was I supposed to know that?"

Ever so slowly, the edges of Jean's lips crept upward. It was kind of sly, that smile. Secretive. I liked it. Except then she placed her hands on her scarily large belly, rubbing in small circles.

Still pregnant. Right.

What the hell was I doing here? Apart from making an ass of myself. It was all Jean's fault. Something about her messed with my head. I was all strung out, my throat tight and raw. I needed fresh air, pronto. "Anyway, can't stand around yapping all day. These boxes okay here?"

"Yes, thank you," said Jean. "I'll get everything sorted how I like it later."

Good enough. I made for the door, Andre close behind me. My feet moved faster and faster, needing to get away from that woman and her whole knocked-up situation. Coeur d'Alene had plenty of female residents. Not all of them could have heard bad stuff about me. If, on the off chance that I couldn't find a girlfriend in town, well, there was always Spokane.

I quickened my pace, seized by a new sense of direction. I had a plan. One that did not include Jean Antal. In the future, I'd just stay the hell away from the woman. Problem solved.

"Smooth," said Andre as we were jogging down the stairs.

"What?"

Smirking, he just shook his head.

"Fuck off," I grumbled.

The idiot roared with laughter.

Nell came charging down the steps, red ponytail swinging and fury burning bright in her eyes. "What the hell do you think you're doing?"

"Helping to move Jean in."

"I saw the way you were looking at her." Her finger jabbed me in the chest.

Andre turned and kept walking. Coward.

"What are you talking about?"

Nell put her hands on her hips. "That woman has had enough crap in her life. This is a fresh start for her and you are not going to ruin it."

I had nothing.

"Only you would hit up a heavily pregnant woman for a fling," she said, voice heavy with disgust. "Like she doesn't have enough to deal with already."

"I've got no interest in the woman," I lied.

"You better not." Her shoulders lowered a little. "Stay away from her, Eric. Or else."

CHAPTER THREE

"Why the pout?"

I put down the glass I'd been polishing and not very success-fully smothered a yawn because it'd been one hell of a busy night. I was beat. "Huh?"

"You've been cleaning that same glass for ten minutes and pouting the entire time," said Alex, watching me over the top of her laptop. "I want to know why."

"Men don't pout."

She blinked. "Sure they do."

I frowned, turning to my brother, who'd just finished serving someone at the other end of the bar. We didn't look much alike, Joe and me. I was more *GQ,* he was more lumberjack. I might have been lean, but he just looked plain mean with the beard and bulg-ing muscles. Happily, he was more of a teddy bear than an actual grizzly.

"Set your woman straight," I said. "She just accused me of pouting."

Joe strolled closer. "Men don't pout. It just isn't done."

"Oh really?" The pretty little brunette narrowed her eyes. She wasn't my type, but she and my brother were happy together. De-spite a rocky start, which I maybe unfortunately had something to do with. Long story, but completely not my fault. Alex cleared her throat, sitting up straight on the stool. "And yet, your brother's been pouting since I got here an hour ago. Please explain."

"You're wrong." Joe shrugged.

"How so?"

My brother crossed his big arms over his chest and gave a mighty sigh. "It's like this, Little Miss. Men don't pout . . . we brood."

"That's right," I said.

"To even suggest that we would pout is an affront to our masculinity."

"Yeah." I nodded. "What he said."

"Everyone knows brooding is very manly. Lots of testosterone involved."

"Especially when I do it," I added. "The word you were looking for was probably 'smoldering.'"

Arcade Fire played over the sound system while Rosie and Taka finished clearing the tables. Lydia was busy at the front desk; Boyd and the kitchen kid tidied up out back. Nell had gone home around nine once things started to slow. A party of eight and some couples were the only customers left this close to midnight.

"You're both full of shit." Alex bit back a smile. "You know that, right?"

"Now then, no need to get all cranky just because you were wrong," I said. "I accept your apology. You obviously didn't know better."

"Apology." She snorted. "Yeah right. So why were you doing this manly brooding—sorry, smoldering, Eric?"

My turn to sigh. "No reason," I said, and turned the conversation toward Joe. "Hey bro, something I wanted to ask you. That new tenant, Jean, is basically right above us. Now I know you said you soundproofed it all, but the thing is that she's pregnant, and I was wondering if we should be easing up on the music volume, at least when it gets late on weeknights."

Joe shook his head. "I guarantee you she cannot hear a thing, except what's drifting through the window."

"Just because she's pregnant doesn't mean she needs to be wrapped in cotton wool, you know," Alex chimed in.

"I know that." I scowled at her.

"See, pouting!" she said, pointing her finger at me in glee.

"Gee, babe, you're right," agreed Joe, the jerk, his voice thick with mock concern. "That actually does look like pouting."

My scowl deepened.

"Come on, man," said Joe, being serious. "It's Thursday night, you're behind the bar, and the place has been pumping all night. And you look like a kid whose puppy died. What gives?"

I sighed again, my shoulders slumping. "I don't know . . . just something Nell said today. Well, she's been on me for a while."

Joe and Alex exchanged looks.

"It's nothing really. Stupid. Don't worry about it."

"Okay," said Alex before taking a sip of beer.

"But, you know . . . just out of interest," I said. "Do you think I'm a manwhore with no concept of responsibility, incapable of having a meaningful relationship, who just uses women because I wouldn't know real commitment if it bit me on the ass?"

Alex's eyes went real wide.

"That's what Nell says, huh?" asked my brother in a low voice.

"Basically." My tongue pushed at the inside of my cheek. "Sometimes it varies, but pretty much. Yeah."

"Wow," said Alex, staring down at her laptop.

"Just today, she called me a fuckboy. Can you believe that?"

Joe let out a low whistle.

"I mean, you two probably know me best," I said. "She's out of line, right?"

Alex's mouth opened, but nothing actually came out. Same with my brother.

"Right?" I asked again, frowning.

Still nothing.

Fuck's sake. "Come on, I am always up front with women. I tell them straight out, I'm here for a good time, not a long time. They know what they're getting into."

After a moment's hesitation, my brother nodded. Sort of.

"Exactly," I said. "And I'm responsible. I always cover my shifts, I work hard."

"Ye-ah," said Joe, dragging the word out for some damn reason.

Alex winced. "Apart from the other week when you wanted to take that girl kayaking."

"Once," I said, holding up a finger. "Big deal."

"Though there was that woman from the liquor company a fortnight back," said Joe. "What was her name?"

"Jesus, I can't remember. So I left work early. Once." I rolled my eyes and added another finger. Two. So what?

"And the times when you're running late because you forget to set your alarm," said Alex. Fast on her way to no longer being my favorite sort of sister-in-law.

I scoffed, but added another finger to the tally. "Two or three times, maybe. Everyone does it."

"Yeah, but every week?" Alex cocked her head.

"She's got a point, bro." My brother nudged me with his elbow. "Probably add a couple more fingers."

I scowled.

"We're going to need your other hand," she said. "Because do you remember last month when—"

"That's enough," I snapped, crossing my arms over my chest. "I don't want to talk about this anymore."

They both shut their mouths, giving each other one of those looks. Couples were downright creepy the way they could do that mind melding shit. Talk about unnatural.

Slowly, I shook my head. "Can't believe you both think she's right."

"No . . ." Joe grabbed me by the shoulder, giving it a squeeze.

I shrugged him off. "Yeah, you do."

His girlfriend kept quiet. Last time I give her free drinks.

Arcade Fire faded into The Killers and not even an old favorite song could help. All agitated like, I smoothed back my hair, redoing the ponytail. "Unbelievable. Even my own fucking brother thinks I'm useless."

"Man, come on. I did not say that. I think . . ." He paused. "I think you do your best."

"Yes." Alex clicked her fingers and pointed at me. "Exactly. You do your best, Eric. Everyone knows you're making a real effort. You haven't even screwed any of the waitresses for months now. No one could expect more."

"Jesus, are you serious?" I asked loudly. "You both think my best sucks."

More denials and other bullshit, but I was done. Finished. Also, people were now watching. Curious eyes sizing up the drama, customers and staff. Awesome.

"You close up the bar." I grabbed a bottle of single malt from off the shelf. "I'm out of here."

Someone said my name and Joe did more sighing and fuck them all. I needed some space. Bottle in hand, I left.

"Eric?" asked a startled voice.

"Hmm?" I shoved my hair out of my face, pulling the door to my apartment closed behind me. Out of the blurry, low-lit hallway came a woman with concerned eyes. "Jean. Hey. How you doing?"

"Better than you, by the look of it." She pulled her baggy cardigan tighter around her, covering the tank and yoga pants combination passing for pajamas. Her feet were bare, toenails painted Smurf blue.

"Cute toes," I said, giving her a grin.

"Been drinking, huh?"

"Just a little," I said. "Where are my manners? The bottle's back inside. Did you want some?"

"Baby on board." She pointed to her belly. "Remember?"

"Right. I remember." The smile fell off my face. "So what are you doing out here?"

"I could ask you the same thing."

"Yeah, but I asked you first."

All casual like, I leaned against the wall. Not falling over like a sloppy drunk. But it seemed the world had started turning a little fast or something. Standing upright wasn't as easy as it should have been. Guess liquor and gravity didn't really mix. I don't normally drink alone, but between Nell's and Joe's and Alex's bullshit, I needed a drink. Or two.

Anyway, it's possible I may have overdone it a little.

"Just walking up and down the hall. As you do at two in the morning."

"I was going to go for a walk too," I said. "Outside. Get some fresh air. You want to come?"

"Thanks, but I'm dead tired and not really dressed for it." She rubbed her tummy. "Plus it's cold out there."

"You're used to Florida weather." I chuckled. "This is only autumn. Wait 'til winter. Why'd you move here anyway?"

"Honestly, I don't know." She shrugged. "I met Nell on the internet. We started chatting on a pregnancy site and the way she spoke about this town just kind of drew me in. And I thought, why not?"

"Because you're heavily pregnant and alone?"

"Besides that."

I just looked at her.

"Things in Florida weren't great," she said, taking her time, obviously choosing her words with care. She glanced up and down the hallway, as if to check there were no other ears listening in. "Actually, that's kind of an understatement. My parents didn't handle the news regarding my pregnancy very well. I get their point, I was basically fresh out of college, just starting to get my life together."

"Mm."

"They wanted me to give the baby away." She frowned at the thought. "Even lined up a couple from their church to adopt her and everything. They were very persistent, but I just couldn't."

"I'm sorry."

"Yeah." She sighed. "Me too. Most of my friends had moved away or were busy living their lives, so I didn't really have a lot of people I could count on. Fortunately, my gran didn't agree with Mom and Dad. Unfortunately, she was very ill. But when she passed she left me some money. Of course, that made things even worse with my parents . . . I didn't want to raise a child around all that negativity."

My heavy head floundered, empty of any comforting words.

Eventually, she made a humming noise. "Anyway, the baby started kicking and woke me up. I don't usually lurk in hallways at stupid hours of the morning. But if I move around for a while things usually quiet down again and this hall is longer than the one in my apartment."

"Huh."

"Nice face." The woman laughed.

"What?"

"It's the thought of the baby kicking, isn't it?" she asked. "I don't think you could look more disgusted if you tried."

Shit. "No, no. I'm not disgusted. That's . . . that's a terrible thing to say."

"You're doing it again right now," she said. "Every time you look at my belly you go sort of green like you're about to hurl."

"No-o-o."

"You do, Eric. Trust me on this."

I exhaled. "You're wrong. I think it's beautiful, life and everything, you know?"

Her dark brows crept together.

"And you, making that life is . . . wow."

"Oh really?"

"Absolutely." I nodded. Then stopped since that made my head spin in a not-good way. "You're beautiful and the baby is . . ."

"The baby is what?"

"Um. Awesome. Yeah."

Now her brows were one dark line. "I don't think you should be going for a walk. How much have you had to drink?"

"I'm not going to drive. Now that would be irresponsible."

"Wait." Her chin rose. "Is 'going to go for a walk' code for 'off in search of booty'?"

"No. Why would you think that?" I scowled as I figured it out. "Hold up. Nell's been saying shit about me to you, hasn't she?"

"Well, you know." Jean stood with her feet apart, rocking back and forth. "Nell and I are friends so I can't really repeat what we talk about. That would be breaking her confidence, and not okay."

"She did." I hung my head. "I knew it." My knees gave way and I sank to the floor. Fuck it. It was more comfortable than standing anyway. "So now I have to put up with it from you too."

"Put up with what from me?"

"You think I'm a useless manwhore too." Knees drawn up, I let my head fall back against the wall. It kind of hurt. "Everyone does. I'm the worst, just ask my family and friends."

She opened her mouth, then closed it again.

"Eric, she doesn't think you're a bad person."

"Save it."

A pained groan. "Come on, you're wasted. Time to sleep it off. Things will look better in the morning, I promise."

Either the lights had gone out or I'd closed my eyes. Hard to tell which. Maybe I wouldn't bother going for a walk after all; every inch of me felt heavy and tired.

"Eric, get up."

"I'm fine here," I mumbled morosely. "Don't worry 'bout me."

Some sighing. "Maybe I should wake Andre or your brother, get one of them to help me get you back inside."

"No, don't." Slowly, painfully, I crawled back up onto my feet. Everything seemed fuzzy and horrible and sad. Real sad. "See, I can stand on my own."

"All right."

"I don't need them."

"Okay." She held her hand out. "Keys?"

"Huh? Oh. Right."

Blessed with sobriety, Jean got the door open in no time. "Come on."

With one of my arms over her shoulders, she directed me toward the bed. Her head turned this way and that, checking everything out. Old framed collectors' edition LPs and the state-of-the-art record player. Thing looked more like a sculpture than something to spin vinyl on. The fully stocked bar cart in the corner and my sprawling gray sofa that matched the dark walls. A lamp shone dimly. Mood lighting and nothing more.

Jean was looking around the bedroom with interest and a slight smirk on her face.

"What?" I demanded.

"Nothing." She sighed. "But for someone who objects to being labeled a manwhore, your whole apartment looks designed for seduction."

"It's all part of the overall package." I defensively waved an extended hand at my five-hundred-thread-count sheets. "If a girl comes back to your room, you've got to show her a good time. That takes attention to detail. Clothes. Ambience. Lighting. Music. The whole experience. You've got to do it right." I tried to puff out my chest a little, which was tricky given that I was still half-leaning on her for support. "That's like a point of principle with me."

"I have noticed that about you. You're very principled," she said, turning to dump me across the bed.

"Don't sound so sarcastic." The mattress bounced beneath me, making my head spin even worse. "Whoa. Everything's spinning."

"Come on, get your legs up on there."

I grumbled, but did as told.

"You're going to bed wearing all your clothes?"

"Depends." I gave her a sexy smile. "You want to undress me?"

"No. I don't think that's a good idea."

Whatever. Her loss.

"Let's lose the boots though, huh?" Without another word, she started tugging at the laces. "You'll be more comfortable."

"Thanks for this. You're real nice, Jean."

"You're welcome."

"I'm not nice."

She dropped one of my shoes on the ground. "You're not so bad."

"It's okay. You don't have to paf . . . pass . . ."

"Pacify?" she suggested.

"Yeah. You don't have to do that to me." I laced my fingers over my chest and stared at the high ceiling. "Even my own brother and his girlfriend think I'm useless."

Not commenting, she got to work on my other boot.

"I can sort of see why. Obviously, getting Nell pregnant wasn't so good."

Both her mouth and eyes opened wide. "*You* got her pregnant?"

"Not this time. Last time, when she and Pat were broken up." I grabbed a pillow and shoved it beneath my head. Might as well be comfortable if I was going to bare my soul and shit. "She lost the baby in a car accident. I thought Nell would have told you all this."

"She mentioned a miscarriage, that's all." In slow motion, she set the boot on the floor. "Eric, I'm so sorry."

"'S okay." The less said about that the better.

Her eyes turned liquid in the low light and she sat on the edge of the bed. With both arms, she kind of hugged her belly. "God, that's so sad. You must have been devastated."

"It wasn't looking like I was going to be much of a dad."

"The baby hadn't even been born yet. You might have been great."

"I had a book."

That was the single best thing I could say for my parenting potential. I had a book. On pregnancy and the first few months. The darn thing wasn't even half-read. Joe had gotten it for me. Got me a whole little library of them actually. Each less read than the one before.

Pathetic.

And if it sounded pitiful to my own ears, I could only imagine what Jean thought of me. For a while she said nothing, just sat there while I stared morosely at the ceiling, wishing we had never started this conversation. Maybe everyone was right and I was the worst. Dwelling on my failings was infinitely preferable to thinking about the baby.

She exhaled. "You and Nell . . ."

"It was an accident," I said, voice barely louder than a whisper. "She and Pat had broken up and she wasn't taking it so well. You know, they've been together since we were kids. No one saw their split coming."

Jean said nothing.

"One night after work, Nell was really laying into the booze. She didn't want to drink alone so I stayed back with her." My whole memory of that night seemed surreal. "Pat had been busy with other women and that hurt her real bad. I was her revenge fuck, really. Her way of getting back at him."

Jean's face was blank, eyes watching me in silence.

"We'd all been friends a long time. I should have said no, but . . ."

Her face tightened, little lines appearing, and she rose to her feet.

"Please don't go," I said, the words bursting out of me. I rose up on my elbows, breathing fast. "I just don't want to be alone." Alone with the remnants of Glenlivet.

Maybe a minute passed and she still said nothing. We just looked at each other, two veritable strangers talking by my bed in the small hours of the morning. Not an unusual occurrence for me, but doing it fully clothed was a first.

"I won't try anything," I said.

She huffed out a laugh and patted her belly. "Oh, I know you won't."

"Sorry I said you were huge. You're still beautiful."

Her brows rose.

"I mean it."

"Thank you." After giving me a long look, she wandered

around to the other side of the bed and sat down with her back to the headboard. "I'll stay for a little while."

"You will?"

A one-shoulder shrug. "Apparently, the baby likes listening to you feeling sorry for yourself. She hasn't kicked since we came in."

"Glad my whining is doing someone some good."

She laughed quietly.

"A little girl?" I asked. "Is that what you said?"

"Yes."

"Huh." It was probably the booze in my system, but the whole idea made me feel strange for some reason. "Nell's was a girl too. I mean, mine. Nell's and mine. We didn't find out until after the accident and the miscarriage. A little girl."

Jean smiled sadly, and a hand reached across to squeeze my shoulder.

I didn't need her sympathy. I didn't need anyone's sympathy. Head turned to the side, I gazed at her bump, mostly in curiosity. "Where's the father?"

"He's not in the picture." She licked her lips. "I just, he was someone I met out one night. It wasn't anything serious, you know?"

"Sure."

She huffed out a little laugh. "Of course you know."

"We're all adults here," I said. "Mostly."

"Yeah, mostly."

"So you had a nice night with him and then . . . surprise?"

"Yes. Big surprise." She looked away. "Guess the condom broke or something. That'll teach me not to be on the pill as well. I freaked out like you wouldn't believe. Then came denial; I must have done about a dozen pregnancy tests. But they all came up positive."

"Mm. What then?"

"Then . . ." She sighed. "I thought really long and hard, I guess. It wasn't an easy decision to make. I had no way of getting in touch with the father. We'd had an okay time together, but he wasn't someone I wanted to see again."

"No?"

"No," she said. "He was a nice enough guy. Fun, very handsome, interesting to talk to. But he was a good-time not a long-time kind of guy. I asked around at the bar where we'd met. He wasn't a regular, though. I can't really imagine that having a baby with me would have been his idea of a *good time*."

I kept my mouth shut.

Her gaze tightened, searching my face. Not in a good way. My already upset stomach sunk even further. I had the worst fucking feeling that I knew exactly what she was thinking.

"I remind you of him, don't I?" I said.

She nodded. "Yeah, you do."

"Why did you flirt with me in the bar then?"

"Good question." She licked her lips. "You made me feel pretty, I guess. Reminded me of what my life used to be like."

I said nothing.

"Maybe I should have tried harder to find him, but then my folks started complicating everything further." Her forehead lined. "I could deal with only so much at one time."

"Fair enough."

"Let's not talk about him anymore."

"Okay." I stared up at nothing a while longer. "Does it feel like there's a freaky alien inside of you?"

"A freaky alien?"

"Guess she doesn't burst out of your chest all gory like in the movie. . . ."

"Jesus. I knew you couldn't stay nice about her for long." She frowned. "Look, I understand now why you're a bit freaked out by babies and pregnancy. But that doesn't mean you get to be a jerk about her."

"What are you talking about?" I demanded. "I'm being totally normal about it. Her."

"So you're just a jerk in general?"

I closed my eyes. "That seems to be the general opinion, yes."

"If I believed that, I'd leave your drunk ass alone on this bed."

But she didn't leave. I could feel her presence next to me. I sighed. "Thanks for not leaving. Even though I remind you of him. Christ, that sucks."

"I shouldn't have said that, I'm sure you wouldn't—"

"But I did," I interrupted. "You were going to say that you were sure I wouldn't bail on my responsibilities, right?"

She said nothing.

"That is exactly what I did, Jean. No need to be polite about it," I said. "I'm an asshole."

Silence.

"Under different circumstances, I'd definitely be hitting on you right now."

"Well, some credit goes to the baby with regards to that. Her presence making me less available to your romantic overtures."

"My romantic overtures?" I asked with a lazy smile. "Who says that?"

"I do. It's the polite way of saying playing naked." The laughter in her voice would have gotten one hell of a reaction from me if I hadn't had so much to drink.

"We would have had fun together."

"You think so?"

"I know so."

"You're that good, huh?"

Eyelids closed, I smiled some more. "Our chemistry is that good."

"Hmm."

"You know when you meet someone and there's just that feeling?"

She didn't respond.

"It's like it's fate. There's just that zap in the air and you know it's got to happen eventually. And when it does, it's going to be spectacular." I opened one eye, beyond pleased to see her trying to hide a smile. "Right, Jean?"

"Wrong."

I just waited.

"It's definitely not happening between us under current circumstances, so what does chemistry matter?" She wriggled a little, getting comfortable, and avoiding looking at me in the process. "Close your eyes, Eric, go to sleep. I'm not babysitting your drunk ass forever."

"I appreciate you being here," I mumbled.

"Couldn't very well leave you all alone in the depths of your alcohol-induced despair."

"Funny, normally I'm trying to get rid of a woman by this time," I said. "Not begging one to stay."

She just shook her head. "So not happening for so many reasons."

"And you are beautiful."

The woman looked to heaven. "Sober or drunk, you are full of it. You get that, right?"

"I get that I'm right. Yes."

"Puh-lease. I'm okay looking."

"You're fucking gorgeous."

"Does that include my belly?"

I cleared my throat. "Sure."

"Real believable." She laughed. "Go to sleep."

"Fine. Doubt me, I don't care." I puffed up my pillow, settling in for the night. Morning. Whatever the hell time it was. My buzz was starting to wear thin, tiredness kicking in. " 'Night, Jean."

" 'Night, Eric."

CHAPTER FOUR

Karen arrived ten minutes late in a tight skirt. Her long hair hung loose and her sweater top hung off her bare shoulder. I'd always heartily approved of her belief in showing plenty of skin. No matter the chill in the night air, here she was with those long legs. It'd been a month since Jean sat by my bedside while I fell asleep, drunk off my ass. Not my finest moment. In the meantime, our paths hadn't really crossed. I'd been busy and I guess she had too. As for dealing with Nell and everyone else's low opinion of me, I had a plan.

"All right, I'm here." She paused, flashing a megawatt smile at the man on the other side of the bar. "Hey, Vaughan."

"Hi, Karen, how are you doing?"

"Great! How's your music going?"

"Good." The tattooed redheaded musician gave her a polite smile. "Played some gigs over in Montana last week."

Like just about everyone else in this town, we'd all known each other for years. Vaughan and I had been tight in high school, but shit had gone south after graduation. We were getting on okay these days. Despite him also settling down and getting serious about everything. He and Lydia had been engaged for a year or two now. I didn't know what the holdup was on the wedding. He worked in the bar when he wasn't off playing guitar. I don't know if it was wise, but we'd pretty much wound up with most of our staff being old friends.

"Ready to head upstairs?" Karen asked, stepping closer. Her arm brushed against my chest and the open invitation in her eyes almost made me rethink my plan.

Like I might have mentioned, we were very friendly. But only in a certain mutually beneficial way at times suitable to both of us. Usually. Still, if I was going to try dating someone, I figured it wouldn't hurt to know ahead of time if that someone and I got along between the sheets. Plus Karen was available. She was between boyfriends, so, win/win. A nice, good-looking local girl who enjoyed fucking. A strong starting point if ever there was one.

With the goal of a relationship in mind, I quashed out the rising surge of lust. It wasn't easy, given Karen's inviting eyes, and the fact that it had been a while since I'd last hooked up. Almost a whole week. But I ignored my simpler urges and focused on the plan.

"Actually, I was thinking we could sit down for a while first," I said, leading her to a candlelit table in the corner.

Her pert nose wrinkled. "You want to sit down?"

"Sure. Why not?"

Apparently there were a lot of reasons why this was a bad idea, because she took a deep breath and opened her mouth to start in on them.

I got there first, however. "We've been friends a long time, Karen."

"Yes, but—"

"It occurred to me that we've never really just hung out together."

She blinked.

"You know, had a drink, and talked and stuff." I pulled out her chair, being the perfect gentleman. That'd show Nell. And you could bet she was in the kitchen right now watching . . . judging. Lydia too, most likely.

"You want to talk?" Karen plonked down in the seat, wrinkles lining her usually smooth forehead. "What about?"

I took my seat opposite. "Ah, well. Anything really. How's your work going?"

"The diner's fine."

"Great." I nodded. "And your family?"

"Fine."

Oh shit, what to ask her about next? It struck me I actually didn't know anything about her family, which made it hard to figure out a follow-up question. Equally though, it seemed a bit awkward to admit that, after the years we'd known each other, I didn't even know if her parents were local or if she had siblings.

The long line of her throat rippled as Karen swallowed and came to my rescue. "Um, how are your parents?"

"Good, thanks. They're actually on vacation in Hawaii right now."

"Lovely."

"Yeah. Mom's been looking forward to it for a long time."

"Right. Wonderful." She paused.

I was stuck for a conversation topic again. Damn it. Dating was harder than it looked. Normally I only ever had real conversations with our close-knit little group. Apart from that, I just flirted with the ladies, which was a game I knew well.

Hopefully Rosie would come take our order soon. Alcohol as a social lubricant could only help.

"Everything's okay with this place?" Karen saved the conversation again. She was clearly better at this than I was. Thank God somebody knew what they were doing.

"Absolutely," I said. "The bar side of things is running smoother than ever. Nell and Lydia have been sourcing more local organic produce to feature on the seasonal menu."

"Mm."

"Things are . . . good."

We both let our gazes wander, taking in the room. The Dive Bar was only half full, what with it being early in the week. Depeche Mode was playing. Lydia must be in charge of the music. We each took turns to keep things fair. Boyd's headbanger shit could be a little hard to handle, however, so we only gave him an hour or two a week.

Fingers fussing with the napkin, I slumped my shoulders, trying to loosen up. It wouldn't do to let anyone know how on edge I was. Jesus, it wasn't like I'd never met a woman for a drink before. But it had never been with a view toward anything long-term. Wonder when I should broach the subject of her and me being something serious.

"Have you ever eaten here?" I asked finally, winning at conversation. Someone ought to give me a gold star. Or a cookie. Or a drink. A drink would be nice. Where was Rosie to take our order?

"No, I haven't."

"Now that's a damn shame. We need to fix that pronto."

A hint of a smile curved the edge of her lips. "People tell me the food's delicious."

I outright grinned, always pleased to hear good feedback. "It is."

"A lot pricier than the diner, though."

"Well, it's a different kind of dining experience."

Nothing from her.

"You know?"

All expression had fallen from her face. "No, I don't believe I do."

"Don't get me wrong, the diner does great basics," I said. "Your pancakes in particular. Man, I could eat a truckload of those things and still come back for more. They are superb."

"Basics?"

I shrugged. "Yeah."

"And you're what? Gourmet I suppose?"

Damn. "Well . . ."

"Just because you cover your pizzas in arugula and other fancy shit doesn't make you better than us, Eric."

"I don't think we're better than you." Though I did really. The Dive Bar was a work of art. In comparison, the diner had all the style and atmosphere of a hot dog stand. "Calm down."

"Not everyone wants to hang out with hipsters."

"Hey, now. We're not—"

"Whatever," she snapped, obviously done with this line of conversation. Which was fine with me, given I didn't want to get into a fight about the relative merits of our workplaces. "Is this food you're talking about going to come soon? I've only got an hour before I'm meeting a friend at the gym."

"You're meeting someone else tonight?"

"In an hour, yes." She nodded. "So every minute we spend sitting here is one minute that we're not . . ." Her voice trailed off suggestively.

I smiled. And then remembered that screwing her was not the goal here. "Maybe we should just enjoy a nice meal now and reschedule for a time later this week?"

"I don't want to reschedule," she retorted. "If you're not in the mood, then whatever. But did it even occur to you to call me and let me know that you wanted to change things up?"

"No." I shrugged. "I figured you'd be pleasantly surprised. Chicks dig romantic dinners. Everyone knows that."

"Funnily enough, women aren't that big on being called chicks."

"Right," I said. "My mistake."

She crossed her arms, glaring at me.

"So, who are you meeting at the gym?" I asked. "Anyone I know?"

"One of the girls from work."

"Great." Fake smiling made my cheeks ache. "What else do you do when you're not working or hitting the gym?"

"When the weather's good I like to go hiking and I help out with a youth group at the church," she said. "I visit friends and I'm also a member of a knitting group. Right now we're working on blankets for the children's ward at the hospital."

"Wow."

"Grandpa has chronic arthritis so I often hop over to his place to help out. Make some meals for him or just hang out and watch documentaries. He loves that English guy, David Attenborough." She stared off at nothing. "And I watch my nephews some nights so my brother and his wife can go out."

"Huh. You really do a lot."

She shrugged. "I keep busy. What about you?"

"I work here of course." I nodded, trying to think of what else apart from women occupied my time. Something that would compare to Karen's achievements. "Yeah, a lot of the time you can find me here at the bar. Really just . . . working, you know?"

"And?" she asked, eyes glazing over.

"Okay. Well, I hang out with friends."

Nothing from her.

"Yeah." Shit. "Oh, often Joe and I go jogging. There's that too."

"Uh-huh."

And all conversation ground to a halt once again. We both just stared at each other while all around us the world carried on. Music played and people talked. People who actually had a lot to say to each other, I guess.

Karen set her hands to the edge of the table. "This isn't working."

"No, this is great."

"Eric, we've been bumping hips on and off for years and you've never felt the need to ask me a personal question," she pointed out. "Why now?"

I raised my chin. "Better late than never, right?"

"Wrong."

"But—"

"Enough, I have to go." The woman jumped to her feet in exasperation, making her chair skid back noisily, drawing plenty of attention. "I knew this was a bad idea. We have sex sometimes, Eric. That's all. We don't *talk*."

"But we could!" I stood up as well, just trying to usher her back to sitting. We could at least do this without causing a scene.

Her whole face screwed up. "What we have is just fine."

"Sure, yeah. I just thought . . ."

"What? You thought what?"

"Well, don't you want maybe something more?"

"No, Eric. God, do I have to spell it out?" Her gaze zeroed in on me. "We're boring each other stupid. And even if we did have stuff to talk about, I don't want a guy like you for a boyfriend. In a couple of days, you'd have changed your mind, gotten distracted or whatever. You're just not boyfriend material."

And with that, she stormed out. Awesome.

Meanwhile, Rosie stood nearby with her pen and pad in hand.

Because more witnesses to my humiliation would just be wonderful. The shit Karen had said echoed round and round inside my head. How wrong could one woman be? Just because she crocheted socks for orphans or whatever. I could totally be a decent boyfriend. With a little practice.

"Bit too late for that," I said, nodding at her order pad and slumping back down into my chair.

"Sorry." Her mouth skewed, dark skin glowing in the candlelight. "Date didn't go so well?"

"What gave it away?" I growled.

"Being an ass to me will help you how, exactly?"

"Sorry, Rosie." I slipped my hand underneath my long hair, rubbing at my neck. "Maybe they're right. Maybe I am just shit at this and everything else."

She sighed and took the newly vacant seat opposite me. "Nell's been at you again, huh?"

I didn't even bother to answer.

"I thought she'd eased up since you started turning up for your shifts on time."

"She did. A little."

"You know, she loves you, Eric," she said. "You're like family to her. She just has a difficult way of showing it."

"Like ripping into me?" I slouched back in the chair. "Bitch of it is that everyone agrees with her. They all treat me like I'm the idiot child obsessed with pussy."

"So prove them wrong. If it bothers you, do something about it."

My forehead wrinkled.

"Though changing just to prove someone else wrong is kind of stupid," she said, chewing at her bottom lip. "You have to want to do it for your own happiness."

"Fuck. I don't know what I want."

"Well, are you happy?"

"I thought I was, until everyone kept pointing out how crappy I am," I said.

Rosie might have been the same age as me, but she'd been married for years and had about three dozen children or something. Don't ask me how she managed it all. If anyone was going to give me advice worth listening to, however, it would likely be her. So I stayed put. Nearby, Lydia handed out meals to a table while Vaughan stayed busy at the bar.

"You could keep cruising along," she said. "Working here, picking up women, and spending all of your money on nice clothes."

"Hey," I objected. "I paid my brother back the money I owed him. Downgraded from a very sweet muscle car to a piece of shit to do it too."

"Good for you."

"There's nothing wrong with wanting to look presentable." With a hand, I smoothed out the creases on my plain white button-down. Designer, of course. Quality mattered. Some fuckers wouldn't know good design and fabric if it smacked them in the face. "I stick to my budget. Lydia helped me work one out a while back."

"That's great. Very adult of you."

"Why thank you."

For a minute, she mused this over, staring at me. "Do you want to know what I think?"

"No one else holds back. Why the hell should you?"

She gave me a mysterious smile. Like she knew everything, while I knew nothing. I could have pretty much already told her that.

"There's no such thing as becoming an adult. It's all a state of mind," she said, leaning closer across the table. "You never reach some magical age and go . . . oh my god, I'm so adult. I couldn't be more grown-up if I tried."

I chuckled. "No?"

"Nope."

"How does this whole life thing work then, oh wise woman?"

"You get your shit together and meet your responsibilities," she said.

"Huh."

"A century ago, everyone knew how they were expected to behave and if you stepped over the line, that was it. You were out. But things are different now." She stared me down, gaze deadly serious. "People are more open minded, mostly. Though quite a few could do with a healthy dose of personal growth and empathy in my opinion. But we have so many options, there's so many things we could do with our lives. Honestly, it can get a little confusing."

I kept my mouth shut because she wasn't wrong.

"Be kind and if you say you're going to do something, make sure you do it." She sat back in the chair, crossing her arms over her chest. "Do with that what you will."

"Basically, don't be an asshole and pay my bills on time?"

"Yep."

"And that's the path to happiness?" I asked.

Rosie frowned. "Not exactly. That's probably the path to getting everyone off your back, though. As for all the ladies . . ."

"Sex is a perfectly normal and healthy pastime."

"True. But you should respect the women you sleep with."

"Come on, I do," I complained.

"Do you really?"

"Yes." I waved an arm at the door my date had just exited. "As Karen just demonstrated."

"The girl who stormed out in a huff just demonstrated you respect women?" Her eyebrows arched. "How do you figure that?"

"Because everyone always acted like it was just me who wanted to keep it light, as if the chicks would rather something more substantial," I grumbled. "But as Karen just made clear, that clearly overestimates my capacity to be seen as a potential partner."

Rosie frowned, her forehead crinkling in thought, as if surprised I was making sense. Frankly, I had been half-hoping for a robust rebuttal, where she assured me I was excellent boyfriend stock. Her thoughtful silence spoke volumes. "I've got to get back to work. Try not to worry too much about what Nell says. Understandable given how things ended last time."

The old familiar feeling of guilt sat inside me like a stone. "I know."

"In a way, I think she's found her happy and now she wants the same for you. To find someone who makes you happy . . ." Rosie stared off at nothing. "Though you shouldn't make someone else responsible for your happiness."

"You're talking in circles. Again."

"Hmm. You know, if you're serious about this," said Rosie, "I'm willing to consider setting you up with one of my friends."

"I don't know." I scratched at my stubble. "All of this soul searching and trying to date is making my head hurt."

"If it's confusing you that much, maybe you should just take a break from sex and women."

I paused, thinking it over. "Yeah. Maybe I should."

"Oh my god, Eric." Rosie howled with laughter. "That was a joke. You, go without? Never going to happen."

"It could." Talk about a complete and utter lack of fucking faith in me. Sheesh. "I mean, just because I haven't ever tried taking a break doesn't mean I couldn't."

She laughed some more, wiping away tears as she got to her feet. "You're hilarious. Hang in there, Eric. I have faith in you. You'll figure it all out. Not that I'm convinced we ever really stop trying to figure shit out. You just move on to new problems."

"Rosie, I love you. You are a dear and valued friend," I said. "But please stop talking now."

Away she went to check on her tables. Thank God. Still laughing, but whatever.

If anything, all of this supposed good advice had just confused me even more. Wise words, my ass. Also, I completely failed to see how keeping it in my pants would make me a better person. Or the alternative, putting a leash on my dick and handing over all ownership to one woman. Pretty sure monotony and monogamy sounded similar for a reason. But what the hell, I was willing to give the first option a go just to see. If only to now prove both Nell and Rosie wrong about me. So there.

Giving Vaughan a chin tip and still not looking over at Nell (or Lydia, just to be safe), I put on my new gray merino cardigan and headed out. There was kind of a gap in my schedule given the time I had intended to spend with Karen. What a schmozzle that turned out to be.

Things were quiet out on the street. Peaceful. The shadows of bare tree limbs waved in the cold wind. Time to start getting out the winter gear. I shoved my hands into the pockets of my black jeans and raised my shoulders, bracing myself against the chill. Luckily, I only had to walk the block.

Pat was open late, still at work in the tattoo parlor. Andre's music shop, however, had been closed up tight. I'd only just stretched out my hand to reach for the door to the apartment entrance when a flash of movement inside caught my eye. Long legs in blue jeans and a pair of fluffy fire engine–red boots. Those could only belong to Jean. Quickly, I ducked around the side of the building, out of sight.

So maybe the reason mine and Jean's paths hadn't crossed in the last month might have something to do with me avoiding her. Between her being pregnant and therefore definitely unsuitable for dating despite her being both hot and nice, and my making a drunken ass of myself, avoiding her seemed best.

She stepped outside, humming some tune, and headed toward the Dive Bar. Probably picking up takeout for dinner. Or perhaps she'd have a chat with the girls, hang out a while. I usually found something incredibly important to do in the basement or back office when that happened. A matching red sweater covered her top half and I think her bulge had gotten bigger. Don't know for sure. But she'd definitely started waddling a little. It was cute.

Out of sight, I watched until she disappeared into the bar. Yes, I hid, spying around the corner like a creepy perv. This was what my life had become. Pride didn't even matter anymore. Maybe the whole no-sex thing would be easy since I seemed to be accidentally crushing on the wrong woman. Especially since I reminded her of the missing father of her child, apparently a total fucking jerk. Awesome. I bumped my forehead against the cold brick wall.

"You're one sorry fuck, Collins," I muttered to myself. And it was all too true.

Hours later, I just couldn't get to sleep. It'd been happening often lately. Seemed like most nights my mind just wouldn't shut up.

It was pure happenstance that I picked up the book. I had done some sit-ups and push-ups for a while, trying to wear myself out.

Nothing much on TV interested me and it wasn't like I kept a variety of reading material around.

Yet, somehow, I wound up sitting down with the pregnancy book my brother had bought me a year or so ago. Back when becoming a father had almost been a reality. God only knows why I picked it up. Well, first I had to fish it out from the bottom of my bedside drawers, of course. It's not like I kept it on the coffee table or anything. But for an hour or so, I read about women in their last trimester. What the baby was up to and everything. It was actually kind of fascinating. I even read a little of the chapter about giving birth. That's where it turned kind of horrific. If sex caused all that, maybe keeping it in my pants was the way to go. Still, lots of questions came up, and most of them made me feel queasy. And I couldn't help but wonder if Jean knew exactly what she was in for, and if so, how the hell she slept at night at all. The changes happening inside of her, what including a baby in her life would mean. It was all so big. Hell, it was huge.

I lay there for a long time just wondering how she felt about it all. Not that I'd ask her.

CHAPTER FIVE

"You're pouting again," said Alex.

"Am not." I sat alone in the backseat of my brother's truck, looking up from my cell to scowl at her. Pouting. Not that I'd ever admit to it.

"He totally is." Alex turned her attention back to the road, before gesturing to my brother. "Check him out, Joe."

"I would," said my brother. "But I can't see shit."

"Least you're not in a dress," I mumbled.

"Shut up." Alex sighed for the hundredth time. "You both look great. I'm a costuming genius."

We pulled up at a red light and Alex took the opportunity to ignore me while fussing with her long black wig. Outside, streetlights cast yellow circles in the dark. Few cars were on the road. Due to the Dive Bar schedule, we tended to have our private Halloween Party after hours on a weeknight. We'd shut early-ish, say about nine o'clock. Then everyone would head over to Vaughan and Lydia's place since they were the only ones with a house—and enough room.

"Next year, I'm picking what we go as," I said.

"Fine," she said.

"You look great as Morticia, babe." Joe reached out, blindly searching for her knee to pat or something. I couldn't quite see from the backseat, but I believe his hand might have landed more in Alex's groin area given the way she squeaked.

"Easy there." She hastily moved his grip to more child-friendly territory. "And thank you."

"Just one question," he said. "How am I supposed to drink anything with all this hair in my face?"

"I'll put a straw in your drink and lead you around all night so you don't bump into things." The light turned to green and Alex accelerated. "Don't worry. I've thought this all out."

I chuckled. "Beer through a straw. Way to go, Cousin Itt."

"Shut up, Wednesday," Joe growled. Or, at least, I think he did. It was kind of muffled from behind all the hair brushed over his face. The black Ray-Bans holding his 'do in place really made the outfit. Of course, all the hair only covered him to his shoulders. So not a true Cousin Itt. Black jeans, boots, and a Henley shirt completed the outfit. He'd gotten off easy, because God only knows how anyone would put up with a wig that reached the floor.

"I'm not afraid to get in touch with my feminine side." Returning to reading on my cell, I played with one of my braids, swinging it back and forth. "Could have done without the tights, though."

"It would have looked stupid with just your hairy legs sticking out from under the dress," said Alex. "Plus, you'll be warmer."

I grunted.

"What's got you so enthralled back there?" she asked.

"I'm studying."

"Studying what?"

"Brushing up on my dating technique for when I finish my sex ban and get back into the game."

"The fact that you're referring to women as a game makes me wonder if you shouldn't make the break from sex permanent," said Alex.

Joe snorted. "Still can't fucking believe you're doing that."

"Believe it," I said.

"Are you going to buy yourself a promise ring?"

I gave him the bird.

The asshole roared with laughter.

"Anyway, I'm learning from one of the masters back here, you might say." I slid the screen up, moving onto the next email. "Very smooth the way you got her talking about her life and everything. Got to say, I'm actually impressed with you, brother."

"The fuck you reading?" Joe turned his head, trying to look back at me. It obviously didn't do him any good since he shoved the sunglasses on top of his head and pried apart his styled hair. He glared out at me with one eye. "Man, those better not be the messages between me and Alex."

The woman herself flashed me a foul look in the rearview mirror.

"Oh, I'm sorry," I said. "Are you complaining about me reviewing my own dating profile, done under my name, with my picture on every message?" Joe had wooed his girl via the internet and the name and face on the dating site profile had both been mine. Another long story. "So, what . . . the ratio is like two general questions to a sex one. Something like that?"

Joe tore the hole in his curtain of hair wider. God only knows what his girl had used on it to get that effect. But it couldn't be good for his hair follicles. "Delete those right now."

"About when do you think you're supposed to ask about her family and stuff? I'm just not sure about that personal shit." I wrapped one of my braids around a finger. "And do you use the same jokes on each girl or come up with new material?"

"I'm going to fucking kill you."

"Never mind," I said. "I'll work it out for myself."

Suddenly, the car pulled over to the side of the road and

screeched to a halt, throwing me against my seat belt. A car sped past, horn blaring. Fair enough, Alex's driving was not the best.

"Eric?" Her voice was strained.

"Yeah?"

"Please don't read those," she said. "I realize they're in your name and that your brother was dubious as hell to do that. But they're still extremely private and I would very much appreciate you deleting them. Immediately."

"Geez, everyone's always on me for all the one-night stands, and then the moment I make the effort to improve my boyfriend-material status, you're all jumping down my throat. . . ." My words dwindled off. They were both still glaring at me. When riled, it turned out that Morticia and Cousin Itt made a pretty fearsome set. I looked to heaven. "All right. Fine."

"Thank you."

People. Jesus. Always so overly sensitive about everything. It annoyed the absolute crap out of me. But happily, the car started moving again and we were on our way. Halloween decorations filled the yards of just about every house we passed. Pumpkins, gourds, and plastic skeletons, white sheets strung up to resemble ghosts. On the actual day, there'd be all of the trick-or-treating and a parade downtown. Not to mention all the hot babes using the opportunity to dress up as slinky devils or cute angels. It was a pretty great time of year.

Looked like everyone had already arrived at Vaughan and Lydia's. They had a small bungalow a few streets back from Sandy Beach. Vaughan, Nell, Joe, and I had all grown up in the area. Before the big money people moved in and built their mansions on the waterfront.

"Help me out with the drinks," said Joe, feeling along the side of the truck for the load in the back.

"What the hell are you going to do all night not being able to see?"

He shrugged. "I'll manage."

"You're pussy whipped."

"Yeah and you're an asshole," said my brother, with no real anger in the words. "Can't believe you were reading those messages."

Instead of answering, I grabbed a case of beer.

Fake gravestones filled the front yard. Big ugly black plastic spiders decorated the side of the steps while bats dangled overhead. Strings of party lights in the shape of skulls and glowing cobwebs hung in every window. The place looked cool, the bass line from Stevie Wonder's "Superstition" thumping through the night air. Classic Halloween musical goodness.

Alex wiggled up to the front door in her tight, long, black Morticia dress, leading Joe via the finger tucked into his belt. Before she could raise her other hand to knock, Lydia threw the door open.

"You're here!" she said and smiled.

"Happy Halloween." Alex kissed her on the cheek. "You make a hot dead Rosie the Riveter."

"Why thank you. You look rather delectable yourself."

Joe shuffled inside. "Hi."

"Cousin Itt," said Lydia. "I like it."

"Hey." I grinned as she took in my knee-length black dress with its prim white collar. "It was Alex's idea. We're doing an *Addams Family* thing."

"You look great." She laughed. "I need to find my cell and snap some pictures. Beer can go straight into the kitchen. Thanks."

"Sure."

"Oh, and the real live Rosie's got a surprise for you."

"What?"

"I'm not telling. Go ask her yourself." Lydia's gaze was distinctly amused.

Shit.

A decent crowd had gathered, staff, their significant others, and a few frequent customers of the bar. After dumping the beer in the kitchen as instructed, I made my way through the gathering, smiling and nodding. I winked at Taka when he made a sarcastic comment about my legs and frock. The dude was just jealous, and fair enough. Not everyone could pull off Wednesday Addams with three days' worth of stubble.

As it turned out, I didn't have to go in search of Rosie. She found me.

"Eric!"

"Hello, you . . ." I tilted my head to the side, taking in her outfit. Heavy black eye makeup and glossy green lips. Random bandages were strategically wrapped around her with a white top and pants beneath covering her curves. Hope her husband knew he was a damn lucky man. "Are you an Egyptian mummy, Rosie? Is that what I'm seeing here?"

"I'm a hot mummy. The 'hot' bit is important." She dragged another woman forward by the arm. "And this is my friend Natasha. She's an aesthetician. Owns her own business over in Spokane."

So Rosie definitely didn't believe me about the sex ban. What a surprise. No matter, I could talk to a woman without trying to bed her. This could happen.

"Hey," I said.

"Hi. Nice to meet you." The tall, beautiful Latina woman saluted me with her almost empty cider. She wore a colorful print dress and her dark hair was piled up on top of her head and filled with big bright plastic flowers. Also, she'd penciled in the middle of her brows making it look like she only had one long hairy uni-brow. Just like that artist . . . damn, what was her name?

I clicked my fingers, forehead scrunched up.

"Frida Kahlo," supplied Natasha.

"Yes! Frida Kahlo. You look great," I said. "Nice to meet you too, Natasha."

"And you're from *The Addams Family*." She nodded. "Very cool."

"Thanks," I said. "My brother's girl gets all the credit, though. She was in charge this year."

"Alex is lovely." Rosie patted my cheek, beaming. "I've been telling Natasha all about you."

"Grrrreatt," I said, feeling ever so slightly fucking awkward. Rosie's eyes drilled into me, pointed and expectant. God help me. She'd gone ahead and set me up with one of her friends after all. Without any warning or even a heads-up. I leaned into Nata-sha. "What *did* she tell you, just out of curiosity?"

Natasha laughed. She had a pretty smile and an infectious laugh. Maybe Rosie hadn't completely messed this up. I never set an actual time limit on the sex ban, now that I thought about it. If Natasha was willing to wait a couple of weeks, just long enough for me to prove myself, this might work. Then maybe we could date. Serious like. Sure, why not?

"I didn't say anything too bad, I promise," said Rosie. "I like you with braids. You should wear those to the bar."

"I dunno." I shrugged, playing with the end of one again. "Don't you think they're more of a casual look?"

"What if you added ribbons?" asked Natasha.

I made a humming noise, pretending to think it over. "That might work."

Both women laughed.

"More drinks required," declared Rosie, releasing her hold on her friend before bustling over to the fridge.

I followed. "Allow me."

"Relax, I got it. You want a beer?"

"Please."

She opened one of the Ninkasi Total Dominations and handed it over. A nice IPA from Oregon and my particular donation to the party bar. Lydia had also liberated some wine from the bar, cider, and a couple of bottles of liquor earlier in the day. Along with some non-alcoholic options, of course. The house had been fully stocked.

"You want one too, Vaughan?" she asked our co-host, who had just appeared at my shoulder.

He nodded, then mumbled to me, "Cool dress."

"Thanks." I looked him over. "What the hell are you supposed to be?"

"Sasquatch. But the head was too fucking hot to wear so I dumped it." He pushed a hand through his still damp red hair. "The full body fur suit is bad enough."

"Go stand out in the cold for a while."

"Andre and I are about to," he said. "He came in a white Vegas Elvis costume. Rhinestone belt and all. Polyester from head to toe."

"That is not a breathable fabric."

Natasha chuckled and I smiled at her. The woman seemed nice. Very nice.

"Have you two met?" I asked. "Natasha, this is Vaughan. He's terrible, you won't like him."

"We've met already," said Vaughan dourly. "And she found me to be delightful and said Lydia was a lucky woman to have me."

I raised a brow at Natasha in question.

"Delightful. Absolutely," she dutifully repeated.

"You know, next year I'm going in drag too and wearing a bikini," said Vaughan. "Get a long blond wig. Come as Pamela Anderson."

"We'll all look forward to that," I said, keeping my face straight. "Maybe you could consider shaving first? Full body wax?"

Rosie snorted. "You definitely should. Natasha can do it for you."

"I have many male clients." Natasha grabbed another cider. "Be happy to help you."

"Thank you. But not a chance," said Vaughan. "Wax scares me. If Eric can get away with Wednesday Addams with stubble, then you can all just deal with me in my natural glory."

"By the way, Pamela Anderson wore a one-piece on *Baywatch*. Not a bikini," said Rosie, passing the man a beer.

"Thanks," he said. "Is a one-piece comfortable?"

"Probably more likely to give you a wedgie."

Natasha nodded. "God knows what it would do to the rest of your goods."

"Damn," said Vaughan. "Might have to give it some thought."

"Wear a dress," I suggested, doing a twirl. "Skirts are cool."

"Good idea. I better circulate and find Andre before he tries to climb onto the coffee table and sing 'Hound Dog' again. Later." Vaughan disappeared off into the crowd.

As per usual, the kitchen remained prime real estate with people constantly coming and going. Rosie might be keen on setting me up with a friend, but she stayed close, keeping an eye on things, making sure I behaved. She and Nell too, bless them both for their confidence in me. Nell's bump had been dressed up as the Death Star. Which meant Pat must be the Darth Vader hanging with Joe in the living room.

Nell's reaction upon hearing about me taking a break from sex had been about the same as Rosie's. In fact, she'd almost fallen over, she'd been laughing so hard. I was a little worried she'd go into early labor. Still, the lack of faith was about what I'd expected. Since one article I'd read on the web suggested reclaiming your chastity could be a purifying experience, it gave me plenty of extra incentive to just stay the hell away from the woman. I didn't need that kind of negativity in my new, purer, temporarily celibate life.

I didn't feel any more enlightened—yet. Surely that would come.

Meanwhile, Natasha and I chatted, standing in an out-of-the-way corner. Mostly we talked about the recent change of premises and expansion at her business. The woman had a sharp mind to go along with her beautiful body. I could learn a lot from her. Back when we first opened the Dive Bar a few years ago, I didn't know shit about running a business. Nice to know I could appear halfway intelligent on the subject now. Or I knew when to nod, at least.

Another drink went by and we were standing close, speaking in low voices. Everything looked good, from the way she kept placing her hand on my arm to the warmth in her eyes.

"I don't believe you." A familiar laugh filled the air and my head shot up. Jean. She entered the kitchen with Andre hot on her heels.

"It's true," he said. "I met the king."

"You must have been like two years old."

"Younger. He made a huge impression on me, changed my whole life."

"Oh, obviously." Jean paused briefly when she spotted me. Her bump had been transformed into a colorful goldfish bowl care of the print on her T-shirt. She even had sparkly themed hairclips. One was a fish, another some shiny green weed, and the last one a little plastic castle. "Eric. Hi."

"E." Andre gave me a slap on the arm. "Looking good. Very pretty."

I smiled. "Those are some serious big-ass sunglasses, man."

"The king doesn't mess around when it comes to eyewear." He held out his hand to Natasha. "Hello, I don't believe we've met. I'm Andre."

"Natasha." She gave it a firm shake. "Nice to meet you."

"Natasha is a friend of Rosie's," I supplied. "And Natasha, this is our neighbor, Jean. We all live in the Bird Building above the bar."

Jean murmured hello.

"Well now, don't you look nice," I said. "Very fishy. But like, in the right way. Not slimy fishy. Or suspiciously fish. Glamorous fishy."

Her smile widened. "Thanks. I dig your hair."

I turned my head so my braids swung about. "Getting a lot of compliments about the 'do. Think I'll have to wear it like this more often."

"Anyway . . . I was just going to grab myself a juice."

"I can get that for you."

"No, I don't want to interrupt," she said, the smile slipping from her face. "You and Natasha were talking."

"It's fine." Getting drinks was my thing, after all.

With an army of red Solo cups waiting on the counter and the fridge fully stocked, I handed her a drink in no time. Andre and Natasha started chatting. Talking about town, their favorite Frida Kahlo paintings, shit like that. The man was being his usual super-smooth and friendly self. He pretty much had the market cornered on nice guy vibes. His boyfriend-material ranking had to be pushing eleven. It normally would have bothered me, but the strain in Jean's smile worried me more.

"You okay?" I asked.

"Yeah. Couldn't be better." She took a sip of her drink. "How have you been?"

"Busy, you know."

"Right."

"Yeah, really busy. Work and stuff."

"Okay. I'd wondered if you'd been away or something," she said. "I hadn't seen you around . . ."

"What, you think I've been hiding from you or something?" I laughed a little too loudly. Shit. "Anyway, how are you? You've been good?" Dammit. I'd already asked that.

"Sure. Very good."

I nodded.

"So, aren't you going to tell me I look like I swallowed Saturn or something?"

"Certainly not," I protested. "The Atlantic maybe, but not Saturn. It wouldn't fit the fish theme you've got going on."

"He better not say anything," said Andre, rejoining the conversation. "You look absolutely wonderful. Glowing and then some."

My friend needed to go away. But the look Jean gave him in response to his compliment was more sibling style than anything. Not romantic. Or at least, I'm pretty sure it wasn't. It better not be. For heaven's sake, the woman had enough on her plate without Andre trying to suck up and get into her pants. Because of course my concern was solely about her.

"Of course she looks wonderful," I muttered. "I wasn't going to say anything like that."

"When are you due?" asked Natasha, bypassing the weirdness.

"Another month." Jean sighed. "I can't wait."

"Make sure you put your feet up and get lots of sleep while you can. My sister, Isla, had her first almost six months ago," said Natasha. "I don't think she's had a minute's rest since."

Jean's eyes brightened. "Congratulations on becoming an auntie."

"Thanks." Natasha slipped a cell out of her pocket and pulled up a picture of a cute little kid with jelly or something smeared over his face. "His name is Henry."

"How sweet."

"Only a month to go. Wow," she said, her gaze taking in Jean and Andre. The cell disappeared back into her pocket. "You both must be so excited."

Andre's mouth opened, but Jean got there first. "No. We're not together. I'm going to be a single parent."

"You're doing it alone?" Natasha's eyes widened. "I hope you have lots of help."

"I'll be fine."

"Fine? Forget that. You'll be great." I grabbed a ghost-shaped cookie off a plate on the counter and took a bite.

"I guess so." Natasha did not look convinced. "But Isla has her wife, who is very supportive, and they're still struggling. Henry has trouble settling at night and some days it seems like he cries nonstop. There's nothing wrong with him, he's a perfectly normal baby. They were just totally unprepared for the amount of work involved. And the lack of sleep."

I gulped down some beer, watching Jean out of the corner of my eye.

"Honestly, I don't know how they stay sane," she continued. "Isla said she went three days without a shower, just because she couldn't find the time and energy. It kind of restores my faith in humanity that so many people get through it, raise emotionally and physically healthy children, and actually go back for more."

"Oh, I agree. It's big, having a baby, becoming a parent." Jean stroked her belly. "Huge, really. But I'm looking forward to it."

"You'll be fine," I said.

"You're braver than me." Andre pretended to shiver. "My cousin got ripped apart down there having her two. For some reason she felt the need to tell me about it in gory detail."

Jesus. "Real sensitive, man. Also, you don't have a vagina so I think you're pretty safe."

His gaze darted to Jean, remorse filling his eyes. "Shit. Sorry."

"No problem." Jean shrugged. "Everyone has stories. I've heard lots of them."

"My sister said once you've got your baby in your arms, you don't even remember all that," said Natasha. "But still, go for the epidural. She said it made all the difference."

Jean took a sip of juice, apparently unperturbed. "Oh, I'm planning a natural birth. Drug-free."

"Seriously?"

"I've done a lot of research and I think it's the best option for me and my baby."

The whites of Natasha's eyes were like twin moons. "You *are* brave. I'd be yelling for painkillers as soon as the first contraction hit. Actually forget that, I'd book a nice neat cesarean."

A trace of a frown creased Jean's brow. "I think recovering from surgery and dealing with a newborn would be extraordinarily difficult."

"My mom would help," said Natasha.

"Yeah, but that's precious bonding time you're giving up with your baby."

"I'll make it up later. Better that than the alternative."

Jean raised her brows and shoulders. "Everyone needs to decide what's best for themselves. It's great that we've got options these days, right?"

"Right," I interjected.

"Absolutely," said Natasha. "But you don't want to be too set in your decision-making. That's where Isla went wrong. Their whole plan went out the window. Like someone had just tossed a grenade into their life."

A tinge of doubt crept into Jean's frown. Dammit.

"Not that I'm planning on having children anytime soon," said Natasha, shaking it off. "I've got other things I want to do with my life."

Again with that not-quite-right smile from Jean.

"Anyway," I said, leaning back against the counter. "Enough about babies. Why don't we talk about something—"

"Personally, I think drugs are your friend," said Andre, wiping sweat from his brow. Even the Elvis hairdo seemed to be wilting thanks to the heat from his polyester suit.

And honestly, I could hit something. How often did Jean have to put up with having everyone's opinion shoved down her throat?

"Drugs are not always your friend," I said. "This wisdom comes care of years of experience behind a bar. What kind of dumbass talk is that?"

"All right," he amended. "In *some* situations they are definitely your friend. I mean, babies are tiny. But still, when you think of where they have to exit . . ."

"Again with you not having a vagina or a clue."

Andre chuckled. "And you have these things?"

"Is the costume confusing you? How much have you had to drink exactly, man?"

"Relax, Eric," said Jean in a low voice, giving my hand a quick squeeze. "It's fine."

Andre gave me a look like "what the fuck is your problem." Idiot. A muscle in my jaw had started to tic, and my eyes could not possibly have been friendly in return. It's not easy to pull off an intimidating glare when you're dressed like Wednesday Addams, but I'm pretty sure I managed it.

"I'm going to get some fresh air," said Andre, grabbing his drink off the counter.

Natasha perked up. Her gaze might have flicked to Jean squeezing my hand. "I'll come too."

"Great."

Off they went together, Andre and my supposed date and yet another might-have-been future girlfriend. Terrific.

Meanwhile, Jean just looked at me.

Next she attempted a smile. "That was a little awkward."

"People and their fucking opinions," I grumbled. "I'm so sorry about that crap they said. Maybe I should go have a word with Andre."

"No, don't say anything. They didn't mean any harm. And it's not your fault." She sighed, short fingernails tapping a hectic beat against her side. "Really, you don't need to defend me. I'm fine."

"I know, but—"

"I'm fine."

"But—"

"*Eric.*"

Okay, so she didn't want me to try and fix it. Anything I said at this point would probably be wrong, so I drank my beer. And Nell said I never learned anything.

"I can be a bit of a control freak, so what?" She shrugged. "No one thinks it's weird to be meticulous about your finances, but invest time and energy into seriously planning the delivery of your child—one of the biggest events in your life—and people think you're crazy."

I kept my mouth shut.

"If they'd really bothered me, though, I'd have shut it down or walked away. But at least they weren't rude about it," she said, staring off at nothing. "Anyway, it kind of comes with the territory. You know, I've had complete strangers stop me at the grocery store to lecture me about things or try to feel up my bump."

"Jesus."

"I realize most people don't mean any harm. But even so." She shook her head. "I don't know what it is about pregnancy that makes everyone lose their minds and think they need to get involved. Well, not everyone. Some people."

I frowned, highly pissed off on her behalf.

"But Andre and Natasha were just . . ."

"Speaking out of their asses?"

She snorted. "A little. Maybe. Yeah."

"Don't know why the concept of you making up your own mind about things is so damn hard," I said. "Idiots."

Jean ducked her head, but not fast enough to hide a grin.

What a win, I'd made her smile! Immediately, my shoulders started relaxing, the anger easing back. Around us the party kept on keeping on, music blaring and people chatting. Given that I hadn't come tonight with any expectation of hooking up with anyone, I hadn't lost anything. Though Natasha was a nice-looking woman. I couldn't help wondering what she'd have been like in bed. Bossy, probably. Which could be fun for a while.

"Why don't you go talk to her?" asked Jean.

"Hmm?"

"Natasha. Go talk to her," she repeated. "You know, before Andre and I came over, you two looked cozy."

"Nuh. I'm good right here."

She cocked her head, eyes amused. "What, you're going to waste the party hanging with the grumpy, hugely pregnant female all night?"

"Yeah, I am. If she'll let me."

"Seriously?" Little lines appeared between her brows. "I can go chat with Nell. Because I'm warning you, watching me knock back juices in between running to the bathroom to deal with my thimble-sized bladder is going to get boring."

"Boring? You kidding me? We just nearly got into a knock-down fight," I said, wiping imaginary sweat off my brow. "God knows what could happen next. If someone gets in your way when you're rushing to go pee, there'll be rock and roll wrestling in the hallway or something."

"Yes, I can totally see that happening."

"My money's on you, of course."

"Damn right it is." She cradled her belly with one hand. "You're a good friend and a good man, Eric Collins."

"Uh . . . I don't know about that." I tugged on one of my braids, then winced. "You haven't been in town long."

"Shut up. I'm paying you a compliment."

"Yeah. Okay." Maybe she was right. I had been pretty restrained when it came to thinking R-rated thoughts about the woman. Guess that was sort of a start on my path to manly betterment? I don't know.

"Anyway," she said. "Don't argue with me. I'm pregnant, I know things. Mostly about leaking bodily fluids and strange internal happenings. But I know other things as well."

"Whatever you say." I tapped my beer against her glass of juice. The faint curl of her lips held all of its usual appeal. Christ, if only she wasn't knocked up. And if I'd wished for that once, I'd wished for it a hundred times. "Happy Halloween, Jean."

"Happy Halloween, Eric."

CHAPTER SIX

It was about twelve o'clock on a Wednesday night, a few weeks after Halloween. I finished locking up the Dive Bar. With Nell off sick with a bad cold, I'd had a busy couple of days. I stayed back to catch up on the inventory and a few other jobs. Having the place all to myself sometimes was good. The bar had its own feel after closing time, with only the quiet shadows and the glimmering steel to keep me company. But I'd run out of tasks, and was facing up to the short walk home and the nightly battle to get some sleep. I didn't know what was wrong with my head lately.

Maybe I'd wind up watching late-night TV with Jean or something.

After Halloween, I'd given up avoiding the woman. Especially since her pacing the hallway and my recent insomnia often seemed to happen around the same time. A few nights now we'd wound up chatting or even hanging out for a while. Though the last time it'd happened, she'd made me chamomile tea. And it tasted like shit.

I smiled at the memory, humming a tune. A bit of Bowie, because Bowie was king despite being from England. As I switched off the last of the lights, the bar area still gleamed in the low light, polished and ready for tomorrow.

Snow drifted down as it had been doing on and off for the last week or so. I shoved my hands into the pockets of my leather jacket, hunching down to protect myself against the cold. Keys jangled, hitting the pavement. Someone standing down the street a little started swearing up a storm.

"Jean, that you?"

Bundled up in gloves, scarf, woolen hat, and a thick jacket, she stood beside her SUV, glaring at the offending key fob lying on the ground. With her belly plus all of that padding, her chances of easily retrieving it had to be nil to none.

"Let me." I jogged over and picked them up, handing them back to her.

"Thank you."

"Everything okay?"

Her face looked pale and drawn in the street lighting, her hand rubbing at her lower back. "Yeah."

"Yeah as in no?"

She started to smile, then winced. "I've had this pain in my back all day and it's getting worse. Think I might go get checked out just in case."

My blood turned to ice.

"Don't freak," she chided. "It's probably nothing."

"If it was nothing, you wouldn't look so worried and you sure as hell wouldn't be out here at this time of night."

"It's too early for it to be anything. I've still got over three weeks to go."

I held out my hand. "Give me the keys. I'll drive you."

"That's nice of you, but not necessary. You've been working all night; you're tired. Go to bed." She pressed the button, unlocking the doors. "I can drive myself."

"If you're in enough pain to need to go see a doctor, then you're in too much pain to drive. I'm taking you."

"Eric . . ."

"Remind me again how much experience you have driving in fresh snow?" I asked as the white stuff drifted down around us. If it wasn't for the stressful occasion, it probably would have looked pretty on the stray hairs spilling out from beneath Jean's hat. "Because you get this kind of weather all the time in Florida, right?"

"Ha-ha."

I just looked at her.

"I've got my bag of kitty litter and a little shovel in the back," she said. "I'll be fine."

"Eight months pregnant and you're going to push yourself out of a snow bank?" I started rubbing at my chest because no shit, the woman was giving me a heart attack. "Please let me take you, Jean. I'm not going to be able to sleep worrying about you otherwise."

She still hesitated.

"Please."

After a heavy sigh she handed over the keys. "I hate it when you're right."

"Really?" I frowned at her words. "When have I been right before?"

Busy climbing into the passenger seat, she didn't bother to answer. I carefully shut her door before heading over to the driver's side. Immediately, I got the seat warmers and heat going.

"Quick, say something terrible," she said, resting her head back against the seat. "I get weirded out when you act all nice."

I gave her a look out of the corner of my eye. "You really do look like you swallowed Saturn now."

"That'll do it," she said. "You sure you're not too tired to drive?"

"I'm fine."

Hell, seeing her out on the street, face lined with pain . . . I couldn't be more awake. Jean might even be in labor. Just the thought of it fucking terrified me. I pulled out onto the road, driving slowly enough to put a grandmother to shame. Luckily, at that hour of the night, the streets were mostly empty.

Over on her side of the car, Jean twisted her fingers together, frowning hard.

I gave her hands a squeeze. "Try and relax."

"I've been trying to relax for hours. It's probably nothing, right?"

"Absolutely," I agreed. "Still weeks to go before you start looking like a planet-swallower. But it's smart of you to get checked out just in case."

Her frown didn't ease.

"Think they'll let us hear her heartbeat? That would be cool."

"Probably," she said. "You're going to stay?"

I shrugged. "If you don't mind. I mean, I don't have to come into your exam or anything. Don't mean to invade your privacy."

"I know."

"Though I guess I could just sort of slow down near the hospital doors while you jump out. That's another option," I said, anything to lighten the mood. "You'd be up for that, right?"

"Ha. I could just roll right in."

"That's the spirit."

Never in my life had I driven with such care. Talk about precious cargo on board and conditions being shit. The snow was getting heavier. And none of that nice, light, fluffy, pretty stuff anymore. This ice meant business. Thank God I hadn't left the bar any later and missed her setting off on her own. Fuck, just the thought . . .

"She can't come yet," said Jean, stroking her stomach, looking far more relaxed. "Nell's my birthing buddy and she's sick."

"Is that the only problem? I can catch the baby, no worries."

"I'd like to see that." A bare hint of a smile graced her pretty

face. There and gone as we passed beneath a streetlight. "You realize there's blood and gore involved. And a baby."

"I have nothing against babies."

Jean winced suddenly, breath catching in her throat. "Damn."

"Your back?"

"Yeah." She shifted in the seat, trying to get comfortable. "Heat
packs only worked for a while, but I didn't want to take anything.
It'll be nothing, though. Probably just a muscle acting up or something. No way is she coming yet. I mean, she's breech."

Breech position. I frowned, forcibly wrenching up the relevant
information from the pregnancy book Joe had given me. The last
time I tried this had been high school. "So she still has to turn
around?" I asked. "Her head's facing up?"

Jean nodded. "I'm going to go talk to the specialist this
week."

Jesus. "Okay. Well, we'll be there soon and the doctors will get
you settled."

She gave a small nod while I silently throttled the steering
wheel. Not going any faster because no way was I taking any
chances. In the accident when Nell lost her baby, Joe said the car
had come out of nowhere. No fucker was catching me unawares
tonight. Still, it would be a hell of a relief to see her safely delivered to the hospital. Even in the dim light her face still looked pale
and strained. Meanwhile, all of my bravado hid a churning stomach and dry mouth.

"You've got your bugout bag, right?" I asked.

"Bugout bag? You mean my stuff for the hospital?"

I shrugged. "Yeah. That."

"Having a baby is not the end of the world." Her brows tucked
in. A hint of a smile remained, however, so I wasn't completely in
the shit. "Eric, I'd imagine the supplies required to handle an
apocalypse would be quite different."

"Not really," I said. "I mean, in both cases you're going to need underwear."

"How about maternity pads as opposed to matches?"

My smile was a flash of teeth, grabbing hold of anything to lighten the mood. "Sure. But I bet you've packed a nice warm blanket."

"A baby blanket."

"That'll do."

"I'd need to shrink by about half before it would do me any good. And I didn't pack—" Her words came to an abrupt halt as another grimace crossed her face.

Nearly there, dammit. "What didn't you pack?"

"A gun."

"That's easy," I said. "Just brain the zombies with a rattle or something."

"It's a zombie apocalypse now?"

"Is there any other?"

The sound she made might have been laughter if she hadn't been in so much pain. God, seeing her like that . . . we might not have known each other for long, but it still sucked. Why couldn't men just have the babies? Surely that'd be easier than watching someone you cared about going through this shit.

And the silence only made it worse. "So you're going to name her Erica, right?"

"Dream on," said Jean.

"Eric-arella?"

Another of those shaky laughs.

"Eric-ina and that's my final offer."

She just looked at me.

"Oh come on," I said. "That's a nice name. It just rolls off the tongue."

"You're crazy," she said, breathing heavily.

The hospital sign lit up the night like a beacon. At last. I headed straight for Emergency, crawling around the ice-slick corner. As soon as the hand brake was on, I jumped out and ran around to the passenger side. She'd opened the door and begun the awkward process of climbing out.

"Easy." I took her elbow, holding her steady while she found her feet.

"You can't leave the car here. It's an ambulance spot."

"I'm not going to," I assured her. "Don't worry, Jean. You go in and start getting things moving and I'll go find a spot."

"Right."

"All good?"

Teeth sunk into her bottom lip, she nodded.

"Be right back. Two minutes tops."

With a hand braced on her lower back, she waddled a couple of steps toward the emergency department's sliding glass doors. Then stopped.

"Crap," she mumbled, looking down.

"What's wrong?" I rushed back over to her and followed the direction of her gaze. Liquid had started pooling around her feet. A cold wind froze me, inside and out. "Tell me you wet yourself."

"No, I ah . . . that's not what happened."

"Fuck."

We rushed through the doors. Despite the circumstances, she was moving fine, but I kept one arm loose around her waist, just in case her legs gave way. Inside, a few people occupied chairs in the waiting area, the place largely deserted at this hour. Behind a big reception desk, some admin or nurses or whatever they were busily worked away on computers.

"Help," I yelled. "Her water's broke."

"Eric, calm down."

"I'm perfectly calm." I was not even remotely calm. "Somebody help!"

"She's coming early," said Jean, as if what was happening were finally hitting home. "Okay. No big deal."

A middle-aged woman over at reception gave us a patient smile. Obviously completely misunderstanding the situation. Or she was on drugs. I don't want to be judgey, but it could be either. Jean was about to push out a kid, for god's sake. Maybe the woman needed some visuals.

"She's in labor. Are you seeing this?" I pointed first to Jean's swollen middle, then to the growing puddle on the floor. Still no one started running. "Jesus. Why is she acting like this happens every day?"

"Because it does."

I just frowned. "Who should I call? Who do you want me to call?"

"Oh . . ." She paused. "No one. No point involving Nell, given her flu. Besides, I've got my plan. I'm okay."

"Hey, how are you doing?" A young woman in medical scrubs approached us with a smile. "Things are happening, huh?"

"Yeah," Jean said a little shakily.

"Contractions?"

"I'm not sure. I've had back pain all day."

"All right."

"It's not like I'm feeling any urge to push or anything."

The woman nodded. "I'm going to go get a couple of pads for you, okay?"

"That would be great." Jean gave the puddle she still stood in a foul look. "Thanks. Eric, can you please grab my bag out of the back of the car? I really need a change of pants."

At last, something I could do. And I did it with all due haste. Christ, my heart was still slamming around inside my chest. About a bucketful of adrenaline had to be pumping through my system.

All around, the snowstorm howled. Thank fuck we'd made it here without any trouble.

I quickly collected the little but tightly packed overnight bag, slammed the back of the SUV shut, and headed back in, not caring that my car was still in the ambulance zone.

"What a mess," Jean said as I approached.

"Don't worry about it."

"Bathrooms are just over there," I heard the nurse say as she returned. "You feeling okay to walk with me around to maternity?"

"Yes, that's fine." Jean searched through her bag for fresh underwear and pants, then ambled over toward the bathrooms.

"This is your first, huh?" the nurse asked as she returned to my side. Kristen, according to her name tag.

"What?" My brows jumped. "No. I'm not the father. Jean's just . . . we're friends."

"So you're her birthing partner?" asked the nurse.

I paused for a moment in the face of the official designation. But Nell was out, and in the car Jean had seemed happy enough about me being there for the event. "Yes," I said. "Yes, I am."

"Why don't you park the car then? We can't have the vehicle blocking the emergency entrance. I'll be taking her straight to maternity and you can meet us there. Annex A, level two."

I focused on the closed bathroom door. To leave Jean felt wrong, scary almost. But Nurse Kristen seemed all kinds of calm and capable. She definitely wasn't hiding a chainsaw or anything under her scrubs, so I guessed Jean would be okay with her. And medical types obviously knew shit about babies and pregnant people.

Deep breaths. "Yeah. Okay. I'll do that."

"Good," she said, wandering back to wait for Jean.

While I didn't mean to skid the wheels tearing out of the emergency zone, a little bit of smoke might have happened. Never mind. Parking the car seemed to take forever. Ditto with figuring out where they'd hidden maternity. The place wasn't a hospital so much as a giant maze. Honestly, walking into fucking Mordor would have been both faster and easier. Seemed likely the kid would be born, grown-up, and have gotten a college degree before I arrived.

I finally found the right wing and yet another reception desk. Trying to catch my breath, I said, "Hey, I'm looking for—"

"It has to be natural," insisted a loud voice from a nearby room. "I have a birth plan."

"Never mind."

The guy sitting behind the desk stood and said something, but I wasn't stopping for anybody.

Inside the big beige room, Jean lay on a bed, legs spread wide. Totally pantsless on account of the hospital gown. Thank fuck for the sheet draped over her knees. We might be friends now, but I'm pretty sure she didn't want me seeing all that. I didn't really have time to freak out further, however. Two women stood beside her, one holding a small machine to her belly. Both wore serious faces.

"Your baby's heart rate is low. We're concerned about how much oxygen she's getting," said the one holding the machine. She sounded authoritative. The doctor, maybe.

Jean's lips quivered, eyes filled with liquid.

I rushed to her side. "What's going on?"

"They want to do a cesarean," she said, grabbing hold of my hand. In her other, she held a crushed piece of paper. Her birthing plan, without a doubt. Pain creased her face, sweat beading on her forehead.

The doctor continued on, her eyes kind though her expression seemed set in stone. "As I've explained, I think it would be safest."

"You're with Miss Antal?" asked the second woman. Another nurse; this one's tag read Madelaine.

"I, ahh." My eyes drifted to Jean.

"Yes," she said, almost impatiently. She had bigger things going on than my status, after all. "He's my partner here."

And they could take that however they liked. If she wanted me there, then there I'd be. No way she should be going through this alone. I squeezed her hand.

"I realize you'd hoped for a natural birth," said the doctor. "And I understand this is a shock to you, but it's my recommendation that we proceed with a cesarean. As I said, if you agree, we'll have the anesthesiologist in shortly to do a spinal block."

Christ, it was all happening so fast.

Jean was shaking her head against the doctor's words, but her eyes were full of doubt. She looked up at me, pain and indecision wrinkling her forehead. Jesus. Things were bad if she was looking to me for advice. I wished I'd read every one of those damn pregnancy books five times, cover to cover.

It was all I could do just to meet her eyes in what I hoped was a supportive way, but I felt totally useless. Jean's fingers squeezed tighter and tighter. She could break my hand for all I cared. Grind my bones down to dust. At least then I'd be doing something.

Finally, she nodded. "All right."

"I'm assuming you want Mr. . . . ." The nurse nodded in my direction.

"Eric," said Jean. "His name is Eric and yes, I want him to come in."

"Come with me, please," directed the nurse. "We'll get you prepped."

She took me into another room and gave me a hair cover and a white coverall thing to wear. A few ties and it was covering up my existing apparel. This was a good thing—the designer jeans and flashy shirt I had been wearing behind the bar really didn't fit the occasion. I got it all done as quickly as possible. Away from Jean, I almost wanted to hurl. It was easier to be brave when she was right there needing someone to be strong and keep their shit together.

"Eric, if you're ready I'll take you in," said the nurse, reappearing.

Frankly, if we were going to wait until I was genuinely ready for something like this, it would be another twenty years or so. And involve Joe buying me another dozen books on the subject. And me getting a couple of shots of liquid courage for good measure. That last was a particularly good idea. Where was a barkeep when I needed one?

But there was no alternative, so I simply nodded, and off we went.

A green sheet hung halfway across Jean's body, blocking our view of everything from her chest down. She too wore one of the hairnets, along with a hospital gown. A heart monitor thing had been clipped onto one finger and a drip inserted into the back of her hand. I stood beside her, still not vomiting despite all the busy medical people, the sight of syringes and blades, and the smell of antiseptic. Yay me.

"Don't touch anything green," directed the nurse. I'm not sure what her name was. In fact, I don't even think I was seeing straight.

I grasped Jean's hand, my palm maybe slightly sweaty. "Can you feel anything?"

"Nothing down below," she said. "Everything's going to be fine."

"Yes."

"You don't look so good." Concerned eyes gazed up at me. "Are you going to faint?"

The doctor chuckled. "We're not picking you up if you do."

"Some hospital this is," I mumbled, before saying in a firmer voice, "I'm fine. Are they getting your baby out for you, or what?"

"Don't you worry about us," said the doctor, giving me a quick look. She wore a surgical mask, but I think a smile was happening beneath it. "You just concentrate on staying upright."

Christ. "I'm fine, really."

Jean gave my fingers a squeeze. Dammit. I was meant to be comforting her, not the other way around.

"You still haven't given me your final decision on her name." I forced a smile. "It's not too late, you can still use one of my extraordinarily helpful suggestions."

"Very kind." Her pretty face had relaxed since the anesthetics had kicked in, but worry still filled her hazy gaze. The woman seemed sort of stoned. "Can you see anything?"

"No."

Beyond that sheet, things were happening. Things I did not want to know about and definitely didn't want to see. Whatever they were talking about and doing, I blocked out. Only Jean mattered.

"You'll look after her, right? When she comes out?"

"Absolutely. Didn't I tell you about those books I read on this? I'm probably better qualified than the doctor."

Her smile was only fleeting, but it was better than nothing. "I can't move."

"I'll look after her."

She took a deep breath, eyes liquid. "Okay."

"You're going to be fine."

"Everything's going well," confirmed the nurse. "Keep her calm, Eric."

"Right, sure," I said. "Ah, how about Wilhelmena?"

"W-what?" asked Jean.

"Or Henrietta. That's a good one."

Her face creased. "Where are you even getting these?"

"Not a fan of the classics? Something more hippy, maybe?" I rubbed her knuckles with the pad of my thumb. "Like Rainbow or Sparrow or River."

No reply.

"I know! How about Moon Unit or Diva?"

"So much no," she whispered.

"Oh come on, those are Frank Zappa's daughter's names," I said. "If it's good enough for Frank—"

"Can you see her yet?"

"Not yet." I concentrated on keeping both of us calm. Nice and relaxed. Everything good. "I really think you're being too harsh on my choices of baby names."

The nurse snorted.

Jean huffed out a breath. "I don't even know who Frank Zappa is."

"He's one of the greats of American music," I said. "How can you not know Frank Zappa?"

"Don't let them take her away from me."

I nodded. "No one's taking her anywhere. Got it. Ready to hear all about the greatness of Zappa?"

She said nothing. I took that for a yes and kept talking, speaking absolute shit, on and on. It turns out that barkeeping skills actually do come in handy in real-life situations. Nonsense tumbled out of my mouth, silly trivia on Zappa's role in Deep Purple's rock anthem. On and on I went, losing track of time. There was only the professional murmuring of the medical team, Jean's worried but dazed face, and my own faux-cheerful ramblings. Two minutes might have passed, or twenty. I went on talking right up until an extremely pissed off little cry filled the air.

"Wow. She sounds mad."

"She was very happy in there," said the doctor, still busy behind the sheet. "But it was time to come out. Congratulations, Jean, you have a daughter."

"My baby," whispered Jean, her voice equal parts awe-filled and tired.

They carried the wailing baby to a table off to the side. Another midwife or doctor or whatever checked her out.

"I want to see her," said Jean, arching her neck, trying to watch everything going on.

Past the sheet, the doctor looked up. "You need to stay still, Jean."

"Here she is." The nurse arrived back and rested a tiny bundle wrapped up in a blanket beside Jean's face. "Eric, can you hold her?"

"Me?"

"You'll be all right," she insisted. "Just slip a hand under her neck to support her head and another beneath her body."

Bomb squad people probably felt this kind of fear. Oh so fucking carefully I took over control of the tiny angry person. Her little face was bright red, dark eyes accusing.

"It's okay, Ada," said Jean, tears spilling down her face. "Mommy's here."

And just like that the baby stopped crying.

"How'd you do that?" I asked in wonder.

"She knows my voice. Don't you, baby?"

"Wow." The bundle in my hands wiggled a little. But nothing else happened. "Ada, huh?"

"Yes. It was my grandmother's name."

"Sure I can't sell you on Moon Unit? Last chance."

Jean just gave me a tired smile. "Ada, meet Eric. Eric, this is Ada."

"Ada." I sighed, smiling too now. "Amazing."

CHAPTER SEVEN

"She's judging me."

Jean, lying exhausted on the hospital bed, just raised her brows. "How exactly is she judging you?"

"The look she's giving me is totally judgey." I frowned back at the baby lying in my arms. I'd been holding her on and off for hours now. Turned out, the longer I held her, the less scary it got. It was kind of silly to be afraid of something so small. Or at least, that's what I kept telling myself.

Initially, I'd been terrified that I'd drop her or damage her in some way. I'd had to remind myself it wasn't the first time I'd held something fragile and precious. The top shelf back at the Dive Bar had a bottle of cognac that was worth more than I was, and I could spin that baby over my wrist without a second thought. Not that I'd be spinning Ada, because fragile.

"To her, you are just a weird blob," said Jean. "She can barely even see you."

That might be it, unless . . . "Maybe I made a bad first impression. I think I swore. That might be why she doesn't like me."

"She likes you just fine. And I think she was probably more occupied with the whole welcome to the world thing. Highly doubt her mind was on you at all." Jean released a heavy sigh. "They haven't given me nearly enough pain meds for this conversation. You know, I just had a baby taken out of me. Why are we even talking about you?"

"I'm keeping you distracted. What sounds like narcissism is actually strategic kindness." I rocked on over toward the bed. Ada liked being rocked even if she didn't like me. "What would you like to talk about?"

"I don't know."

"Are your stitches hurting? Do you want me to get a nurse?"

"No." Another sigh. "I'm just tired and feel like crap."

"Still bummed about the delivery? I know it didn't go according to plan."

"A little, but that's stupid. I mean, she's a beautiful healthy baby."

"Jean, you're allowed to feel however you want."

"Hmm."

Guess she really had cut ties with her old life. Because she hadn't called anyone, not even her folks. I couldn't help but wonder if she thought about Ada's biological dad at all. The dude was missing out on a lot. A whole new life that he'd contributed to coming into the world. Maybe it's how he would have wanted it. The idiot didn't know what he was missing out on.

"You'd been thinking about it, planning it all, for months and then it went sideways on you," I said. "The whole thing was pretty scary. It's okay not to like how it happened."

"I guess I thought I'd just be glowing with motherhood or something by now." She lifted a hand, stroking the baby's cheek. "She is beautiful."

"She really is," I agreed. "Judgey as all hell, but the gorgeous chicks always are."

Jean chuckled, then winced. "Ow. Don't make me laugh."

"I wasn't trying to make you laugh. You just have no respect for my feelings." I turned away, hiding a smile. Don't think I'd ever been so bone-weary tired, yet so wide awake. The new mother, on the other hand, had dark bruises beneath her eyes, her face pale. Not good. "Why don't you try to sleep? I'll wake you if she needs you."

"I slept a little in recovery. I'm fine."

"Remember everything the nurse talked about," I said. "You need to be careful. This is some serious sh— . . . stuff you just went through."

"I know."

"Then there's the pee and poop thing."

"Oh my god," said Jean, color rising to her cheeks. "Can we not talk about me using the bathroom? Can I be allowed that small amount of dignity?"

"Sorry."

Jean nodded with a frown. "There's so many rules. How the hell am I supposed to avoid stairs living in a second-floor apartment?"

"It'll be okay," I said. "We'll all help with getting whatever you need."

She didn't respond.

"Lots of other people make it through this and you can too," I said. "Look at Ada. You made her! This pretty much makes you Wonder Woman in my eyes."

Her face softened.

"Hey there." Nell swept into the room, face alight at the sight of the bundle of joy. Pat was behind her, weighed down with bags of stuff and flowers. "Here she is. Hi, you gorgeous little girl. Give her to me before you drop her, Eric."

"I'm not going to drop her." Jesus. I thought about mentioning the cognac, but decided against it. Reluctantly, I handed her over. "And her name is Ada. Watch her neck, she's floppy."

"Ada—that's a beautiful name. And I know how to hold a baby, Eric."

"Hi, Pat," said Jean, giving him a vague smile.

"Nell checked with the doctor, she's not contagious or anything," he said. "But I'll stay over here just in case I am."

"Okay. Thanks."

The man leaned against the doorway, watching us with interest. Seeing Nell and me fussing over a baby had to stir up all sorts of weird shit for him. Whatever his thoughts were, however, the bushy black beard hid them well.

Nell's face crumpled. "I'm so sorry I wasn't there for you."

"It's okay," said Jean. "Turns out Eric makes an excellent birth partner."

"She's the most precious thing I've ever seen," said Nell, eyes wide. Never missing a chance to change the subject once someone is saying something nice about me.

"Isn't she beautiful?"

For a while, the two women gushed over the baby. Then Jean moved on to recounting the birth in great detail. I took the opportunity to grab a seat and close my eyes for a second. That's all it took. Next thing I knew, Pat was shaking me by the shoulder.

"Damn." I wiped a hand over my face. "Did I fall asleep?"

"You need to go home and get some rest," said Jean, busy nursing Ada. And when I say nursing, I mean breast-feeding. With breasts and everything.

I did my best to keep my eyes on her face and no lower. But oh my god, Jean's breasts. Only in my dreams had I imagined getting to see both of them, let alone a glimpse of one. And maybe it was because of the pregnancy or the body preparing for the breast-feeding or whatever, but they were as full and round as imaginable. To have my dream come true in this context was all wrong. But for fuck's sake, I was a guy who liked women. The bulk of my life I'd been taught that when given the opportunity, you looked at a woman's breasts—whether pumped-up cleavage, tantalizing half-see-through blouses, slick wet bikini tops, or (when the fates really smile on you) beautifully bare breasts. You ogled them, appreciated them, played with them, and pretty much made them your best friends. Frankly, if the girls want to show them to me, then I want to look. I'm open minded like that.

Except, not here. Not like this. This was all so very wrong.

In the end, I settled for staring at the puke-green wall over her shoulder, and tried to remember what Jean's question had been. About getting some sleep. Not about breasts or fullness or nipples at all. "Yeah, good idea."

"Are you okay to drive?"

"I can drop you back if you want," said Pat, still leaning against the door frame, tatted arms crossed.

"Nuh, I'm good."

Apparently, along with missing the initial baring of the breast, I'd also been asleep long enough for Nell to have put the flowers in a vase and for Jean to have unwrapped about a bazillion presents. Ada let out a lone wail of despair and Jean fiddled with her boob, getting the baby going again. Such pale creamy skin. I swear I didn't mean to, but it was just human nature to glance at what was going on, right?

I was going to burn in hell.

"Poor baby," cooed Jean. "It's okay."

How could it ever be considered okay to put such gorgeous breasts out on display and expect me not to look? Was I a superhero or something? No, I was not. Some days being an adult was really hard.

"You're turning red," said Nell, looking at me. "Are you sick or something?"

"I'm fine."

"Oh god." She slumped dramatically in her seat. "You're not actually embarrassed by seeing a woman breast-feeding, are you?"

Even Pat snickered.

"I am not."

Jean fussed with her top, covering up a bit more.

"Shit. Don't do that," I said. "I mean . . . I didn't mean to make you self-conscious."

"Breasts are for feeding babies." She frowned at the bed, not meeting my eyes. "You do realize that that's their primary purpose in life, Eric?"

"Absolutely," I agreed.

"I'm not trying to put on a show for you here or anything."

"I did not think that for a minute." I clasped my hands together because begging occasionally could be quite manly. Or just necessary. "I'm an animal. Please forgive me."

"Idiot," mumbled Nell.

But the hard line of Jean's mouth had softened. "Go home and get some rest."

"Yeah," I said, slowly rising out of the chair. "Will do."

"Thank you for everything," she said, gazing so damn sweetly at me. Obviously tired and in pain, she was still so damn pretty propped up on the hospital bed with her baby in her arms. The most perfect thing I'd ever seen.

And my heart hurt. It felt swollen and sore like it was about to explode. Maybe I was experiencing cardiac arrest or something. If so, totally in the right place.

"Eric, are you sure you're okay to drive?" she asked.

"Yeah, yeah. Fine." I rubbed at my chest, picking up my coat. "I'll ah . . . see you later."

Pat gave me a chin tip. Nell said nothing.

"I'll visit," I told Jean, delaying. Because for some reason, walking out the door seemed wrong. Like seriously the worst idea I'd ever had. Which made no sense considering some of the dumb shit I'd pulled over the years. Take the time I got pulled over for driving dangerously. Last time I let a girl go down on me while a car was in motion ever.

"I'd like that." She smiled.

"Sure."

Everyone just looked at me, waiting.

"Right," I said, nodding to myself. "Later."

I forced myself to march out of there. Out of her room and then out of the hospital. Every step taking me farther away from all the weird feelings Jean and the baby seemed to inspire. Jesus, it was no big deal. We'd just been through some shit together, that was all. Perfectly normal to feel a bond and get a bit emotional. But now it was time to go back to the real world. Back to my life. Hell, I was due back at work in eight hours.

Outside, I took a deep breath, the bitterly cold air like a slap to the face. Sure, I'd visit her. Absolutely. We were friends, after all.

And I meant it . . . at the time.

CHAPTER EIGHT

"Wow." I nodded, polishing a glass. "It was intense."

"Sounds it." Joe's eyes were wide. "Alex and I have talked about having kids someday, but the thought of her going through that. Of being in so much pain." He shook his head.

"The baby was real cute though . . . after they cleaned her off and everything."

My brother laughed.

"It's true," I said. "At first, she just looked like a really angry tiny red monster. Like something out of a B-grade horror film. You know those ones out of the eighties with the bad animation?"

"Maybe don't repeat that in front of anyone else, okay?"

"I won't." I scowled. Jesus. "And it was only at first. Her pint-size arms were flailing and she was screaming her head off. Once they got her cleaned up and she calmed down, she was fine."

"I'm sure little Ada appreciates your tick of approval." He smiled. "Did it help put you off sex?"

"I don't know about that. Definitely gave me a healthy respect for women, though."

"Mm."

It was near closing time, everything winding down. The Dive Bar had had a busy night. I'd slept all day, before starting my shift in the evening. Vaughan had offered to cover for me, but I knew he and Lydia had plans. Nell was back at work in the kitchen, though she'd spent half the night showing people pictures of Ada. I didn't bother looking. Seeing as the baby only had three settings, asleep, confused, and enraged, and I'd seen them all.

The last of the customers headed out into the night and Rosie locked the door. At last. I took the opportunity to pour myself and Joe a drink.

"Top shelf?" he asked. "What's the occasion?"

"We're wetting the baby's head, of course."

"Of course."

I'd no sooner rolled the first sip of whisky over my tongue than Pat knocked on the door. Taka let him in. First he headed over to say hey to Nell, then leaned against the end of the service counter, out of the way.

"Pat," I called out, setting a third glass on the bar and pouring a couple of fingers. "Come join us."

Joe shot me a look. Surprise or caution or what, I don't know.

"We're wetting the baby's head," I informed Pat once he'd taken a seat at the bar. "It's tradition."

"It's a vague excuse to drink," said Joe with a laugh.

"Whatever. Works for me." Pat raised the glass to us both. "To Ada."

We all drank. And this felt good, it felt right to try mending fences with Pat. Someone new had been born into the world today, and somehow that seemed to reset things. Anyway, after everything we'd been through over the years, it was time. No one could doubt that Nell and I had been a hell of an accident. A gigantic mistake. Whatever you wanted to call it.

"How are you holding up?" he asked, gaze serious.

"Um, fine." Weird question. God knows I've pulled off more than a few all-nighters over the years. And under much more dubious circumstances. So I was doing great. I'd even skipped some sleep to pick up a toy for Ada at the local toy shop. It would be past visiting hours by now, of course, but I was pretty sure I could charm my way past a few nurses to drop it off. "You?"

A vague smile. "Eric, you lost a child last year. And last night, you watched someone else's baby being born. I'm asking if you're okay."

I blinked, surprised. "Right."

My brother had gone strangely quiet. Fair enough, this wasn't what I'd been expecting either. But I thought it over for a minute, giving the question its due.

"I'm okay." I straightened my shoulders. "It was heavy, but it's all good. I mean . . . I'm glad they both got through it okay and there were no major problems or anything. That's what matters, right?"

"Sure," agreed Pat, clasping his tattooed hands together on the bar. "But if you needed a couple of days, no one would blame you."

Shit. This was not what I'd been expecting when I invited him over for a drink. It was stupid to bring Nell's miscarriage up. This was totally different. The time with Nell, I hadn't even been around. That was why it had happened, after all. I hadn't been there to pick up Nell after work, so Joe had had to drive her back home. But this time was different. This time when it mattered, I was there.

"I'm not too busy," continued Pat. "The parlor can close for a few days and I'll cover for you."

"Not a bad idea," said Joe. "I've got a few jobs on, but Vaughan's home for a while. Wouldn't be a bad time to take a break."

"Um, look . . ." I said, taking a deep breath. "Appreciate the thought, but I don't need any time off or anything."

Pat just shrugged.

"Sure about that?" asked Joe. "He's right. I should have thought of it myself. But no one would blame you for wanting some space. A bit of time to get your head around it. I can see if Dad could take on a couple of the jobs and join you if you wanted company."

"I don't need any fucking time off." My voice tensed, despite my best efforts to stay chilled. "Thank you, but no. I'm good."

Neither of them spoke.

"Look, can we just relax and enjoy the drink?" I asked. "Let's celebrate the arrival of little Ada. That's what I want to do right now."

"Sure." Pat took another sip. "Jean said you nearly fainted like some girl."

I snorted. "I've spent the last twenty-four hours seeing what girls can do. That's no insult, my friend."

Tongue digging into his cheek, he grinned. "True enough."

"I'd be taking every damn drug they'd give me and crying for more," said Joe. "Probably begging for my mommy. Shit like that."

"Hell," I said. "I nearly did all that and I wasn't even the one giving birth."

"To women." Pat raised his glass and we all toasted.

I cleared my throat. "But, Pat, if you pass out while Nell's pushing your baby out into the world, reasonable or not, we're going to give you shit about it for years. That's the god's honest truth."

"Forever," corrected Joe.

"Right, my bad. Forever."

"Assholes." Pat chuckled. Then he fixed me with his gaze. "It was really that intense? I mean, they showed us a documentary at the hospital class the other night. But it didn't seem *that* bad."

"Wait for the real thing," I said, voice serious. "There are no words."

"Damn," he muttered, going a little pale.

"Ah, true fear. Now you are beginning to understand." I laughed. "My work here is done."

With a dour look, Pat flipped me off. My brother started laughing too, thumping the bar with the flat of his hand. What can I say, a tired crowd is an easy one to entertain.

"You got him scared," said Joe, sipping at his drink.

"I'm not scared." The big, hairy, tattooed dude shook his head. "It's just . . . so long as Nell's okay, everything'll be fine, you know?"

"Absolutely," I said without hesitation. "And she will be. The baby too."

"Yeah." Pat shook off the worry, raising the glass again. "Guess we should drink to Jean too."

"To Jean." Joe and I tapped our glasses against Pat's and drank.

"Doctor said she and the baby should be home in a few days."

"Great," I said, but I didn't think it would be quite so soon. She just had an operation, after all. I'd been rejigging my schedule to fit a few more visits in.

"I guess you'll be going to go up to the hospital to see her tomorrow before you open the bar?" asked Joe.

"Apparently, he's quite the birth partner." Pat grinned, scratching at his beard. "Half the nurses thought he was the father."

Something squirmed in my gut. "I'm obviously not the father," I said, shuffling my feet. "Of course I'll visit her sometime. I mean, why wouldn't I?"

"Does it feel like there's a bond there now, after seeing her through the birth?" asked Pat.

"I dunno." I shrugged. "I just happened to be there. It's not a big deal."

Joe scratched at his jawline. "You think she'd have expectations?"

"Jean's not like that," I said.

"She is alone."

I scowled. "Don't be an asshole."

"Can't see her trying to latch onto him or anything," said Pat, intervening. "She's nice."

My brother didn't seem convinced. "You have to admit, man. You do have a soft spot for the woman."

"So?" I snapped. "I might have said I'd help her out, but . . ."

"You did?" Joe's eyes were wide. "Maybe Pat's got a point about you stepping back before you get too involved."

"Jesus Christ." I hung my head, bracing my hands on the bar. "Why are you making this into such a big deal?"

"Because babies are a big deal," he said. "Are you sure you're not, even a little, replacing the kid you and Nell lost with Ada?"

"*What?*"

"It's just a thought."

"Well it makes no damn sense."

"Okay," he said. "Calm down. I just know that what happened with Nell messed you up. Don't want to see you getting involved with Jean and the baby for the wrong reasons and getting hurt."

I had nothing. Absolutely nothing.

Pat just raised his brows. "Fucked if I know. Figured I'd check to make sure you were okay with everything, that's all."

I picked up a glass and a cloth and got to polishing. Anything to keep my hands busy. "I thought it was the bartender's job to hand out bullshit advice. Not the idiots on the stools. Stop freaking me out."

"You're my brother," said Joe, unrepentant. "I'm supposed to worry about you."

The silence that followed was all kinds of screwed up. Same as my brain. I didn't do complications. At least, not to this degree. Surely Jean didn't expect anything big from me. Being the first person to hold Ada after the doctor had been nice and all, but it didn't mean I needed to glue myself to her and her mom. I wasn't a part of their life, not really. Would Jean think I was? Then what if she started relying on me and I let her down?

Shit.

All Joe and Pat had done was confuse the crap out of me. I needed better friends. And why did everyone else have to barge in on the scene, with their expectations and worries and demands? Jean and I had done just fine at the hospital without anyone else there. "I think I might just send some flowers."

I gulped down the last of my drink. Why the hell Pat had felt the need to bring up the accident last year and Nell losing our baby, I don't know. "Yeah," I said, warming to the idea. It felt safer, less complicated. "Flowers are nice, right? I mean, if they're going to be home in a few days anyway there's no need to be rushing over there again."

"Sure," said Pat, looking about as convinced as my brother.

"Won't she be expecting you?" asked Joe.

"Come on." I laughed. "Jean and I are just friends, neighbors. I'm glad I was there to get her to the hospital safely and everything, but honestly, we barely even know each other. There's no need for me to be hanging around, getting in the way."

Neither of the knuckleheads in front of me said a thing.

"Probably even be weird if I kept turning up."

Joe mumbled something. It sounded vaguely agreeable.

Then Pat raised his glass again. "To you being there to get her safely to hospital," he said. "Sometimes, despite everything, things can go right."

I forced the whiskey down, ignoring the continuing weird sick swirling feeling in my stomach. Everything was fine. Tomorrow, I'd definitely order her some flowers. Problem solved. Because the fact was that whatever weird bond or whatever I'd thought I'd felt with Jean and Ada, it was just a passing thing. A part of going through the whole birth and everything with her the night before. If I started blowing it up in my head, trying to make it into something more . . . that would just be stupid. Like the woman didn't have enough going on with a newborn baby and recovering from surgery.

Nuh, Nell and Alex would be all over her, wanting to help. She didn't need me. In fact, things would probably just be awkward if I was around. Being the birth partner had complicated things. I'd been her only option for getting to the hospital and staying with her through it all. It felt like it should all be significant, but the fact is, it wasn't.

I don't fucking know. My mind was a mess.

"Maybe getting my vacation days out of the way before Nell goes off to have the kid is a good idea," I said, tightening my ponytail. It had nothing to do with Jean, really. Things were bound to get busy with Nell off on maternity leave. It made good business sense. "I'll talk to Lydia and Nell about it. See what they think."

Joe nodded. "True."

"Yeah, we'll see." I shrugged. "You know, a little time away might be good . . ."

"Nice tan," Jean said, three weeks later.

So I may have run away to California to hide for a while. Like a manly man. Or like an absolute ass, I don't know. "Did you get the flowers?"

"Yes. Thanks." She had to raise her voice to be heard over Ada's wails. She stood in the doorway to her apartment, kind of gently jiggling the baby in her arms. "When did you get back?"

"A little while ago." Two minutes, give or take a couple of

seconds. Long enough to dump my bag at my place, hear the crying, and come knock on her door. I was truly pathetic. So much for staying away. If the woman kneed me in the balls and left me crying on the floor, it'd be no less than I deserved.

"Did you have a good vacation?" she asked, voice a little cool.

"Sure, great," I said, playing it down.

She just nodded, saying nothing.

"Sorry I didn't get to say good-bye." I raised a shoulder, hesitating. "Pat and Joe didn't have much going on and were able to cover for me. Made sense to just go. Quickly. You know, business wise . . ."

"Right."

"Lydia's going to have some time off now that I'm back," I said. "It's not just me that's getting away for a while. Regular breaks make for better mental energy and everything. Particularly for people in management positions. Very important to step back and refresh yourself . . . yeah."

She just blinked.

"What's up with her?" I cocked my head, getting a look at Ada's tiny screwed-up face. "Man, she's grown."

"It's been three weeks." Jean smiled tiredly at the baby. "As for why she's crying, I think our country's current political situation is really getting to her, you know? As a woman, she feels underrepresented and forgotten. It's upsetting."

"She's a sensitive kid."

"Yeah. That or she's overtired and can't settle. Take your pick." Jean yawned, mouth splitting wide. The bruises under her eyes and general pallor of her face were disturbing. She looked seriously run-down in her yoga pants and flannel shirt. Not that she didn't also look kick-me-in-the-ass gorgeous. Funny how sometimes you can really see people properly only when they are at the end of their tether. As if all the wear and tear just strips away the superficial crap.

She stepped back. "Well, good to see you."

"I missed you two," I blurted out, then frowned.

Jean's head shot up, surprise in her gaze. "You did?"

"Yes. A lot. Much more than I thought I would."

"Oh." Her smile was slow, even a little wary. "We missed you too."

"Good. I mean . . ." My brain searched for words and came up empty. I had no damn idea what I meant.

"Why are we standing in the hallway? Come on in." She stepped back, wandering into her apartment. "Oh, wait. Scratch that. I forgot that the hallway is much nicer than my apartment."

"I don't mind. Really."

She bit her lip. "Just be warned, it would seem my neat-freak days are far behind me."

And the woman wasn't lying. Inside, the coffee table was buried beneath a pyramid of laundry, while empty take-out containers from the Dive Bar littered the kitchen counter. At least Nell was making sure she ate.

"It's bad, I know." Jean didn't sit, walking back and forth amongst it all with practiced ease. Ada kept on crying. "Everyone in the building has invested in earplugs. I hope someone thought to warn you."

"It's fine."

Another yawn.

"How have things been going?" I leaned against the wall. Easier than finding somewhere to sit.

"Honestly?" she asked, patting the baby's butt.

"Always."

"S. H. I. T."

I winced.

"She won't sleep for more than a couple of hours. At first it was because I had trouble feeding her." Jean's shoulders slumped. "She wouldn't latch on right and my nipples were like something out of a horror movie, all cracked and bloody. Also, I say 'nipples' in front of random men now. It's kind of my thing."

"We all need a thing."

This time the smile was even smaller than the last. "Now I think she's just gotten into a bad routine."

"I'm sorry."

"It's not your fault." Her eyes were bright with unshed tears. "I totally get why they use sleep deprivation as a form of torture now."

Jesus. While I'd been partying in California, having a great time despite continuing to live the celibate life for some reason, Jean had been going through hell. And I'd promised to help her. I was the fucking worst. Seriously, the woman should have slammed the door in my face.

"Unfortunately, breast-feeding was a total disaster," she said. "I really wanted it to work and the midwives and even a specialist were trying to help me, but . . ."

"You did your best."

Her gaze narrowed. "How do you know?"

"Because I know you," I said, guilt clogging up my mind. "I know you want the best for your baby and would have given it your best shot."

"Maybe. If anything, having a baby has taught me exactly how little I know. These things are meant to be natural, and I feel like such a failure. Like I should win worst mother and most useless boobs of the year awards or something." Her eyes went glossy with tears and she sniffled. "Sorry."

Ada's cries picked up in volume.

"Anyway, she's on formula now. Something needed to change and Nell talked me into giving it a try a couple of days ago." She rubbed her cheek against Ada's little head, gaze sullen. "She's still not happy, though. But at least she's putting on a little weight."

"You're both still alive and in good condition. Don't be so hard on yourself."

Jean snorted. "It does feel like survival of the fittest some days."

"Let me take her." I stepped forward, hands held out. "Please? It's the least I can do after disappearing on you. You take a break, I'll walk her around for a while."

"Oh. I didn't mean to dump my sad story on you." She took a deep breath, visibly pulling herself together. "Alex and Nell have been helping me out a huge amount. People have been really kind."

"But you need some sleep, right?"

She just frowned. "You only just got back."

Honestly, I was kind of kicking myself, wishing I'd never left. But I couldn't tell her that, it would be too weird. Hell, what about me glomming onto Jean and her baby wasn't? "I basically spent three weeks lying on the beach with my board next to me. Onshore wind and the swell was nothing. I think I caught four good waves the whole time."

"Do you surf well?"

I shrugged. Some things just come easy. "I'm better at snow-boarding."

"Right." She seemed bitter about something. "What else did you do?"

"Checked out a few new nightspots. Did the rounds, you know."

"Yeah?"

"L.A.'s always crazy good fun. Love the place."

She nodded.

"Got invited to a really great launch party for a new vodka," I said with an easy smile. "Man, they went all out. Had this amazing band, women doing that burlesque dancing, fireworks, you name it. The party didn't stop until four in the morning."

"Huh." She studied the ground. "Sounds amazing. A lot more fun than we've been having here."

Shit.

"Actually, it wasn't that good," I backtracked. "I mean, the vodka itself was so smooth it was bland. At what they wanted to charge per bottle, a total waste of money. I only drank it 'cause it was free. And the appetizers were all these weird little mushroom things. Not good."

"Mm."

"Weather was kind of average too. Basically the whole trip was crap."

She cocked her head. "Are you just saying that to make me feel better?"

"No."

The woman did not look convinced. Fair enough.

"Anyway," I said, moving things along. "Trust me, I'm rested up and ready to spend some quality time with Ada."

"You're sure?"

"Yes."

Her brows remained drawn in, gaze doubtful. "I guess we can see how it goes. If you're sure."

"I'm sure."

Eventually, carefully, she handed the baby over. Ada hiccupped, then stared up at me with big surprised eyes. After that, she recommenced sounding off about how bad she felt about everything. Apparently, this was extraordinarily bad. Okay. I'd done this holding her thing before. Everything would be fine. Nice and slowly, I lay her tummy down over the length of my arm, putting my hand on her back, all the while keeping a gentle grip on her wriggling little body. One of the baby books had suggested the position and total success. I aced it. Even if Ada was still bawling.

"We're okay here. I read some more about rocking babies to sleep. Apparently this position can be highly effective. We'll just hang out right here," I said. "You try and get some rest."

"I can't just dump my baby on you."

"Yeah, you can. I'm here now and I want to help. Please?"

"All right, if you're sure."

"Try taking a nap. If I mess up, you're just in the next room." Instead, Jean looked around. "I should really tidy up."

"Hey, you can't function on no sleep," I said. "You know that." At last she said, "Okay. All right. Just for a little while." I nodded.

"She's just had a diaper change and been fed. Come get me if you need anything."

"Got it."

A little line appeared between her brows. "Okay."

"You can trust her with me. We'll be fine."

"I know," she said. "You were almost the first person to hold her. I do trust you."

"I know where to find you if she decides she hates my company or something. I haven't forgotten how judgmental she can be."

"Sure." Not even an attempt at a smile this time. But slowly, gradually, Jean headed toward the bathroom connected to the bedroom. She looked back no less than eight times before finally disappearing inside and closing the door.

"Phew," I muttered. "I thought she'd never leave. Okay, Ada. What's the problem here?"

I rocked back and forth, softly jiggling her like her mom had. One of the books suggested babies liked a bit of pressure or firmness on their stomach, so hopefully lying along the length of my arm would soothe her a little. Hopefully.

"You need to go to sleep, baby girl."

She ignored me and bawled on.

"I did miss you," I said. "Sorry I wasn't around. Truth is, I really did have a good time in Cali. Getting away from everything for a while was exactly what I needed. Things had just gotten so heavy. But I didn't forget about you, I promise."

Small pitiful cries continued.

"Looks like you've been giving your mom a pretty hard time and you're not all that happy about the state of things either." I rubbed her back. "So what are we going to do, hmm?"

Damn she smelled good. Baby powder and soap or something.

"You know, this is pretty weird, you and me hanging out together," I prattled on. I don't know why, except that her incessant crying seemed to demand some sort of response, and speaking bullshit was all I had. "Don't take this the wrong way, but I never even wanted to have kids. Never wanted to be a father. Children only get in the way, tie you down, and they're expensive as all hell. Not really my style."

Her cries went down a bit in volume. Highly doubt her agitation had much to do with me anyway. More like she and her mom were both upset and overtired, stressing each other out. The book said that sort of loop could occur. Babies could be very emotionally tuned in to their caretakers.

"So anyway, there I was staying in the most amazing beach house. It belongs to this sort of friend of mine," I mumbled, keeping my voice low and hopefully soothing. "You wouldn't like him, he's a bit of an idiot. Though a very rich one. But I mean, he hits things with sticks for a living. How dumb is that? I'm much cooler, right?"

Apparently, Ada had no thoughts on the matter.

"So he was away on tour in Europe or something stupid. But he said I could crash at his place for a while." I stared out at the softly falling snow. "It was much warmer there. Still some girls in bikinis and everything. I caught up with a couple of friends and checked out a few bars, you know. Did a bit of shopping, stuff like that."

Ada sucked on my arm, which was slightly gross, but whatever made her happy. A thin line of drool dripped down onto my jeans.

"Nice," I said. "You're a very classy girl and don't let anyone ever tell you differently. Now, where was I? Right. My trip. So I took a look around town, hit some of the new hot spots. But this is the really weird part. You ready?"

She made no response. Still, she was struggling with how to bawl about life at the same time as sucking on my arm, so at least the volume had turned down a little.

"I just . . . I kind of panicked for some reason. Don't tell anyone this, okay? That's a pretty safe bet with you, I think." I sighed. "Like, I was worried about you guys. I wanted to see you and your mom. But I didn't at the same time. Again, don't take any of this personally."

Still no response.

"Then, see what I did? The minute I get back, I'm knocking on your door. Can't stay away." I shook my head. "Crazy, isn't it? You think maybe my mom dropped me on the head when I was little or something? Might explain a few things. Just joking, you'd love my mother. She's a great woman. I'm sure you'll get to meet her sometime soon if you haven't already."

Nothing.

"Ada?"

Carefully, I lifted her so I could see her face. Sure enough, her eyes were closed, her chest rising in deep even breaths. Amazing. I'd bored the baby to sleep. My internal pain meant nothing to the kid. This just confirmed my beliefs about not talking about life stuff. Nobody wants to hear it.

A door cracked open and Jean tiptoed out, eyes wide. "She stopped crying."

"Shh," I whispered. "I thought you were getting some rest."

"I brushed my teeth." She sounded weirdly satisfied.

"For the last five minutes?"

She nodded serenely. "First time in days. Gross, I know." Her chin tipped toward Ada. "Is she . . . ?"

"She's asleep."

"Good job," she said. "Now we have to try to put her down in her cot without waking her up."

"Why do I suddenly hear the *Mission: Impossible* theme song playing in my head?"

Jean laughed softly. The nicest thing I'd ever heard, aside from the blissful sounds of Ada not crying. "That's pretty accurate, actually."

"Babies are intense."

"You have no idea."

And it took three tries. She kept startling and waking, upset with us for trying to put her down. Hey, if I was her, I'd want to be cuddled and carried around constantly too. It was probably extremely soothing. But in the end, the baby was in her cot, eyes closed, fast asleep. I quickly gathered up the old food containers to take Jean's garbage down. Since the contents of my fridge included two beers and some moldy cheese, a food run was required. Sure, I could eat at the Dive Bar. But I wasn't ready to end my downtime, away from everyone.

Still feeling like the king of the world, I left. It was good to be home.

They cornered me the next day, right before my very first shift back. A sure sign of bad things to come. The three of us crowded into the small dingy office in the back, Lydia sitting behind the desk at the computer. Since she handled the bookkeeping, this made sense. Nell carefully lowered herself down into the seat beside me, hands laced over her growing belly.

"What's going on?" I asked, not the least bit seeming afraid because that wouldn't be manly. No, fuck that. I was edgy. Edginess was manly. "What do you want to talk to me about?"

"What do you think we want to talk to you about?" asked Nell, a ginger brow elegantly raised.

"I don't know."

"How'd things go in California? Fall off the no-sex wagon yet?"

"No, I did not." I held in the "so there." Very mature of me, I know.

"Damn, he's telling the truth," said Lydia. "I owe Vaughan five bucks."

Nell sighed. "I owe Pat a lap dance."

"You've all been betting on me?" I spluttered.

At least Lydia had the grace to look ashamed; Nell held her head high. "Yes. But that's not the reason for this little talk. Been up to anything else lately we should know about, *Eric*?"

"I don't know. Jesus." I inched up in the seat just in case an emergency bolt was required. She couldn't possibly know about me and Jean. Not that there was a me and Jean. All we'd done was hang out and I'd rocked the baby to sleep. I was innocent. Mostly.

Nell's gaze narrowed.

"What?" I asked. "What have I done? Just tell me."

Lydia slumped back into her seat with a sigh. "Nell, stop playing with him. Honestly, you are such a sadist."

The edge of Nell's lip curled up. Evil woman.

"Not funny," I groused.

"An interesting thing happened yesterday," Lydia said, fiddling with a pen on the desk.

"Nell went down to the crossroads, bargained with the devil, and got her soul back?"

Faster than the speed of light, she punched me in the arm. Bam. The woman might be pregnant, but that didn't slow her down one iota. I doubt Ali would have braved the ring against the woman.

"Ouch!"

Lydia smacked the palm of her hand against the table. "Enough. We should be able to have business meetings without insults or violence. Please."

Silence.

"Sorry," I said eventually. Because someone had to be a grown-up. Sad-ass day when that someone was me.

"Nell?" asked Lydia.

"Oh, all right. I'm sorry." She exhaled. "Let's get on with this."

The look Lydia gave us both spoke strongly of grabbing us by the ears and banging our heads together or something. Hard to blame her. She cleared her throat, setting her shoulders. "The thing is . . . we got an offer on the Dive Bar."

"What? Who from?" I asked, startled.

"A well-respected local businessperson," said Lydia.

"The owners of the resort," Nell chimed in.

My face tightened, I could feel it. Brows pulling in, forehead stiff. "Huh."

"It's a good offer," said Lydia.

"How good?" I asked. She gave me the figure and I swayed slightly in my chair. "Jesus. That is good."

Nell scowled. "My bet is they want to be top dog in town. We've established a reputable upmarket restaurant and bar so they swan on in and try to take it off our hands."

"You don't want to sell, then?" I asked.

"Do you?"

"I don't know." I thought of life without the Dive Bar. What a huge change and not necessarily a good one. "I mean, the money would be nice. Guess I could get a job somewhere else."

"The money would be nice," agreed Nell glumly. "Pat and I could buy a bigger place. Something with more room for a family, you know?"

"Yeah." I scratched at my chin. "What about you, Lydia?"

"I'm sure I could find something to do with the cash," she said. "But do we really want to give up this place?"

For a long moment, we all stared off into space, deep in our thoughts. It was a lot to take in. A lot to consider.

"What would happen to everyone else?" I asked. "Rosie and Boyd and everyone?"

"Apparently, the new owner would assess them for suitability."

"They'd lose their jobs?" I swore quietly.

"Not necessarily," said Lydia. "Hopefully, they'd be given interviews for the positions and their prior experience would weigh in. They wouldn't necessarily be out of work. But ultimately, that would all be up to the new owners. We just don't know."

"Pat's keen on the idea of me maybe taking some time off after the baby's born. Financially, I'd be able to do that if we sold." Nell placed her hands over her stomach. "Maybe stay home until our baby was ready for kindergarten. Maybe have another child in the meantime."

"Is that what you want?" I asked.

"Good question. It would be nice to have a bit less responsibility for a while. Anything would be an improvement over managing this place." It might have been my imagination, but it felt like Nell's eyes flickered in my direction.

"I'm not sure I could work for someone else again, here or somewhere else," said Lydia. "It was so horrible being at the real estate agency, having those assholes just fire me like I was nothing. Being in charge of myself, having a say in everything . . . I like it. Chances are, the first time anyone gives me crap about something, I'd tell them to get screwed."

Nell snorted. "Yeah, me too."

"So we start up somewhere else?" I shrugged. "It's an option."

"There'd be limits on our ability to do that. How soon and how close to the Dive Bar," said Nell. "They'd legally tie us up to protect their interests here. Make sure we don't steal any of the customers."

Lydia nodded.

I cocked my head. "I don't know how I'd feel about just walking away, you know? Would they let us work for them?"

"Back to what Lydia was saying." Nell pointed in her direction. "Eric, would you really be able to handle someone telling you how to run *your* bar? Telling you what you could and couldn't do?"

"You do that already."

She snorted. "Not even remotely to the extent that another actual manager would. And what if they want to make their imprint on the place, alter things, and redecorate . . . change the name, completely transform the vibe of the place?"

"You're right. This is the Dive Bar," I said, more than a little outraged. "This place has been the Dive Bar since back in the seventies or so. There's real history here. Sure it's largely cheap beer and gaudy, shameful shit. But it's still real local history."

"They'll change my menu," said Nell.

I frowned. "So? You change the menu all the time."

"It's different when I do it. For starters, I know what I'm doing." She crossed her arms. "They'll probably be like those idiots who are all, 'And here's a serving of organic chicken breast in a fresh crumb mixture served with golden potato spears and a liquid tomato salsa and a sprinkling of microgreens.'"

Lydia gave her a blank stare.

"Chicken nuggets with fries, ketchup, and a sprig of parsley on top," I said, having heard this particular rant of Nell's previously. Several times.

"Oh, right." Lydia nodded. "Pretentious assholes are the worst."

"Exactly!" Nell raised her hands. "So wrong."

"Practically speaking, though," said Lydia, "we could all get jobs elsewhere and it is a lot of money. Vaughan and I could pay off the house. That would be a huge weight off our shoulders. Go on a trip, maybe."

Nell bit her lip. "Yeah. It's a lot of children's school fees and books and everything. Eric, you could buy an even bigger and better muscle car penile-enhancement vehicle. A real chick magnet."

"Don't talk about my genitals. That makes me uncomfortable."

This made her laugh.

"So, mostly no?" asked Lydia, gaze moving back and forth between Nell and me.

I raised my brows and Nell winced. "Maybe?"

"So, partly yes?"

Again, we both hemmed and hawed.

"Okay." Lydia rapped her knuckled against the desk. "Decision made. I'll tell them we're considering the offer, but won't be rushing into anything."

Nell nodded. "Agreed. Eric?"

"I can live with that."

"If they don't like it, too bad." Lydia grinned.

CHAPTER NINE

"Thing is, I honestly don't know what I'd do with myself." It was around lunchtime, the next day. I'd spent the last twelve hours running the question over in my mind.

Jean kept on packing the dishwasher. "With all your experience, you'd be able to get another job without a problem."

"Yeah. Probably." I lay on my back on the living room rug, a cushion beneath my head and Ada lying on my chest. The perfect way to chill when I had stuff on my mind. Seemed I'd traded women and whiskey for spending quality time with a baby and her awesome mom. Even more surprisingly given my history, it was more than fine with me. "I think she's trying to gum a hole in my shirt."

"Wait 'til her teeth come in. Then she'll do your wardrobe some damage."

"Little girl, that's a Black Sabbath tour shirt you're attempting to eat," I said. Then I frowned. "Hmm. Actually, that's probably kind of appropriate, in a heavy metal kind of way. Carry on."

"Put her on her blanket under the baby gym if you want."

"Nuh, we're good." I patted Ada on the back, ignoring the dribbled-on wet patch of shirt sticking to my chest. Gross, but whatever. If you liked the baby, you could apparently put up with the weird and disgusting.

"You're not ready to try something else?" asked Jean. "Move on to a new challenge?"

I sighed. "There are times it gets boring behind the bar, sure. But everyone that works there, our regular customers, they're like family. Well, Joe *is* family. But Boyd and Taka and everyone too."

"So don't sell."

"But it's a lot of money."

"Big decision." Dishwasher packed, she stood and stretched her back, a hand to her lower stomach for support. "I'm not sure what I'd do in your position."

"How're your stitches and everything?"

"Good. The doctor's happy."

"Good."

Ada made a little grunting noise, her face creased. Next, a truly awful smell filled the air. Oh no. No, not on me. Even if there was a diaper and baby suit between me and the possibly toxic mess, it was still way too close.

"Your daughter wants you," I blurted out. "Quickly. Please."

"Hmm?" Jean wandered over, her gaze on Ada. And then her nose wrinkled. The mom's, that is, not the baby's. Ada was still busy doing her thing.

"You take her," I said.

"Ha. You're a fair-pants friend, Eric Collins." She picked up the baby, raising her to her face. "You smell bad, my darling. Are you poopy? Are you?"

In reply, Ada sucked on her fist.

I shook my head. "Jesus. I'm sorry, but that smell is shocking."

"I think you should change her." Jean smiled because she was evil. "It'll be a growth experience for you."

"No, thank you. I am a conscientious objector when it comes to growth experiences."

"Oh, come on. Be brave."

"Another time. Or possibly never. Let's wait and see."

I climbed to my feet, following them into the nursery. But at a safe distance. Not that anywhere in the apartment was safe, care of what was going on in Ada's pants. Hazmat suits would probably be required. Some emergency Febreze would also be great.

"Coward," taunted Jean, laying the baby on the changing table and getting busy. "My respect for you just plummeted."

"Come on, at least start me out on a wet diaper. Something low-key."

"Your bestie Eric is not coming through for you," she told Ada.

"Hey, come on. That's just mean."

"It's the truth."

"I let her dribble on me."

"What's a bit of spit between friends?" Jean laughed quietly, making faces at the baby. "Let's get you cleaned up."

"She's so tiny. Where did all that even come from?" I asked, mildly horrified. Okay, lots horrified. Hell.

Safer to distract myself with the newly crafted ambience in Ada's room. Farm animals had been painted on the walls. A cow, duck, dog, pig, and hen. Alex's work, I bet. The animals were over the top deliriously happy, their eyes huge and smiles wide. Maybe the grass on their farm was the special stuff. Brilliant colors splashed around the room: wooden furniture with bright yellow sheets, blankets, and stuff. It was cute.

"Shouldn't you be on a date or something instead of hanging out with us?" asked Jean over her shoulder. "Not that I object to you hanging out with us, but I'm sure you have better-dressed and better-smelling options."

I lifted a shoulder. Fact was, I'd just spent three weeks away from them and largely been fucking miserable and worried. It was the plain hard truth. As vacations went, running away to Cali had been a bad idea. I hadn't meant to change my priorities and world-view, it had just happened. Jean and Ada were important to me and that wasn't going to change anytime soon. Time to accept it. They didn't replace the baby Nell and I had lost. They were new and special in their own way. "I'd rather spend my downtime with you two. If that's okay?"

"Sure it is." Her smile was something else. If the room hadn't already been duck's-butt yellow, that smile definitely would have lit the space up. It made me feel things. Complicated things best set aside. The woman was barely getting enough sleep to string a sentence together. Me putting the moves on her would be selfish and stupid. Even I could figure that out.

"And she's good to go," said Jean, swinging the baby back over my way. She pulled at her somewhat straggly ponytail. "Would you mind hanging out with her a bit longer so I can take a shower and wash my hair?"

" 'Course not," I said. "Go for it."

"Are you going to run if she poops again?"

"Maybe," I joked.

Jean sighed. "For clean hair and a shower that's longer than a minute, that's a risk I'm willing to take."

"Go ahead. We'll be fine."

I lay Ada on the blanket under her baby gym and sat down at her side. Mostly, she waved her arms about, occasionally swatting some of the toys, and blew bubbles. No idea what the toy turtle dangling on a plastic cord had done to her, but she really gave it a whacking. Possible future in boxing for the kid, if she was willing to work on her form.

"Hands down, you're the prettiest girl I've seen all day," I told her.

She really was a damn cute kid with her chubby cheeks. It would be cool once she started to smile. The book, however, said that didn't tend to happen for a few more weeks. She hadn't been swatting away for long when I heard the front door open and close.

"Hello?" I called out, leaning over to try and check out more of the hallway.

Nell walked in, loaded down with a couple bags of food from the restaurant. Guess Jean had given her a key. At the sight of me, her two brows formed one vaguely threatening and most definitely unhappy mono-brow. "What are you doing here?"

"Visiting."

"Jean's in the shower?"

"Yes."

Her gaze flicked to the baby, because I obviously couldn't be trusted with shit. Let alone something as precious as Ada. Then she started unpacking the food and putting it into the fridge. Taking out the old containers and chucking them in the trash.

"Do you think that's a good idea?" she eventually asked.

"Me visiting?" I rose to my feet, not wanting any hint of cranky around Ada. "Seriously?"

"Yes."

I glanced back at Ada. No change there, she was still happily beating the crap out of her toys. All good. "Nell, what's your problem?"

She shot me a look. I couldn't read it.

"I know we've been through some tough times and I let you down." I swallowed hard. Jesus, just the thought of the accident and her losing the baby and everything made my knees turn to jelly. "I'm owning that. But do you really think I'm out to harm Jean and Ada here?"

"I warned you to stay away from her when she first arrived," she bit out.

"We're friends. Deal with it."

"I warned you—"

"Jesus, Nell." I hung my head. "We're not kids anymore. This isn't the damn schoolyard. You don't get to tell me who I can or can't see."

"She has enough to deal with being a single parent."

"I am not trying to add to her problems."

She huffed out a laugh. It wasn't the I'm-happy-and-having-fun type. "You don't have to try, Eric. It's just who you are."

"Christ."

She said nothing.

"Jean and I are friends. End of story," I said. "If you don't like it, I honestly don't care. That's your problem, not mine."

A muscle twitched in her jawline. "I'm just trying to protect her."

"What have I done to hurt her, hmm? Tell me."

"What you always do. Anytime the heat is on, you're out," she said. "Take just zipping off to California for a few weeks."

"Are you blaming me for being around her, or for not being around for her?" I snapped. "Make up your mind."

"You'll screw up eventually, Eric. You can't help it."

The venom in her voice . . . hell. I rocked back on my heels. "You actually hate me, don't you?"

"No, of course not," she said. "But I'm wary of you. I know you too well to be anything else. And I don't want you hanging around my friend who is young, alone, and vulnerable."

Christ. "I thought we could get along, move past all of this. But that's not going to happen, is it? Maybe we should just sell the Dive Bar."

"Maybe we should." Nell rubbed at her temples, not saying anything for quite some time. The silence was not comfortable. "Look, just promise me you're not going to hit on her or anything."

"Sure." Possibly feeling just a wee bit defensive, I crossed my arms. "I am not going to hit on Jean. I promise."

"Are your fingers crossed?"

"What?"

"You heard me."

Swearing under my breath, I held my arms out straight, fingers splayed. "I repeat. Not going to hit on Jean."

"You really think you can be friends with a woman you find attractive and not want to sleep with her? Really?"

"Yes." My jaw tensed. "I can. Jean has a lot on her plate and I want to help her. We're just friends and that's the way it's going to stay."

Her eyes couldn't have possibly gotten any wider. "God. You actually believe that, don't you?"

I counted to ten. Slowly.

"Come on, Eric, you have to admit this is unprecedented," she said. "You actually caring about anyone outside of yourself."

"You think I can't make decisions with the big head, huh?"

"I know you can't. Especially when you're attracted to the woman," she said. "And I know you're into Jean. The way you behaved when she first arrived was ridiculous. I've never seen your tongue hanging so far out of your head."

I wasn't even going to dignify that with a response.

"Well?"

"If you're convinced I'm so terrible, then why are we even talking about this?" I crossed my arms again. The whole fucking conversation got under my skin in the worst way possible.

"All right, I'll try to withhold judgement."

"Big of you, Nell."

She exhaled. "Fine."

"Fine."

Without another word, she headed on over to play with Ada. I probably should have just left. Only who knew what Nell would say to Jean about me going. Something along the lines of undependable, ruled by his penis, and out to destroy your life, no doubt. Plus, I'd told Jean I'd be here looking after the baby while she took a shower. Screw it, I was staying. The evil ginger woman would not chase me out. Jean and Ada were the best things to happen to me in a long time. Being with them made me feel good, gave me a purpose. They made me want to be better, to do better. No messing around, no sex or anything to make things confused. I was going to be someone they could both rely upon if it killed me.

Decision made.

Except then Jean came out of bathroom wearing only a towel and I really didn't expect my vow to only be friends with her to start killing me quite so soon. Dark wet hair hanging down and cheeks pink from the hot shower. A good amount of leg was on display. Though honestly, even her bare shoulders got me bothered. Nell might not hate me (and the jury was still out about that), but God sure as hell did. I reversed course and headed for the fridge, badly needing a glass of water. Also possibly a kick to the head, which I bet Nell would be more than happy to provide.

"I forgot my robe," she explained.

"No problem."

"Hi, Nell!" she called out, making a dash for her bedroom.

"Hey," said Nell.

The woman was bare-assed naked under the towel and never had I been more aware of that fact. Dammit. I was not going to look again and I was also not going to hit on her. She did have enough going on in her life. We were just friends, which was great because she needed friends, people she could depend on not to make decisions with what was in their pants. And I would be someone she could depend on.

Water gushed into the glass I was holding, my hand shaking. I drank the whole thing down in one gulp. No doubt my liver would thank me. Check me out, getting through a slightly traumatic event, like seeing Jean wet and wrapped in a towel right after I'd promised never to hit on her, without even hitting the scotch. Eric version 2.0 was already off to a great start. Amazing.

The bedroom door clicked shut, and it was safe to look up again.

"Are you okay?" asked Nell with yet another frown.

"Yep."

"Then why do you have that look on your face?"

"Gas," I lied.

"Jesus." She turned away, blinking. "Yeah, I didn't need to know that."

"So next time don't ask."

Ada, cranky about life or something, made a screechy sound.

"I hear ya, girlfriend," I murmured.

"What?" asked Nell.

"Just agreeing with Ada."

Nell nodded. "You are intellectual equals. For now. She'll eclipse you soon, though."

I don't even bother saying "whatever." No point.

By week four of Ada's existence, Jean was about ready to climb the walls. I knew this because she told me so. Repeatedly. Venturing out into the real world was required. She settled on grocery shopping since the only thing in her fridge was food from the restaurant and even great food repeated got boring after a while. Also, some Christmas shopping needed to happen. The big day was only a few weeks away. She'd been all set to go on her own, but I managed to sweet talk her into inviting me along.

"I just feel that you're stereotyping her," I said as we wandered down the grocery store aisle.

"Eric, for the hundredth time, I don't care what you think of her outfit." Jean pushed the cart along like a woman on a mission to buy just about everything. Mostly fruit, vegetables, and ice cream. A good cross section, really. She had my full approval. Not that it was required. "I think it's cute."

"I'm not saying it's not cute." I stopped and waited as yet another woman cooed at Ada. The kid was a girl magnet, I kid you not. Also, I was going through a dry spell. Hell, let's call it what it was, a desert. I was crossing the sexual equivalent of Death Valley, my libido dragging itself through the hot sands. Not even sure why exactly. Something just kept stopping me from following through on getting down with someone. Maybe Eric 2.0 needed to stop and take stock. Get his shit sorted on his own with no distractions. While still keeping his commitments to Jean, Ada, and work, of course.

God, all of this deep thinking hurt.

"She's more of a tiger than a rabbit, you know?" I said once I'd caught up to Jean again. If anything, she seemed amused by the attention Ada and I were getting.

"Did you get her phone number?" asked Jean.

"Hmm?"

"Your new friend." She nodded to the curvy redhead still watching us from over by a citrus fruit display. "You did, didn't you?"

"No." I frowned. "I'm here to help you, not cruise for chicks."

"And complain about Ada's bunny suit."

"I'm offering valuable parenting advice. That counts as helping."

"How's my precious girl?" Jean leaned in, giving the baby currently attached to my front by some crazy harness contraption a kiss. I didn't take the opportunity to sniff Jean's hair, because that would be weird and creepy.

Coconut scented, though, if you're wondering.

"She slept almost a full five hours in a row last night." Jean sighed. "I feel half human."

"I thought I noticed something different about you this morning. You look . . ." What did *just* a friend even say in this sort of situation? That was the question. Everything that normally would have come out of my mouth could easily be misconstrued as a come-on. Which it normally would be. These were difficult, trying-as-all-hell times. Truth was, I'd never seen her look anything less than gorgeous. No matter how tired or messy-haired she got. The woman made my knees weak. But friends probably didn't tell each other stuff like that. "You know . . ."

Her smile was hesitant, waiting.

"Good. You look, yeah, good."

"Thanks."

"But back to these . . ." I held up the pair of fluffy ears attached to Ada's seriously stupid bunny snowsuit. Despite needing every and any distraction, I was pretty offended on the kid's behalf. "Do these say warrior princess to you?"

"Isn't she a little small to be kicking butt?"

"But it's the message you're sending. She should be in like a wolf suit or a dragon costume or something."

With a smile, Jean held Ada's hands. "Fine. Whatever. You dress her next time."

"All right, I will."

She laughed. "Can't wait to see that."

"Why? It's not that hard, is it?"

Jean just shrugged. "I'm sure it'll be fine. Big capable guy such as yourself should have no trouble getting her into her suit. Especially when she's in a foul mood and throwing a tantrum. It's really fun then."

Ada's little feet swung around, one hand waving while the

other got sucked on. When she was all chill and cute, it seemed hard to believe she could ever be all "hell hath no fury."

"Hmm." I tucked the ears back so they didn't hang in her face. "I think your mommy's being mean to me about this whole suit thing, Ada. And I was only trying to stick up for you."

"Not even remotely. Rest assured, you'll know when I'm being mean to you, Mr. Collins." Jean raised an eyebrow. Never had a woman holding frozen chicken strips looked so hot.

Whoa. I stopped, licked my lips. "Will I now?"

"Mm-hmm." With five solid hours of sleep under her belt, she seemed a little more back to being herself. The charming young woman who had swanned into the bar a few months ago.

"Why would you want to be mean to me, when I live only to serve you and Miss Floppy Ears here?"

"Oh, do you now?" she asked, going heavy on the disbelief.

"You know I do."

Jean shot me a megawatt smile this time.

We were not flirting. We were doing something else. Something that felt a shitload like flirting, but wasn't. Because we were just friends. And hey, I'd only been stating a simple fact. "I, ah, did meet someone last night at work who I wanted to tell you about."

Jean's smiled disappeared. "Yes?"

"Her name was Caroline and she's a single mom like you," I said. "She had some interesting ideas for helping Ada go to sleep. About using light to signal that it's bedtime. Basically, lots of sunlight during the day, then use the dimmers at night when you want her to settle."

"Okay," she said slowly.

"You're already putting her down when she's drowsy instead of asleep, so we knew about that one. Same with the baby origami so she doesn't twitch and startle." I put my hands under Ada's little sock-covered feet. She liked pushing against something, test-ing her strength. "But Caroline also suggested avoiding eye con-tact during midnight feeds so you don't stimulate her."

"You talked about baby bedtime routines with a random woman at the bar?"

I shrugged. "Yeah. She was very nice. Gave me her number in case you wanted to reach out."

"Um, I don't think it's me she's hoping will reach out."

"Of course it is."

Jean laughed. "Since when in your experience have women talked to you in the hopes of finding baby playdate friends?"

"Hey now," I said, "just because I'm delightful and ridicu-lously good looking doesn't mean every woman I talk to is only thinking about what I can do for them in bed."

"Hmm."

"You don't constantly think about us having sex, do you?" I asked, already knowing the answer. Because Jean might have flirted with me at first, but those days were long gone. "I rest my case."

Her mouth opened, then closed, her brows drawing closer to-gether. "I'm too tired to think about sex."

"Exactly."

"Besides, look what sex did to me." She stroked Ada's cheek with a finger. "It gave me this beautiful, wonderful, incredibly high-maintenance baby girl. Excuse me if I take a break from all things naked and horizontal for a while. I only just got to stop sharing my body with a little being. I'm not sure I want to open it up to anyone else anytime soon."

"Fair enough," I said. "Now stop saying 'sex.'"

"You stop saying 'sex.'"

"I swear, it's all you ever think about, you ladies."

More laughter. "No, I think about diapers and milk and laundry.

It's a very glamorous life having a baby. God knows how people deal with more than one. They should be given gold medals and cookies."

I grinned.

"Hey, I thought it was you guys," said Andre, wandering up alongside us. He nodded at my chest. "Got something on your front there, man."

"Yeah, thanks," I said drily.

Ada waved her chubby fist and he grinned. "Hey, bunny girl. Cool costume."

Jean gave me a look like, "Andre likes the outfit" so I gave her a look like, "that really just makes my point." And then he had to go and do it. He leaned in and kissed Jean on the cheek. Give me strength. If it had been the baby, no worries. But I didn't even get to kiss Jean on the cheek and we were like besties these days. When I wasn't at work, I was helping her out with whatever she needed. Be it taking out the trash, doing dishes, or hanging out with Ada so she could get stuff done. Hanging with her and Ada was my new happy place.

But as for this whole face-kissing thing . . . fucking outrageous. Andre was seriously crossing a line. Where was Nell to lecture him when he needed it, huh?

"How are you doing?" he asked in a much warmer voice than was required. Making my hands curl into fists.

"Great," said Jean, smiling on. "How about you?"

"Better now that I've seen the two cutest girls in town."

Gag.

I grabbed Ada's cloth out of my back pocket and wiped her chin before an impressively long line of dribble could hit the floor. Obviously, she was as unimpressed by Andre's hustling as I was. The girl had taste.

Jean and Andre chatted for a minute, while I distracted myself by quietly singing Ada some Janis Joplin. "Me and Bobby McGee" was our go-to track, though she also enjoyed "Mercedes Benz." "Cry Baby" would have been too obvious, plus possible subliminal messages that wouldn't end well for anybody. I didn't really know any proper baby songs, but she didn't seem to mind. Jean didn't seem to mind either. She always told me not to stop on her account. And the other day I heard her humming "Mercedes Benz" to Ada as she changed her diaper. Classic rock was everyone's friend. Forget Mariah Carey and her Christmas carols playing over the store's speakers.

"Right, Eric?" asked Andre.

"Huh?"

"She should come to the bar's Christmas party next week," he said. "Jean and the baby, right?"

Jean grimaced. "I don't know . . ."

"Come on." Andre grinned. "You can both be my dates. It'd be an honor."

My heart stuttered. I swear, it stopped for like a second or something. She had been getting cabin fever lately being stuck at home with Ada all the time. Given the frosty weather conditions, it wasn't like even going for a walk was easy.

"It is just downstairs and there'll be plenty of people to help look after Ada," I said.

A kind of light came into her eyes. Excitement, perhaps. "You think?"

"Sure. You should come."

Later I'd kick myself for not asking her before Andre. Later.

"It'll be fun. You'll have a good time," I rambled on. "Stupid of me not to have asked you already. We've just been so slammed at work with all the Christmas party bookings and everything. Damn."

"Snooze and you lose," quipped Andre. Never had I wanted to

kill a friend quite so much. Strangle him with tinsel or something equally fitting for the festive season.

"Okay," said Jean, still a little hesitant. "That would be great. Thank you. We accept your kind invitation."

"Excellent." Andre leaned down and kissed her on the cheek again. Bastard. "I've got to keep going, but I'll see you later."

"Bye." Jean stared after him, wistfully or something. Whatever it was, I didn't like it. "Eric, wasn't that nice of him?"

I grunted.

She slipped one of her fingers into Ada's tiny grip. "We've got a hot date, baby girl."

I was going to smother the son of a bitch to death in his sleep. Either that or insist he join me on the celibacy wagon. Death or abstinence, the man had a choice.

All right, so maybe there was a little jealousy. Maybe Nell was right that I sucked at being just friends. But I gritted my teeth and held back the venomous snipe at Andre burning on the tip of my tongue. Fake it 'til you make it and all that. One thing was for certain, this personal growth thing hurt.

"Come to my folks' place with me, Christmas Day," I blurted out. "You should . . . yeah. No reason to spend the day on your own. Mom would love having you and Ada there. Also, she's a great cook."

Her mouth opened.

"I mean, Dad's a bit of a downer, but you just ignore him. Grumpy old bastard. I mean, if they ever flicked the switch and sent up nukes, he'd probably be like,"—I lowered my voice—" 'about time.' "

"Oh, Eric, I—"

"We should do this. It'll be great. Please?"

"We've already got plans," she said with a wince. "Sorry. Nell already invited us to spend the day with her and Pat. Lydia and Vaughan."

Shit. Too late again.

"She did?"

Jean nodded. "Sorry."

"No worries." I smiled at her so hard my cheeks hurt. "I mean I think it's great that you're getting out and having some fun. Better that than climbing the walls."

"Me too," she said. "This whole mommy business kind of takes over your life, becomes your whole identity. I love Ada. But it'll be good when there's a little room for me to be me too." She paused, frowning a little. "God, she's only a month old. Does that sound completely awful of me?"

"No," I said simply. Honestly, I could hardly get my head around how much of her life Jean had been willing to put on hold. It was almost scary what some people were capable of doing.

The smile she gave me was slow and it spread across her entire face. More beautiful than any dawn I'd ever seen. All I could do was stare dumbstruck at her magnificence.

"Thank you," she said.

I gave myself a little shake. "Hmm? For what?"

"For being you."

"Oh. You're welcome."

Maybe I wouldn't kill Andre. At least, not just yet.

CHAPTER TEN

Lydia and Alex had teamed up to do the Dive Bar's Christmas decorations, spray-painting small tree branches silver and suspending them from the ceiling. Matching paper stars and twinkling lights dangled down among them. We'd gotten a lot of great feedback from customers. It was pretty seasonal-forest spectacular.

"Another jug of the pomegranate martini and two more brandy alexanders," ordered Rosie in her jaunty flashing Santa hat.

"Sure you don't want me to take over?" asked Joe, leaning against the bar.

"No." I shook my head, making my dumbass antlers shake. "Go relax."

Better to stay busy. It kept my mind off how cozy Andre and Jean were looking, chatting over at the long table running down the middle of the room. Generally, Andre was a couple of dates, then move on kind of guy. A few months at most, maybe. Jean deserved . . . no, she needed more than to be some momentary distraction. Also, the woman looked damn good. She'd put her long dark hair up in a bun and wore a red sweater dress. Seasonal yet sexy. No matter how hard I tried to keep my eyes on the job, my gaze kept wandering back to her.

I rubbed at my chest with the heel of my palm. "We got any history of heart problems in the family?"

"Don't think so," said Joe.

Weird. I should probably ask Mom.

Meanwhile, Nell was entertaining Ada. We'd pulled a high chair up to one of the tables in the main dining room, and Ada was soaking in the atmosphere, looking wide-eyed at the ceiling decorations. Boyd stayed in the kitchen, keeping the food coming. Socializing wasn't really Boyd's thing and I could relate. Behind my bar, things just felt safer. I knew where I fit in the whole scheme of things, throwing around bottles and shit, keeping my hands busy filling orders. And it wasn't like Jean or Ada needed me. They were both perfectly fine and having a great old time.

I should be happy for them both. Hell, I should be delighted.

"Got it pretty bad for her, huh?" Joe looked over his shoulder, checking out Jean.

"What?" I sputtered, spilling cream on the counter. A quick wipe and all better. "The fuck you talking about?"

"You realize Andre would back off if you just told him you were serious about her." My brother scratched at his beard. "If you are serious about her. Are you?"

I coughed out a harsh laugh. "When the hell have I ever been serious about anyone?"

"Good point," said Joe, leaning in. "So why are you looking so damn miserable?"

"Well, apparently my little brother's turned into the neighborhood gossip or something. It's got me down."

"Fuck off. I'm being serious."

"Me too."

He scowled. "You're a moody little bitch when you're not getting any. You know that?"

"Don't you talk about her that way," I said, getting angry.

His face cracked open on a smile. "Christ, I wasn't even talking about Jean. I meant you in general, knucklehead."

I ignored the idiot and kept on working. Cream, cognac, crème de cacao, and a sprinkle of nutmeg on top. All good. Oh shit, Rosie had said two. I grabbed down for another martini glass.

"Putting your dick on ice doesn't seem to agree with you," he unfortunately continued. "It's been a while since I've seen you leave here with a woman. You spend all your downtime with Jean and the baby these days."

"I like spending my time with them," I said. "Why don't you worry about your own life?"

"But you've been acting weird for a while, now that I come to think about it." The nosy bastard picked up a toothpick and stuck it between his teeth. "At first, I figured Nell was just driving you nuts. Now . . . something's seriously off and I think I know what it is."

"Ooh, please tell me. I can't wait to hear your wisdom, gossip girl."

He grinned. "You're in love."

Jaw hanging open, I could only stare.

"It's written all over your face," he said. "Every time you look at her I'm surprised you don't start drooling like the baby."

"What's happening over here?" Alex asked, as she leaned against Joe's back, slipping her arms around his waist and squeezing. "Boys, why the frowns? Show me some Christmas spirit!"

"Ho ho ho," said Joe, copping a feel of her ass.

"That's better." His slightly inebriated girlfriend grinned. Next came the tongues and mouths and . . . oh god, I didn't need to see this. Plus, it was unprofessional.

But that was love, them being all stupid and gooey about each other. Jean and I weren't like that at all. Speaking of which, I accidentally glanced her way again, catching her eye. A quick friendly smile and back to work I went. Yeah, everyone could just mind their own business about us. Nothing to see here.

"You're full of shit," I said to my brother. "This conversation's done, Joe."

He licked his lips, holding back the chuckles. Asshole. "Yeah, okay."

"You're wrong."

"Am I? Guess we'll see."

"Excuse me, babe." He gave his girlfriend's arm a pat then rose from his seat and came around behind the bar to take over. "Go talk to her, dude."

"Her being Jean?" Alex asked, taking a sip of Joe's beer. So great that she could join in the conversation.

"We were just discussing the big issues," said Joe. "Life, love, shit like that. You know. . . ."

"Shit like that? You're an absolute charmer, babe." Her nose delicately wrinkled. "Very well, continue on."

"Let's not," I said.

Bad enough my brother felt the need to get all up in my business and start discussing feelings. If Alex started in on the topic, we might be here all night doing quizzes in women's magazines and talking over sad moments from our childhood.

She made a humming noise and turned, looking over to where Jean and Andre were happily chatting again. With half a glass of red wine in her hand, Jean looked happy, relaxed. Which was great. It wouldn't hurt Andre to sit back a little and give her some breathing room, though. Jesus. Talk about being in her space.

"They make an interesting couple," said Alex.

"I don't know," said Joe, making up a jug of pomegranate martini. "Andre's probably just being a good neighbor."

"You don't think he's serious?" I crossed my arms. "Why, because she's got a baby?"

Joe nodded.

"Not so sure about that," said Alex. "I think Eric might have some competition."

"They're just friends. My big brother's reformed," stated Joe. "In case you haven't noticed."

Jesus. Pretty sure a lobotomy would hurt less than listening to this. "I'm taking a break."

I slid behind my brother and got out of there pronto. Fresh air was required, no matter how freezing. Chatter and music filled the room, everyone busy having a good time. No one would miss me. From the rack by the door, I grabbed my coat and slipped outside into the butt-chapping winter wonderland. Times like this, I missed smoking. A good excuse for just stopping and getting my thoughts in order. Not that dying from messed-up lungs would ever be something I was in any way interested in, but you get what I mean.

Nothing much moved on the dark empty street. The sounds from inside were muted, the candles on the tables glowing. Too much was going on inside for me to think straight.

Neither me, nor Nell, nor Lydia, had raised the subject of the offer to sell again. Not really. We'd been tiptoeing around it, pretending it wasn't in the back of all our heads, taking up space. Everyone had been so busy with the Christmas bookings it'd been easy to avoid the subject. Next came New Year's Eve and that always drew a big crowd. Things usually quieted down during January so I guess we'd talk it out then. Maybe. The thought of scattering our patched-together family set my chest to hurting again.

The door opened and Jean stepped out, pulling on her coat. "Hey there."

"Hi. What are you doing out here?"

"Actually, I came out here to ask you that question." Her breath frosted the air, cheeks pink from the heat inside and maybe the glass of wine. "Everything okay?"

"Sure."

"You weren't about to make a phone call or something, were you?" she asked with a faint smile. "Am I cramping your style?"

A sudden urge flared in my mind to lie about some booty call with some hot girl. Better that than for Jean to think I was just standing out here all alone for no reason, like some loser. But I pushed the urge aside. "Cramping my style?" I echoed. "You're the one out on the hot date."

Her puffy turquoise jacket covered her from neck to knee, but she still had to be cold. "Why don't you head back inside? It's freezing out here."

"Soon," she said.

"Ada's dealing with all the noise well."

"I think she's loving the attention." Jean looked through the window, watching Nell hold the baby while Pat had an apparently very serious conversation with the small child. "I worried you were going to give me crap about her reindeer suit."

"Nuh, reindeers have antlers. They can be fierce." I tilted the soft foam antlers on my head in her direction. Kind of underlining my point.

"Ah." She laughed, then sighed. "Are you thinking about the offer for the bar?"

"I was, actually."

"Come to any decisions yet?"

I shook my head. "No, I haven't."

"Sure you're not tempted to sell and buy a bike, hit the road?"

"I'd freeze my ass off doing it this time of year."

Jean looked to heaven. "How about a car then? A very fancy, fast, and cool car?"

"I don't know." I ummed and ahhed for a minute. "Not a bad

idea. But I don't think so. Funny, I always dreamed about getting out of town, heading for the West Coast and living in a big city. Do big things."

"And now?"

"Now, not so much," I said. "The three weeks I spent in L.A., they honestly weren't as great as I'd hoped they'd be. Maybe I've grown out of the bright lights and getting lost in the crowd thing, you know?"

"Yes. I know."

"Or maybe I'm just slowly turning into a grump like my dad. Probably start yelling at people to get off my lawn any day now."

She laughed.

"If we did wind up selling, I think maybe I'd open my own place."

Her smile held a hint of sly. "Be the big boss for real, huh?"

"You know it." I smiled back at her, ignoring the tinge of embarrassment over remembering the shit I'd told her about being sole owner when we met. That was months ago. Things had changed. Mostly. "Though it might not be enough money for that. Also, there could be legal complications over going into competition. Anyway, are you having a good time? How's your hot date going?"

"Great."

"Good." I stared at my brogues. "Yeah . . ."

From inside came the faint sound of a baby crying. Jean turned to go. "She's must be getting tired. I know I am."

"Did you want me to go?" I offered. "Might be able to get her to chill so you can hang out with Andre a bit longer."

"That's okay." She huddled down in her coat. "It's nearly nine-thirty. Way past our bedtime. Well, our official bedtime anyway."

"Okay."

Her smile was soft and pretty as she slipped inside and went straight to Ada. Andre gathered up the baby bag, ready to walk them home. It was weird seeing another man step in, doing the things I normally did for her. Honestly, I fucking hated it . . . big-time. My hands curled into fists, jaw rigid as I watched from outside. People waved and blew kisses, wishing them a good night. Nell probably loved seeing them together. And I wanted to be happy seeing Jean have a good time. But it just wouldn't stick.

If my antlers had been real, Andre would have been in serious trouble.

Christmas and New Year's passed in a blur. First came the traditional Christmas Eve showing of *Die Hard* with Alex joining Joe and me for our yearly ritual. Followed by Christmas Day with the folks. Dad didn't grumble about the state of the world too much and Alex got Mom tipsy, resulting in her telling all sorts of funny stories from when Joe and I were little. Like the time I found out people got wrinkles as they got older and promptly told the sweet old lady next door she was about to die. Clearly I'd always been a hit with the ladies. Altogether, it turned out to be not a bad day. I tried stopping by Jean and Ada's place a couple of times, but my timing was off. They were either resting or out at Nell and Pat's.

The Dive Bar was packed for New Year's Eve. It was insane. Even with Vaughan, Joe, and me all working nonstop, the line for drinks was steady. I staggered up the stairs to home in the small hours of the morning, dead on my feet. Only to find Andre making out with some woman in the hallway that led to my room. That led to Jean's room.

For a moment, I thought he had Jean up against the wall, and my heart seemed almost to stop. But her hair was blond, and she was the wrong height.

Fright turned to anger.

"What the fuck?" I hissed, keys in hand.

"Huh?" He lifted his head from the smiling blonde's neck. "Hey, Eric. Good night?"

"We need to talk."

Pained lines filled his face. "Now?"

"Right now."

The blonde was petite and thin, yet missing all of Jean's curves. Sure, she had a nice face. But where was the character? Jean's sharp nose and wide lips were way more interesting. Andre was a goddamn fool and kicking his ass sounded like a fine way to end the night.

The man licked his lips, fussing with his own keys for a minute to get the door open. "Sorry, Christina. Mind waiting inside for me? I won't be a minute."

"Sure." She shot me a look of displeasure. Whatever.

Once she was gone and the door closed, Andre stood tall, hands on hips. "What's the problem?"

"What's the problem, seriously? How about Jean?"

His brows jumped. "That's why you're cock-blocking me?"

My muscles turned to stone. I was going to kill the shit.

"I escorted her to the Christmas party, yes. You know Jean and I also had pizza together the other night too," said Andre, smoothing back his hair. "Does that mean we're married now?"

"It means you need to show some respect."

"How am I disrespecting her?" He held his hands wide. "She's nice and I like her. Don't even mind the kid, for that matter. But Jean and I are friends, Eric, that's all."

"Does she know that?" I asked.

"Yes."

I just stared at him.

"She's not interested in me like that."

"Hang on," I growled. "Did you make a move on her?"

"No, of course not." He seemed pretty certain and a little

pissed off. Made two of us. "Eric, I think I'm old enough to tell if a woman's into me or not. Though I wasn't looking for anything when I asked her to hang out."

"Then why did you?"

He shrugged. "She's on her own, doesn't know a lot of people. Seemed like the right thing to do."

Meanwhile, the muscles in my jaw and neck felt tight enough to break. "You sure?"

Andre hung his head for a moment, exhaling hard. "Jesus, I had no idea. You really need to talk to her sometime soon."

"About what?"

"Don't try that shit with me," he said, gaze fixed. "You've had your head messed up about her ever since she arrived."

"She just had a baby."

"Didn't stop you from imagining she and I were suddenly joined at the hip, did it?"

Huh. Sort of true. Or definitely true. One of those.

"I sympathize, man. I really do." He put his hand on the door. "But I also have a beautiful woman waiting for me to take her to bed. So you and your problems are going to have to wait."

I hesitated.

"Go and sleep. You need it," he said. "And dude, maybe you should seriously think about getting laid. You've made your point to Nell and the rest of them. It might help you relax."

"Maybe." God knows, just like the song said, masturbation had long since lost its thrill. But now I was pretty much confused about fucking everything. Besides being exhausted. "You're definitely not hurting her by doing this?"

"Not even a little. Night, man."

"Morning."

The douchebag wiggled his fingers bye-bye before disappearing inside his apartment. I lingered in the hallway, lost in my thoughts. Soon enough the sound of feminine giggles and moans started up. And I stood outside his door listening like a pervert. Nice. Though it was probably as close as I would be getting to sex anytime soon, what with my fascination for all things Jean. Fascination wasn't an emotion. It wasn't love or anything. It was just like . . . you know, a thing.

I trudged into my apartment, slipping off my tiepin and unknotting my tie, tossing them on the sideboard. If you couldn't dress up for New Year's, when the hell could you? Next, I toed off my boots and socks, then just kind of gave up on life and getting undressed and fell into bed. Stone-cold sober and alone at the end of one hell of a New Year's Eve party. These days, I barely recognized myself. What a sad sap I'd become.

On the other hand, Andre and Jean were just friends. Excellent news. I fell asleep soon after with a smile on my face.

"It's also her seven-week birthday tomorrow," I said.

Jean looked from me to the bear and back again with Ada gurgling on her shoulder. Hard to tell if she was stunned or pissed. The mom, not the baby. Ada seemed fine about the whole thing and enjoying her midmorning awake time. Though to be fair, Ada had trouble focusing on anything more than a foot away, so probably couldn't even see the problem.

"That's worth celebrating, right?" I smiled. "Jean?"

Her lips parted but no words escaped.

Shit, she wasn't buying it. So I might have gone a little overboard with Ada's Christmas present. How was I to know? This was my first time having anything to do with an infant. Women you could get flowers. So long as you aren't cheap, they're happy. All good. But babies are trickier and I wanted to make an impression. A good one, though.

"It's bigger than her nursery," said Jean, eyes still wide with shock.

"Sorry."

She exhaled. "No, Eric, it's great. Incredibly generous of you. I just . . ."

"A nine-foot-tall teddy is a bit much, huh?"

"Just a little. Not that it's not beautiful."

We both stared at the big fluffy bastard sitting in the corner of her living room. I'd smuggled him into the apartment when Jean was changing Ada in the nursery. Though maybe "smuggled" was the wrong word for something that had to be squeezed through the door. He did kind of take up a lot of space. Oops. "A bit too big."

She nodded. Then she started quietly laughing. "That's the largest teddy bear I've ever seen in my life. I mean . . . it's ginormous. Where do you even get something like that?"

"Ordered it online. I might have gotten a little carried away," I said. "Just wanted her to have the best."

Jean's eyes went all soft and sappy.

"No big deal," I said.

"It's a huge deal. You're very sweet, Eric."

Jesus. I shoved my hands into the pockets of my jeans feeling awkward as hell.

"Is it wrong that I feel like someone needs to make a joke about size?" she asked.

"Later," I said. "Not in front of the baby."

She snorted and kissed Ada's little head. Over on the table, her cell started beeping. "Do you mind?"

I took the baby, getting my first cuddle in ages. "Hello."

Ada stared up at me with her big eyes.

"You know I was reading the other night and the book said you should be seeing things better soon," I told her. "Your fingers will be opening too. What do you think?"

She whacked me in the chest with her tiny fist.

"Don't worry, you'll get there."

Over by the table, Jean had her cell up to her ear, listening. "No, Mom, it's fine that you called."

Anxiety seemed to be flowing out of the woman in waves. If her parents upset her any more I'd have a few things of my own to say.

"Yes, I realize that Grandma leaving me everything upset you," said Jean, her lips a tight line. "Threatening to sue me kind of made that point."

Uh, this was not good.

"Challenging the estate was attacking me, Mom." She sighed. "All right." Pause. "I appreciate the apology. It was an emotional time for all of us." She listened again. "Ada's doing great. I mean, it's hard, working out her sleep routine and everything. But the doctor's really happy with her growth and weight. She's beautiful, amazing. I wouldn't have changed having her for the world." Another pause and her brows rose. "Of course, I'd be happy to send you some pictures."

In my arms, Ada started fussing, kicking her little feet and sucking on her fists.

"What's up, Ada?" I mouthed.

The good thing about babies this age is that there are generally only five things that set them off. Either they're hungry, need a diaper change, are bored, need burping, or are tired. Fuck if I knew which one had her upset, however. So I settled her on my shoulder and gently patted her back. Amazingly enough, the crying stopped.

"Mom, I have to go. I think Ada's ready for a nap." She listened, biting on her lip. "Okay." A pause. "No, I would like to hear from you again." She shot me a smile. It still seemed a little strained. "I'll talk to you later then. Bye."

"You all right?" I asked, rocking from foot to foot to keep Ada happy.

"That was a surprise." Jean headed toward the kitchen to grab a drink of water. "Things were so bad when I left Florida, I honestly didn't know if I'd ever hear from them again."

"It'd be their loss," I said. "Missing out on having a wonderful daughter and granddaughter in their lives."

She shot me a grateful smile. "Thank you."

Ada lay still, slumped over my shoulder. "It's the truth. Shall I put her in her crib?"

"Yes, please," said Jean, heading for the short hallway. "The Eric magic works again."

"My conversation can put anyone to sleep," I said modestly. "It's just one of my many gifts."

Carefully, I followed her into the nursery, and laid Ada on a light blanket so Jean could wrap her up. Ada twitched and made a little noise of distress, but didn't fully wake. Success. We crept out of the nursery, quietly closing the door.

"You going to get some sleep now?" I asked.

"Do I look that bad?"

"No. You look fine."

"The whole yoga pants, old T-shirt, and messy hair thing really works for you, huh?"

I just smiled. The truth being that her whole existence worked for me. Jean breathing and moving and being herself was beautiful in every way. Not that I would be saying that. An expensive giant bear might have been slightly pushing the boundaries, but blurting out sweet nothings would definitely cross a line.

She still seemed tense though, her shoulders tight and gaze distracted.

"You okay?" I asked. "You don't think your parents are going to try and cause trouble again, do you?"

"No, I don't think so." She frowned. "I mean, what can they do? The estate is settled and we're halfway across the country."

"True."

"Mom actually sounded sorry."

"Think they're finally figuring out what they've lost?"

"Maybe." She shrugged, staring off at nothing. "I miss them, you know. Don't get me wrong—what they did, trying to pressure me like that. It wasn't okay. But they're still my parents . . . we used to be so close. And I always imagined them being there as grandparents."

The hurt in her voice slayed me. What would my friends do in this sort of situation? Pat would probably buy me a beer. Slap me on the back a time or two. Ditto Joe. Alex, however, would be all over me with the hugging and caring.

Since it seemed a bit early in the day to try the beer option, I opened my arms somewhat stiffly. "Need a hug?"

"Yes, please."

Next thing I knew, her face was pressed against my chest and her arms were around my waist. I wrapped her up tight, giving as good as I got. Not thinking about the way her curves fit against me, because wrong. Friends didn't do that. I rested my cheek against the top of her head, nudging her messy bun out of the way. Affection with your clothes on could actually be worthwhile. Incredible.

"I needed this," she whispered against my sweater.

Me too. But I kept quiet, enjoying the moment. This was about her, not me.

"I can hear your heart," she said.

"Yeah?"

A nod. Then she sniffed. "I think my hormones are still a bit crazy."

"Sure you're all right?"

"I'm fine," she said. "And I do dig the bear, really."

I smiled. "Good. Next time I'll keep the presents to a more manageable size. Say, eight feet maximum. Definitely nothing over eight and a half. You have my word."

"Great." She laughed. "Um, Eric?"

"Hmm?"

"I think you have regurgitated milk down your back, compliments of my daughter."

Of course I did.

"Come into the kitchen, let me clean you up."

She stepped away and I let her go reluctantly. Best hug of my life, hands down.

"Thank you for the hug," she said.

"Anytime."

"Say . . ." She cocked her head. "Got plans for the next while?"

"Not really. What are you thinking?"

"That some adult time would be wonderful," she said. "Don't feel like watching TV with me, do you?"

I grinned, baby vomit and all. "I'd love to."

CHAPTER ELEVEN

"Ada hated it. Too many explosions."

As part of Jean's getting the hell out of the apartment and practicing taking the baby on expeditions program, we'd attempted going to a movie. It hadn't exactly gone as planned. But then, I was fast learning that things involving infants rarely did.

Joe shook his shaggy head. "No such thing as too many explosions in a movie. Did you even try to explain it to her?"

"They're loud and she's little."

"Amazed you took her in the first place."

"They have special showings where they leave the lights on for people with babies."

"Huh," he said, mixing up a couple of old-fashioneds. "So you left?"

"Nuh," I said. "I just walked back and forth beside the candy shop with Ada so Jean could catch the rest of the movie. She doesn't get out much and it would have been a pity for her to miss the ending. I can see it anytime."

"Good of you."

"Can't believe Ada's two months old already. Seems like just yesterday we were at the hospital and she was being delivered."

"Lot's changed for you with her and Jean around."

I shrugged. "Yeah. But it's all good."

"Well, I for one am very surprised and disappointed in young Ada for not getting into the film." He popped the tops on a couple of beers and added them to Rosie's tray.

"Why is that?"

"I really thought she'd be into *Thor*. Guys with long blond hair are just cooler," he said, tossing his own blond locks around. The dickhead. "Ask anyone."

"Be prepared to wallow in disappointment, bro." I wiped my hands off on a towel. "Ada's an intelligent and discerning young lady who thinks highly of men with long dark hair. She told me so."

Rosie watched us, unimpressed. "You're both such idiots."

"Harsh but true," said Joe.

I smiled. "It runs in the family."

"Pretty sure it comes from Dad's side."

"Probably." I laughed. "Mom would agree with that."

It'd been a great night. Busy, but not crazy stressful. Everyone had been in a good mood. It was close to eleven-thirty and things were winding down now, though the music kept pumping. Nights like this made me glad to own a bar. Or one third of a share in a restaurant and bar. Whatever.

Lydia, Nell, and I had decided to stick with the no decision as a decision regarding the offer on the place. If the resort owners, the people wanting to buy the Dive Bar, had tried pushing us for a definite answer, we probably would've just said no. None of us were busting to be free of the place. But since they were content to leave the offer on the table, so be it. It could sit there until something changed.

If something changed, I mean.

Boyd and Curt the kitchen kid had been taking over more of the cooking duties as Nell's belly expanded. Funnily enough, being heavily pregnant seemed to improve her mood. It was like once the period where she'd lost the last baby passed, she could relax a little. She even stopped riding me so hard about Jean. Especially since I'd kept my word and not made a single move on the woman. I'd mostly made peace with the fact that Nell would never see me as a decent upstanding member of the community. Given how badly I'd let her down, I probably deserved it. Some things weren't so easy to forgive.

"You good here?" I asked, finishing cleaning up my area.

"Yeah. You on for the gym tomorrow?"

"Text me what time."

"Will do," Joe said and nodded. " 'Night."

During the winter, my brother's building jobs tended to slow as working outside became next to impossible. He took on more shifts at the bar to maintain the cash flow. It freed up Vaughan to book more gigs out of state and also meant I was available to pick up the slack in other areas, if necessary. No more doing inventory into the early hours of the morning on my own. Thank God.

Tonight, however, I was free.

A couple of ladies I'd chatted with over the course of the night gave me inviting smiles. I nodded back but kept walking. Honestly, the thought of a random hookup just didn't do anything for me. My dick was still officially out of order, though I had more than a sneaking suspicion it wasn't broken. More like Jean had unknowingly taken my libido hostage. Until I worked her out of my system, I didn't see anything changing.

I started hitting the gym with my brother more often to use up extra energy. My own hand took care of the rest. Given I'd been sexually active since losing my virginity at fifteen, it was weird to take a break. The smell of it, the feel of skin on skin, I missed it all. But there was an upside. Being friendly, as opposed to flirty, made interactions with women interesting. I'd had some decent conversations about various shit. Like I had a bit more room in my head without the need for pussy.

Don't get me wrong, taking a break from fucking didn't make me deep or anything. But enough about the insides of my head and back to reality.

In the office, Curt was pulling on a jacket.

"Finished?" I asked.

"No," he said. "Nell asked us to make an order for upstairs before she left, but we got busy. Haven't had a chance to get away before now."

"I'm heading that way. I'll take it."

Curt grinned. "Thanks."

I grabbed my jacket and picked up the brown paper bags off the desk. "Jean, Andre, or Alex?"

"Jean."

Excellent.

The outside steps were a little icy so I took it slow. Hopefully, Jean hadn't given up on dinner and gone to bed. If my timing was right, she would be finishing up Ada's midnight feeding before her big sleep. Of course, Ada answered to no one, so no guarantees.

When I put my ear to her door, noises could be heard. It was safe to knock.

She answered the door in flannel pajamas covered in hedgehogs. I'd never considered the small animals a turn-on before. But honestly, it was hard to look away, she was so cute.

"Eric. Hi."

"I hear you've been waiting on this?" I held up the order. "Sorry about the delay."

"No problem at all." She smiled. "Are you heading straight to bed?"

"You feel like company?"

"Absolutely." She stepped back, holding the door open. "Come on in."

Subtlety had never been my strong suit. By now Jean should just know that if given the chance, I'd want to be with her. Ada lay on a blanket on the floor, apparently watching a TV show involving colorful balls bouncing around and a soothing voice reciting the alphabet. Weird.

"She was wide awake so I gave up trying to settle her," said Jean, unpacking her chicken-and-noodle salad. "It's her favorite program."

"Remind me to introduce her to WWE sometime."

Jean cocked her head. "Maybe not."

"Okay." I pulled a chair up to the table. "I bet this show would make perfect sense if you were stoned."

"Probably." She laughed. "How was work?"

"Good. Busy."

And right up there with hedgehogs was watching Jean eat. Lips sliding over the tines of her fork and her tongue struggling to keep everything under control. She was hot even with noodles slipping over her chin. Hell, I had to look away before things got uncomfortable.

"Joe is upset Ada didn't love *Thor*," I said, picking at a thread on my jeans. "I think he sees himself as Thor in this scenario."

She laughed. "Tell him I feel real bad for his poor delicate male ego."

"We can't help it." I put my hand to my heart. "We're sensitive creatures."

"Sure you are."

"Meant to ask you, did you hear any more from your parents?" I asked, curious. And maybe a little protective.

She nodded, taking a moment to swallow her food. "Yes, actually. I haven't talked to Dad yet, but Mom's called a couple of times."

"Big turnaround."

She shrugged. "I don't know. She seems sincere."

"Like I said, they're missing out big-time not being part of your and Ada's life."

"Thank you."

I shrugged it off. It was, after all, a simple statement of fact.

"I think they've mostly agreed with all of my big decisions up until this point." She frowned, staring off at nothing. "Guess going against their wishes and keeping my baby caught them by surprise."

"Maybe," I said.

"You know, you guys don't have to keep bringing the orders to my door," she said, changing the subject. "Not that I don't appreciate it."

"Curt often runs things up for Alex." I shrugged. "It's not a big deal. I'm sorry it was late though."

"No worries. Are you sure about delivering?"

"Yeah." I nodded. "Saves you from having to suit up Ada and bring her down."

"That's true," she said, wrapping noodles around her fork. "But I don't have to take it easy on the stairs or anything anymore. The doctor okayed me for everything a couple of weeks ago."

"That's great."

She nodded, finishing another mouthful. "Not that I have the least interest in sex."

Whoa. Where did that come from?

"Even if I did have a partner," she said, waving the fork around. "Can you imagine getting busy after caring night and day for a baby?"

"Hmm." I tried to smile, but it felt more like a grimace.

"It's just so full-on. I mean, where would that energy even come from?" she asked, eyes wide. "Besides the fact that I look like something a cat coughed up on the rug."

"You don't look anything like cat barf," I said, sternly. "I keep telling you, you look good, but you don't believe me."

She barked out a laugh. "I think you're very kind."

"No. Not really."

"They should make up a sex position for new parents," she continued. "The sloth. 'You have my permission. Just hurry up and get it done while I lie here and take a quick nap.'"

"Sounds hot."

"Right? Total turn-on."

"I take it there'll be drool and snoring during this incredible quickie?"

"Oh, absolutely."

I just shook my head.

"Sorry," she said. "I'm probably making you uncomfortable."

"It's fine," I said, not thinking about having any kind of sex with Jean to the best of my ability. My ability sucked. "We're friends. You can talk about anything with me. Even the sloth."

For a moment, she just looked at me. Her gaze full of I don't even know what emotion. Then she sighed. Oh holy shit, that sound. It alone had my dick at half-mast. All the woman had to do was click her fingers and I'd be begging on my knees. Friendship my ass. I was the literal worst.

"Thank you," she said. "Honestly, I'd be lost without you, Eric. Everyone's been great, but you've . . . you've really gone above and beyond. I wish I had a medal or a cookie to give you."

Geez.

"I'm serious."

"Jean. Really, I'm happy I'm here to help," I said, bumbling along, searching for words. "You two, you mean a lot to me. Sorry I disappeared on you when I went to California. That was shitty of me when I'd said I'd be here for you."

"You're forgiven." God, her smile and the soft sweet look in her eyes. Bury me six feet deep, I was officially dead.

"You're not like I thought you'd be," she said, voice low. "That day we met, you seemed . . ."

"What?"

"Well, you're nothing like Nell said."

I turned away. "Shit. Shoot, I mean. Really, Jean, don't get carried away trying to make me into a good guy. I've gone out with a lot of women. Just, you know, having fun. Good time, not a long time, and all that."

"And here I thought you were a virgin like me."

"Smart ass," I muttered. "What I'm trying to say is, with you in the situation you are, a guy like that would be useless to you. You need someone dependable."

She said nothing.

"You deserve the best."

"Eric, having a baby doesn't mean I'm helpless or that I belong on a pedestal."

"I know."

Pink tinged Jean's cheeks. What emotion it was, I didn't know. Suddenly she stood, taking the bowl of salad and putting it back into its container before placing it in the fridge.

"Not hungry?" I asked carefully.

"I'll eat it later." She turned, putting her hands on the kitchen counter at her back.

Neither of us said anything for a minute.

"So, seen Andre lately?" I asked. Just making conversation. Not digging for information at all.

"Um, no. I think he's busy with a new girlfriend." No trace of a frown on her face or anything. Guess he'd been right about them only hanging out and being neighborly.

"Good," I said. "For him, I mean."

"Yes." She rolled her shoulders, stretched her neck. "He's a nice guy."

"He's okay."

She frowned. "I thought you two were friends."

"We are. Sure, I just . . ." I scratched at my head. "Yeah, no, we're friends."

"All righty," she said, gaze confused. "At any rate, I've been thinking. I'd like to make you dinner next time you've got a night off. What do you say?"

Normally I'd run a mile from such an offer. Science (sort of) showed that meeting a woman in a public setting then relocating somewhere private only for the sex portion of the evening was safest. It cut down on opportunities for drama. Excessive attachment and shit like that. If sporting teams were stronger on their home territory, then surely the same applied to women. Only I'd already been in Jean's apartment plenty of times. Hell, I'd even rolled around on her living room floor. Fully clothed. The boundaries in this kind of friendship were far different from what I was used to. But I'd continue to do my best to keep things on the up and up. How I felt about her didn't matter.

"That'd be great," I said. "It's in two days."

She licked her lips and drew a breath, as if she were going to say something big and meaningful. But then didn't. "Okay."

"I'll look forward to it then."

She just smiled.

CHAPTER TWELVE

A tie or bow tie would have been too much. But T-shirt and jeans seemed to send the wrong impression. Like, "Thanks for inviting me for dinner, not that I give a shit." It was a hard call. In the end I settled for navy trousers and a gray sweater. Long hair tied back because Ada was starting to grab at things. A splash of cologne and all good.

Jean opened the door in sweats. "Hey. Hi. Come on in."

"You okay?"

"Yeah." She smoothed back her ponytail, smile hesitant. "We had a bad day, but she's asleep now. She had a mild fever."

"Poor Ada," I said, keeping my voice down. "Want to put this off for another time?"

Jean crawled onto the corner of the couch, knees drawn up to her chest and arms wrapped around them. That she was comfortable enough around me to just be herself got me a little high.

"Or I can grab something from downstairs?" I offered.

"I had such great plans for tonight," she said. "I'd picked out recipes and was going to go grocery shopping and everything."

"You know, I'd be happy with a peanut butter and jelly sandwich."

"Typical." She sighed. "I'm out of bread and I ate the last of the peanut butter for dinner last night. Straight out of the bottle with a spoon. It was glorious."

"Ha. All right, so what have you got?"

Her brows rose. "How do you feel about chicken nuggets?"

"Are you kidding? I love them."

"Right. I'll get them cooking." She jumped off the couch and got busy turning on the oven and stuff. "You find us something to watch."

"Yes, ma'am." I sat down and grabbed the remote, started flipping through the channels. No to hockey, home shopping, news, and cooking. But eventually I struck gold. "*Top Gun*?"

She paused in the act of pouring a box of chicken nuggets onto a baking tray to shoot me a look over her shoulder. "Really?"

"It's an absolute classic," I said. "Come on, you can't not love *Top Gun*. That would be un-American. Tell me you've seen it."

"Have I seen it . . . sheesh." Her lips twitched. "Do you feel the need, Eric? The need for speed?"

"Exactly!"

Giggling, she put a finger to her mouth. "Sleeping baby."

"Sorry, sorry," I whispered.

We settled in side by side with a safe amount of space between us. On the big television, jets flew, doing all sorts of amazing shit.

"What would your call sign be?" I asked.

"Hmm. How about: help, I don't know what I'm doing in this thing?"

I snickered. "Nice."

"Otherwise, I guess I'd have to stick with the Jean Genie."

"Good one." I nodded. "I always wanted to be Maverick."

"It is the cool name."

Of course, we had to sing along with the bad karaoke of "You've Lost that Loving Feeling." It was a must. I may have given

Jean slight side-eyes during the volleyball scene. Jealousy is a bitch. If she asked, I'd be more than happy to get rid of my shirt and flex some muscle for her to ogle. This thought didn't make me feel lame and pathetic at all. Much. The action scenes kept us oohing and aahing, and the soundtrack had us tapping our toes. And seriously, *Top Gun* had been an excellent choice. A great time was being had by all.

Right up until the sex scene. I'd never been so hyperaware that two actors were pretending to get it on ever in my life. We were even munching down on the last of the chicken nuggets by then, and you'd think such a highly unerotic food choice would have helped keep things PG. But it didn't.

"Great song," she murmured.

"Mm."

The screen was blue and gray with the characters in profile and tongues and kissing and oh my god. This was the worst movie choice ever. My dick stirred and my skin tingled. I was such an idiot.

"It's interestingly shot." Jean shifted in her seat. "Very atmospheric."

"Yeah." I searched for something to say. "Really great song. Like you said."

"So great." She nodded, licking her lips and tucking her long hair back. Then she peeked a look at me out of the corner of her eye. "Just . . . great."

Like I'd be checking out the naked woman on-screen when she was sitting beside me. Jesus. Why couldn't they just go back to flying jets and blowing shit up? Or they could kill off the best friend already. Spoiler alert. Yeah, we should maybe fast-forward to that. Surely they had to quit screwing soon.

Jean cleared her throat, squirming some more in her chair.

Meanwhile, I crossed and uncrossed my legs. Nothing felt comfortable.

The damn scene was going on forever. Typical HBO. It just wouldn't end. On-screen, the woman dug her fingernails into the guy's back and he was moving over her and holy shit. Much too much. Was the movie X-rated or something?

I shook my head, turned away.

"I know, it's disgusting," said Jean with a half-smile.

"Like people actually even do this," I joked.

"Right? If someone put their tongue in my mouth I'd just bite it off."

"And you would be well within your rights to do so."

"Incredibly unhygienic," she said.

"God only knows what he's been licking," I said. "Could have been the floor for all she knows."

"Or worse."

"Yeah."

"Body parts are covered in germs and fluids. Just because we can't see them, doesn't mean they're not there." Her face had pinked and she kept biting the side of her thumbnail. "It's all completely gross."

"Totally," I said. "And we don't sound the least bit like twelve-year-olds."

She laughed. "Not at all."

Finally the fucking scene ended and we both sank back into the cushions, breathing a sigh of relief. Post–movie coital trauma or something, I guess. At least it hadn't only been me who'd weirded out. No one warned me watching sex scenes with a female friend would be so hard.

Just really hard.

Jean exhaled quietly. "I think maybe I do miss sex after all."

Kill me now.

"It's still good, isn't it?" she asked. "I mean, I haven't blown it up in my mind into something it's not?"

"Yeah . . ." Shit. "I'm, ah, taking a break right now, so maybe the wrong person to ask."

"You are?" Her eyes widened in shock. "Why?"

I lifted one shoulder, playing it cool. "I don't know. Rethinking life and stuff."

"Wow."

"Hmm." It wasn't a complete lie. Just a partial truth. "No big deal."

She said nothing, going back to staring at the screen. Thank God I'd been let off the hook. Phew. Stuff happened in the movie. I wasn't even really watching.

The trouble happened at work a few nights later.

We were only about half-full, pretty normal for both this time of week and year. I'd been meant to finish at eight, but had hung around to help Joe out for a while. Or just to keep him company. A woman and her friend were hanging at the bar, chatting with us. Basically, we were just having some fun with customers, talking and laughing about stuff. It was harmless. The friend was a bit flirty, but whatever.

Most people, they have a few drinks in them, they get relaxed. Our job was to stop serving long before things got messy.

"You go to Shape Fitness?" she asked, playing with her straw.

"No," said Joe. "A different place."

"Where? Because you two definitely look after yourselves," the woman purred. "I can see that."

Joe smiled, moving on to another job behind the bar. He looked about ready for a break. If I didn't know better, I'd have thought he was taking on all the extra shifts to save up for buying something big. Something for his girlfriend, maybe.

"Thanks," I said. "How's the martini?"

"Dirty always gets the job done." The woman flicked her hair and right on cue her friend laughed hysterically. Christ, the girl almost fell off her stool she was cackling so hard.

I grinned. "Great."

That's the things with puns and jokes, people always think they're the first to tell them. Trust me, as a bartender I can say with absolute authority that they're usually not. Alcohol and subtlety do not go hand in hand. If it did, there wouldn't be cocktails with names like "slippery nipple" and "screaming orgasm." But I'd take getting hit on by some batting eyelashes to being cried on by some poor, brokenhearted schmuck any day of the week. Breakup sob stories were the worst, especially when the person was obviously to blame. Like, I'm sorry she left you because she found out you'd been screwing her best friend, your secretary, and the mother-in-law behind her back. How totally unreasonable of your wife to kick you to the curb. Yeah, no. Still, hazards of the job. It's not all flying bottles and flourished pours, though that's part of it too. Along with giving folks their change in one-dollar bills, of course. Got to get those tips.

Bartending was far from being the worst job in the world. But like anything, it had its highs and lows.

"Let me feel," demanded the woman, waving her hand in the general direction of my biceps.

"Eyes only," I said, before giving them the gun show. Even with the long-sleeve T-shirt, it didn't look half bad. I was actually pretty happy with how my upper arms were going. All of the hitting the gym with my brother to burn off steam I wasn't otherwise using had been paying off.

"What the fuck are you doing?" snarled some guy.

"Huh?"

"Are you flirting with my girl?"

"Troy!" The one who'd almost fallen off the stool from laughing grabbed at the dude's arm. "We were just talking. Baby, I would never—"

"Bullshit." He was big, ugly, and angry. "I knew you were up to something, telling me you were working late."

Add paranoid asshole to the guy's list.

The woman sputtered, shaking her head. But it was the genuine fear in her eyes that got me. Out of the corner of my eye, I could see Joe had braced himself, edging nearer the entryway at the end of the bar. Just in case the guy needed moving on.

"Calm down," I said. "There's nothing to get upset about. Your girl and her friend were just having a drink together after work. Nothing's going on." I smiled disarmingly at the brute. "How about I fix you a drink? On the house, just 'cause we're all friends."

And that's when the asshole leaned across the bar and hit me. Straight in the fucking face. Pain filled my face, and for a split second, white dots covered my vision.

By the time I'd snapped back to reality, Joe was already behind the guy, wresting the thug's arms behind his back. My brother didn't have any proper security training or anything, but he'd had to muscle more than a few guys out of the Dive Bar before. Plus it helps if you're the size of a truck. Once Joe had the guy's arms pinned hard behind his back, the fucker gave up his struggling, and let Joe march him toward the door. The women had scattered, getting out of the way. Which was good. Last thing we needed was someone else getting hurt. Ignoring the pounding in my face and the feeling like my eyeball was about to explode, I jumped over the bar and followed. Moving fast rather than carefully, just in case Joe needed backup.

He didn't. Like I said, sometimes size matters. Joe tossed the fucker out the door.

I covered my right eye with my hand. Ow. "Cock-sucking son of a . . ."

"I called the cops," said Lydia, turning to the kitchen. "Curt, grab an ice pack for his face, please."

A woman was crying. The idiot's girlfriend probably. And the otherwise happy hum of conversation had been replaced by a frenzy of whispers. The bartender had gotten punched in the face. Exciting times! Not.

My brother came back inside, rubbing his arms to get some warmth back into himself. "Dickhead took off in a car. I've got the license plate number."

A wail from the idiot's girlfriend and she ran out too, followed fast by her friend. Good. Not only was my face pounding, but we could definitely do without the drama. Though she and her friend had probably just stiffed us on their bar tab. Dammit.

"Show's over," Rosie announced with a smile. "Sorry about the interruption to your evening, folks."

A heavy rock song was replaced by something a little calmer and happier. The Dive Bar had a playlist for just these sorts of occasions. Eventually, all of the nosy folk who'd left their tables dispersed. Things slowly started to settle back to normal. But my heart was still thumping in my chest, adrenaline pumping around my body. I glared after the dickhead, wishing I'd had a chance to give him one back.

"You all right?" Joe clapped me on the shoulder.

"More annoyed he got the drop on me than anything."

"What can you expect? You're getting old."

I just gave him the finger while he walked back over to the bar. Curt ran over with an ice pack and I held it to my abused eye. Better to hide out in the kitchen until I was presentable again.

"What the hell happened?" asked Nell, moving the ice pack aside for a moment to check out the wound. "No blood. Just swelling and bruising."

I grunted.

"What are you doing? Keep the ice pack on."

"Asshole accused me of flirting with his girlfriend. Then he leaned across the bar and punched me."

"Were you hitting on her?"

"No," I snapped. "Joe and I had been chatting with a couple of women. One tried to get handsy, but I stayed back. She seemed to get the message. No different from any other night."

"Hmm." And you had to know the noise was loaded full of doubt.

"I'm a bartender, Nell. People expect me to talk to them."

"Yeah, but how heavy on the charm exactly were you?"

"Nell, that's enough," said Lydia, her face unimpressed. "Eric's the victim here."

I just shook my head. "Forget it."

Once the cops had been by and I'd given my statement, I was out of there. What a night.

"Talking to people is part of my job, right?"

"Keep still," said Jean, holding a new ice pack to my face since the last one had turned to sludge. I sat slumped on her couch, my head back against the cushion, feeling deeply sorry for myself. All while she played nurse. Or at least, knelt by my side, holding the ice over my eye. Maybe the playing nurse thing was more a figment of my imagination. But it had definitely been worth knocking on her door. If a beat-up face can't get a bit of sympathy from a pretty girl, then life would be too grim to bear.

"We were just having a laugh. I get that it's a fine line between a little harmless flirting and actually hitting on a woman," I said. "I'm not an idiot. Nothing I was doing was crossing that line. I've thought about it, a lot."

"Okay. I know you've been putting a lot of effort into moving away from the whole frequent different sex partners thing."

I nodded.

"Not that there's any excuse to hit anyone anyway," she said. "But if you say you weren't coming on to the woman, then I believe you."

"Nell didn't," I grouched.

"Yes, well. Nell and you have a complicated history." She winced. "It might take her longer to come around. Plus, she's not exactly at her best right now. The pregnancy has her anxiety sky-high."

I said nothing.

"Sounds like this girl is dating a violent jerk."

"Hope she's got the sense to dump his ass," I said.

"I hope she has people to back her up in case he decides to retaliate against her." Jean sighed particularly heavily.

I swear my heart stopped beating. "Did that happen to you?"

"No." She shook her head. "But a friend of mine had some issues with this one guy. He just wouldn't take no for an answer. Kept calling her and stopping by, following her sometimes. It was scary there for a while."

"What the hell makes people act like that?"

"I don't know," she said. "Overblown sense of entitlement? Maybe they just get away with behaving that way so often that it seems like a good bet to them. Some people just seem to think violence is always the answer. Trying to control someone, having someone afraid of them must feel good to them I guess."

I moved the ice pack aside, trying to see her better. Not that it worked with my eyelids all swollen. "I want you to know, I would never want you to be afraid of me."

"I don't think too much investment in a relationship is a character flaw you're ever likely to blunder into." She smirked. "But I appreciate the sentiment."

I frowned. "Not that we're together or anything . . ." Damn. "I didn't mean to say that. But, if you were ever in trouble or anything. If ever someone was hurting you, you know I'd help, right? I'll believe whatever you tell me. I wouldn't doubt you."

Her smile was slow, hesitant. "Thank you, Eric."

"Just wanted you to know."

Silence.

"Is the Advil kicking in yet?" she asked, setting the ice gently back on my eye.

"I'm tough. I'll live."

"Good to hear."

I smothered a yawn. "Sorry. Tell me about your day."

"Ah, well. Today, Ada and I tried our first mommy and me yoga class."

"Did you enjoy it?"

"It was fun." She leaned against my shoulder, relaxing. It didn't mean anything. With the way she was holding the ice pack, resting against me was easiest. Sure as hell, I didn't mind at all. This was definitely my idea of playing nurse.

"Good."

"Going out with her is getting easier with each practice too," she said. "I mean, I still have to carry a crazy amount of stuff. I have three separate bags, one for diaper changes, one for other emergencies, and one for toys and other distractions." She gave the sort of satisfied sigh that suggested she'd itemized and labeled each component to her heart's content. "But it's doable."

"Glad to hear it."

Suddenly, she grabbed my arm. "God, Eric."

"What?"

"I totally forgot I had something to show you. The black eye distracted me. Hold this." Then she grabbed my hand and attached it to the ice-filled facecloth. I did as told and she jumped off the couch, grabbing her cell from the table. Her finger dashed across the screen and then she was holding it up in front of my face.

"She finally smiled?" I asked, incredulous.

"Isn't that amazing?"

There on the small screen was a shot of Ada with her little round face, button nose, the usual drool-covered chin, and a big toothless grin. God, my chest filled with warmth.

"That's so awesome," I said.

"Yeah. It was after a bottle."

"Fair enough, food makes me happy too."

Laughing softly, she swiped through to the next picture. Same grin, slightly less drool.

"She's beautiful, just like her mom," I said.

Beside me, Jean stiffened. "You think I'm beautiful?"

"I, ah—"

"Wait. Stop."

I did so.

"You were just being kind." She sat on the edge of the couch, tossing her cell onto the coffee table. "That never happened. God, how embarrassing."

Shit. Did friends not tell friends they were a goddess sent to an undeserving planet? I mean, Joe, Pat, and Taka would happily slap me on the back and tell me I was a dickhead. Which everyone knew was basically bro code for "I love you" or something like that. Letting them know how I felt about them wasn't a big deal. Dad would just kind of grunt at me, but that was Dad. Surely complimenting a female friend wasn't totally out of the question.

"I've never mentioned that before?" I asked. "Seriously? Thought I had."

She turned to face me, brows drawn in.

"I figured it was obvious. I mean, you just are." I shrugged. "That a problem? I'm not hitting on you either. Promise."

She didn't seem convinced.

"I mean, it's not even about me," I protested. "It's not like *I* think you're gorgeous. You just are. Objective fact. Nothing to do with my opinion. It's like someone saying to Joe that he's tall. And everyone would be like, thanks, Captain Obvious. It's like that."

Yep, good one. Also, I wasn't rambling at all.

And still, she said nothing.

"Christ, I've done the wrong thing again, haven't I?"

"No."

With all of the weirdness in the air, it was hard to believe her. "Thanks for the ice, Jean. I'll, um, let you get to bed."

She stood and so did I, heading for the door. Maybe I'd send Joe a text and ask him to ask Alex if I'd messed things up. Not that I really wanted anyone sticking their nose into what went on between Jean and me. But constantly being confused as fuck got old fast. I'd only come here in the hope of some sympathetic attention to my wounded face, after all.

"'Night," she said, holding open the door.

I just gave her a chin tip and headed for my place. Face throbbing, feet weary, and all around over life. At least until tomorrow morning. I fished my keys out of my pocket and unlocked my front door. Peace, quiet, and darkness. Perfect. Except the door had no sooner shut than someone started knocking on it.

When I opened said door, Jean stood there, eyes huge for some reason. "Eric, I've been thinking . . ."

"Since I left ten seconds ago?"

"A bit longer than that, actually."

"Okay." I leaned against the door frame, crossing my arms and trying to feel defensive. But I could guess what was coming. This was how all my efforts to be friends with a girl were going to end. Having not properly read the how-to-not-be-a-dick manual that everyone else in the world seemed to have a copy of, I'd opened my mouth and screwed the whole thing up. The perfectly fucked ending to a perfectly fucked evening.

Her gaze shifted back to her own door, then to her bare feet, to my face, then off to the side again.

"Jean?" Just get it over with, and let me curl up in a heap in the corner of my bed.

"Ithinkweshouldstartsleepingtogether."

"What did you say?" I leaned in closer. "I didn't quite catch that."

The woman took a very deep breath. "I realize you've been taking a break from sex, but I've been thinking, and maybe it would be okay if you and I were like friends who took things into the bedroom," she said, and then rattled on without pause. "No pressure about the sex or anything. Neither of us are in a place to be thinking long term and we've both got so much going on that attempting a relationship would just be crazy. But I feel comfortable with you and I think that most of the time you feel comfortable with me too. And we both find each other attractive, it seems. At least, you said I was beautiful so I'm hoping you find me sexually attractive as well. If you don't that's totally fine. Like I said, no pressure. Either way, whether we have sex or not, we'd still definitely remain friends. I mean, of course we'd stay friends. You're one of the people I'm closest to here, I don't know what I'd do if we stopped talking, and you're so great with Ada too. She absolutely adores you. So this whole sex thing would be totally separate from our friendship. Or it would be like, an addition to it. But not in the way that I expect it to go anywhere. Just two people who really like each other in a friendly platonic way having sex."

I just stared. No wonder she'd taken a deep breath.

"Wait, does that make sense?" She frowned at her own words. "Platonic sex?"

"You keep saying sex."

"I do, yes."

"My brain kind of got a bit stuck on that." I ran my tongue over my teeth, giving myself a moment to sort it all out in my head. I had failed to grasp the way this conversation was going to go, and it was taking me a moment to catch up. "Platonic friends who have sex . . . that's what you're suggesting?"

She raised her hand, fingers twitching. "Platonic is probably the wrong word there."

"Probably."

"Though in my defense, I'm sure Plato himself would have had sex and he's kind of where the word came from and everything."

"Right. Good that that's settled."

"Um, anyway," she said, taking a step back. "You think about it. I'm going to go back into my apartment now and maybe we'll talk about this later or maybe we won't."

"We'll talk about this later. That's a definite."

"Sure. Okay." Then the woman turned and ran back down the hallway, disappearing into her place. She could really move when she wanted to.

I stood in the now empty space, my brain not only hurting, but quite possibly more confused than ever. Jean wanted to have sex. At least, I was pretty sure that's what her word vomit had been about. Unless the knock to the head had made me delusional.

There was always a small chance. And the woman might think she and I getting horizontal would change nothing. But that was crap. Against all expectations, I'd gotten to a place in my life where I was pretty much best friends with a woman. I loved talking to her. I loved hearing about her day. She was funny and cool and kind and this could ruin everything.

"I should say no," I mumbled.

Dammit.

CHAPTER THIRTEEN

"Hold up," said my brother, forkful of bacon hovering in front of his face. "Eric, are you actually complaining because a woman you're attracted to wants to have sex with you?"

I paused. "Yes."

"Honestly, I don't know what to do with that."

Mom just laughed.

There weren't many topics we couldn't talk about in front of her. After hitting the gym in the morning, I'd ask Joe if he wanted to go talk Mom into cooking us breakfast. Usually, if I gave her really sad puppy dog eyes, she'd cave. Either that or pat me on the cheek and tell me to grow up. There was an even chance of either happening. That was our mom. She'd been a nurse for pretty much forever, so my black eye and pain meant little. Apparently, today had been my lucky day and she'd put out a full breakfast spread. Bacon, eggs, link sausage, biscuits. Meanwhile, Dad was hiding out in the shed making bird boxes or something. I don't know.

"She's going to ruin our friendship," I said, finishing up chewing. "And it'll be all her fault, not mine . . . for a change."

"Don't eat with your mouth open," admonished Mom.

"Nell would skin you alive." Joe chugged down some coffee. "You know that."

"Nope," I said. "I promised not to hit on Jean and I didn't. She hit on me. Therefore, I'm off the hook."

Joe snorted. "Like that'd save you."

"C'mon, nothing I do is going to make Nell happy. I'm over even trying."

"Think you're probably right there," he said. "You've turned yourself around at work, been putting in a lot more effort. I've noticed."

"Thanks."

"You decided to grow up, huh?" Mom smiled. "Good for you. I always knew you were capable of great things if you put your mind to it."

"I'll settle for average things," I said. "Great would probably take took much effort. 'Eric the Adequate,' that's what they'll call me. You'll see."

Mom smacked a kiss on my cheek.

"What about me?" asked Joe. Whiny little jerk.

"Don't worry," said Mom. "You're both my favorite."

I shook my head. "You always say that."

"One day you're going to have make a choice, Mom," said Joe.

She pretended to think it over. "All right, I choose Alex. Alex is my favorite."

I looked to heaven. "That's cheating."

"She's my girlfriend, Mom," said Joe. "Not your child."

"We've welcomed her into the family. She's basically my adopted daughter."

"I can't sleep with my adopted sister," complained Joe. "Don't be creepy."

Mom cackled. Her own jokes amused her. I think I had inherited that trait too.

"You raised me slightly better than that," said Joe.

"I'd hope so." Mom smirked.

We'd grown up in this bungalow near Sandy Beach. The area had skyrocketed pricewise in the last decade or so. No way would we be able to afford it these days. If Mom and Dad ever decided to sell up, they'd probably make a tidy sum. It was a nice house. Though Mom was way more into pastels than anyone needed to be. I'd tried to talk her into modernizing the place, giving it a fresh coat of paint. Little had changed since Joe and I were kids. With the exception of Mom turning my room into a craft room and Joe's into a dressing room for Dad. Apparently, Mom needed the bulk of the household cupboard space for her clothes and crap. I highly doubt Dad minded. Hell, he probably hadn't even noticed. Football and building shit was Dad's whole world. A big part of why we'd never really bonded.

"When do I get to meet your Jean?" asked Mom. "And her baby. Have you got any new pictures to show me?"

"Ada's just started smiling, but I haven't got a picture of her doing it yet," I said. "And she's not *my* Jean. She's just Jean."

"Jean who you're very enamored with and about to get more involved with."

"Who even says 'enamored' these days?" muttered Joe.

Mom ignored him. "Eric, you don't sound like you're ready to take that step with her."

"It's what she wants."

"You know it'll change things." Mom watched me carefully.

"I know."

"How would this work, exactly?" asked Joe. "Just out of curiosity."

"Dude, you want me to explain the birds and the bees to you?"

In response, he gave me the bird. Quite fitting.

"No fighting at the table," said Mom. "Go wrestle in the backyard if you must."

"It's too cold."

"Yeah, Mom," I said. "You trying to kill us from exposure or something?"

"Not right this minute, no," she replied calmly, nibbling on a biscuit. "Eric, I want you to bring your new girlfriend and her baby to dinner some night."

"She's not my girlfriend, Mom. She was very explicit about that. Said she wants a platonic—" I checked myself before stumbling down that path. "Anyway, she just wants to stay friends and I want us to stay friends too. I've never really had a female friend before. Well, Nell and Lydia don't really count. I've never been tight with them like I am with Jean. There's a lot to lose if things go south, you know?" I shook my head forlornly. "It would have been better if she had never made the offer. The thing is just a disaster waiting to happen."

"That's very mature of you, darling," said Mom. "Still, you need to think about the best way of politely saying no. You don't want her to feel rejected, when you're actually doing it because you value her friendship so much."

"What? " I spluttered. "Say no? Why on earth would I do that?"

My brother burst out laughing. "As if."

"The woman wants to have sex with me, and I'm going out of my mind over her." I shrugged. "Besides, who am I to deny her? If everything goes to hell, it'll obviously be her fault. I'm totally in the clear on this one."

Mom just sat there, mouth open.

"Not that *I* would blame her or anything, because she's one of my best friends," I said quickly. "Got to look after her feelings and all that."

"God, Eric turning down Jean." Joe wiped tears from his eyes. "Like that would ever happen. He's been hung up on her for months now. You're hilarious, Mom."

For a long moment, our mom said nothing. Finally, she picked up her cup and took a long sip of coffee, her gaze less than impressed for some reason.

"What?" I asked.

"Nothing, dear." She sighed. "Nothing at all."

Mom's weirdness about the whole situation got me thinking. When I got back home, I texted Jean to see if she was up for a chat. It wouldn't hurt to get a few ground rules established before we started bumping hips. Not that I wanted to delay the bumping of said hips. But with Ada's unpredictable routine, it was possible we wouldn't be hitting the mattress anytime soon anyway.

Hopefully it wouldn't be too long. The idea that we might make an official date for sex and then have to patiently wait until the duly appointed hour was liable to drive me out of my sweet mind. Though given Jean's love of organization and Ada's need for routine that might be exactly how it happened. Guess I could do with a lesson in patience.

I'd barely knocked when the door flew open, Jean standing there with a frown on her pretty face and a baby on her shoulder. "Hey."

"Hi," I said quietly, just in case Ada was on her way to sleep. "Everything okay?"

"Sure."

"You seem down."

"No, no. Come in." She headed back inside, the baby's little head moving as she sucked on her fingers. Jean lay her down carefully on her blanket under the jungle gym. Ada immediately smiled and started laying into her old friend the dangling turtle. Man, she really had it in for that guy.

"See? Violence does make her happy," I said, grinning down

at her. "Don't know why she didn't get into the movie the other day."

"Her moods are mercurial." Jean picked up her cell and pressed play on some baby-friendly classical music mix. It wasn't Janis Joplin, but it wasn't bad. At any rate, Ada seemed content.

"Anyway," I said, exhaling hard. "I thought we should talk."

"It's okay, Eric. You don't have to."

"Huh?"

"Everything's been so good between us," she said. "It was stupid of me to rock the boat. Can we just pretend that me propositioning you never happened?"

"No." I shook my head, adamant. "Absolutely not. That would be like canceling Christmas or breaking a bottle of my favorite single malt."

She cocked her head. "It would be?"

"Yes. It would be terrible."

"Oh."

"You can't just ask me to . . ." I looked down at Ada. "You know. Do that thing. And then change your mind."

Her brows rose in surprise.

"Unless you've actually changed your mind, which would be totally fine," I quickly inserted. "Have you changed your mind?"

She froze.

"Please don't have changed your mind. I'm willing to beg if that would help at all."

"No, that's okay." Her smile was magnificent. Thrilling. Amazing. All of these things and more. The kind of grin to weaken a man's knees and harden his cock. Then she too peeked down at her happily playing daughter and said, "Let's discuss this in the hallway."

"Sure."

The woman grabbed my hand and towed me around the corner and out of the infant's sight, into the little hallway that led to my bathroom. And the bedroom.

"Because we probably need rules and stuff, right?" I asked. My hand was still hooked into hers, making it hard to concentrate.

"Sure."

"Like are we having sex with other people or being exclusive or what?"

"Well, it will be monogamous at my end," she said, shrugging. "Just because no one else is ringing my bells right now."

"Ditto for me," I said. The idea that I alone was ringing her bells got my heart pounding double-time. "How about how we act around other people? We keeping this on the down low? Because otherwise I need to prepare for Nell to try and kill me while making it look like an accident. I'm thinking there'll be an incident with hot oil in the kitchen."

Jean snorted, but she did not try to deny it. "Let's keep it just between you and me."

"Sounds good," I said, trying not to let my relief show through too much. "Though I may have already kind of talked about it to Joe and my mom and Joe will definitely talk to Alex about it if he hasn't already. He's pretty much pussy-whipped when it comes to stuff like that. Sorry."

"So basically word is going to get around?"

"Probably."

Her lips wrinkled, then she shrugged. "Whatever."

"Whatever?"

"Yeah." Out of nowhere, her hands were on me, pushing me up against the wall, and leaning in until her T-shirt-covered breasts were brushing against me. Made it damn hard to think. Christ, the absolute focus in her eyes. "I don't mind if you don't."

I cleared my throat. "I, um, I vote we just tell them all to mind their own business."

"Will they?"

"Probably not."

"Duly noted."

Then her hands grabbed hold of my shoulders and she lifted up, pressing her lips to mine. Her breath mingling with mine, her face so close. Fucking hell, it was perfect and the woman did not mess around. Sweet turned to sin in no time. Mouths open and tongues playing. Our teeth clashed and my palms smoothed down her back, holding her tight. From our knees upward, we were pressed together and I could happily have died.

"You don't mind if we practice a bit before the big event?" she asked, breathing heavily. "It's kind of been a while."

"Whatever you want. Practice makes perfect."

"Thanks."

And then she kissed me again, hard and hungry. Her fingers dug into my hair, the kiss deepening. Ever so slightly out of control, I grabbed at her gorgeous round ass. Something I'd always wanted to do. A tiny voice in the back of my head wondered if ass-grabbing counted for Jean as "practice," and whether I was moving things along a bit too fast. But at my touch she pushed her hips hard forward into me, and my doubts disintegrated. She was as into this as I was. Maybe more, if that was even possible.

Our mouths fused together once more, my hands happily full of Jean's delectable soft rear. Our pelvises were grinding together, the front of my jeans getting damn tight. The woman did things to me. Things beyond my control. Not that I wanted either of us in control right then. No, what I really wanted was to reverse our positions, have her legs wrapped around my hips, and then take the whole grinding thing to the next level. Though even just kissing Jean was a treat. The kind of experience where nothing else existed.

We were halfway through the maneuver, Jean's legs just beginning to lift and spread around my waist, when Ada made some weird outraged yodel kind of yell in the next room.

"Shit," whispered Jean.

"We got a little carried away."

"Just a bit." Then, sadly, she stepped back, straightening her top. The sight of her hard nipples undid me just a bit more. Her breasts would be as nice a handful as her ass. "You okay?"

"Yes. Thank you."

"If you want, I'll show them to you later."

"Sorry, what?" My gaze returned to her face.

Only to have her point to her breasts. "I said, I can show them to you sometime if you want."

"I would like that very much."

"Okay then." She grinned. "Next make-out session, no shirts. Agreed?"

I was a total winner at life. Forget how much money currently sat in my bank account. Ignore my maturity levels and emotional stability or lack thereof. Jean had offered to show me her tits. The year had only just started and mine was already made.

I grinned back at her. "Second base it is."

Ada yelled again and Jean headed her way. Though the sound from the baby seemed more bored than upset or anything. She'd had both of our attention for a minute there, and then me and her mom had disappeared. Clearly not okay.

"Hey, baby." Jean swung her up into her arms. "What's going on?"

Ada gurgled happily once more.

"Oh my god," cooed Jean. "Were you not the center of attention for a minute? That's outrageous. Worst mother of the year. Again. And you're not even a year old yet."

"Hello." I gave the baby my finger to hold onto. Of course, she immediately tried to stick it in her mouth. "Cool zebra-print onesie, baby girl."

"So glad it meets with your approval," said her mother.

"You want me to hang with her while you get some stuff done or anything?"

"Actually, I'd love to go downstairs for a coffee and get out of here for a bit," she said. "We could all go?"

"Sounds good."

"All right, let me just brush my hair." Jean passed me the baby, giving me a quick kiss on the cheek as she did so. "Won't be long."

"Take your time." I settled onto the couch with Ada nestled into my shoulder. "I am completely happy right here."

The next day at work I had a lot to think about.

As I walked around opening the place up, the fingers on my left hand still tingled with the memory of holding Jean's ass. But by 10 a.m. I'd moved on to more pressing matters, daydreaming about how Jean's tits would look, adorned with nothing more than a skimpy bra. The next tasks were to tally the books and restock the bar, which was an opportune time to speculate on what a sight they would be sans bra. Awesome, was my educated guess. Memo to self: don't dim the lights so far tonight that you can't get a good view.

By the time I'd finished with that business, it was late morning. A few young tourists had moseyed in for brunch, and it was game on. I fixed their Bloody Marys wondering how those two magnificent creatures would feel when I finally had them in my hands. Firm and strong, if the memory of them pressing into my chest last night was anything to go by. Not to mention how they looked when she had tried to straighten her top, and those hard nipples pressed out against the fabric. But then, tits were strange and magical things, and sometimes they'd be surprisingly soft and succulent. A box of chocolates and all that. So it was hard to know. And then there was the whole question of skin texture and nipples to be considered. Like I said, a lot to think about.

Oddly, it was turning out that messing around with Jean was twice as much fun as actually having sex with anyone else. After work the next day, I stopped by her apartment. She'd invited me over via text message. Ada was fast asleep and the lights were set to low.

"I was trying for some atmosphere, but it turns out I only own one." Jean pointed to the thick white candle flickering on the coffee table. "Vaguely romantic second base?"

"Works for me."

"Oh, not that I'm trying for romance here," she quickly amended. "That's not . . . damn. I didn't think."

"Jean, relax," I said, joining her on the couch. "Pretty sure that having a candle on the coffee table doesn't equal a long-term commitment or anything." Actually, my entire life history demonstrated as much, but I didn't think that was the best thing to mention right now.

"Okay."

"Though you should keep more candles around in case of an electricity outage or something."

"Yes, I've put them on the next shopping list."

"Or in case of future emergency bases. I don't know if I'd be comfortable moving to fourth base without at least three candles. It just wouldn't seem right."

"Right." She smiled and I just had to kiss her. It'd been far too long since our lips had last met. Like a day and a half or something outrageous.

This part came easily, slipping my tongue into her mouth to caress hers. Then putting an arm around her shoulder and drawing her in close. And in return, she sank her fingers into my hair, holding on tight. Something she seemed to like doing and I certainly had no complaints about. I traced the length of her arm, curved my hand around her shoulder. Our kisses grew hotter, more feverish. But for some godawful reason, I couldn't concentrate on what we were doing. My brain would not shut up. Last time, she'd been so wonderfully greedy. Was I going too slowly for her now? I just wasn't sure at what stage she'd be expecting me to get the whole naked-from-the-waist-up thing going on. What if I moved too soon and messed it up and totally let her down?

Shit, this was confusing.

Also, it hadn't even occurred to me to ask her about her day. I'd barely been able to string a goddamn sentence together since I stepped foot through her door. The woman probably thought I was a useless jerk. Jesus.

"What's wrong?" she asked, moving her lips to my cheek.

"Huh?"

"You seem distracted."

I sat back with a sigh. "Yeah."

"Eric?"

"I'm fucking it up."

She frowned. "No, you're not. Tell me what you're thinking."

I pushed my hand back through my hair with a groan. "Damn, you know, I think I'm actually nervous."

Her gaze widened.

"I'm never nervous. This is crazy." I got to my feet, pacing back and forth, avoiding Ada's jungle gym and the oversized teddy in the corner. "Joe and I have been working out at the gym regularly, I'm in my goddamn prime right now. I dress nice, I have a good job. No mistake, I'm catch."

Jean continued with the saying nothing.

"And I always know exactly what I'm doing with a woman

when it comes sex," I said. "I don't think it'll come as any surprise to you that fucking is my specialty. Right up there with mixing drinks. But talking, telling chicks—sorry, women—what's in my head, communicating my feelings, shit like that—I can't do that. It's just not okay. A bit of foreplay, though? Hell, I'm all over that."

Jean still said nothing.

"This makes no sense," I berated myself and continued my pacing. But maybe on some level, it did make sense. It was different this time. Maybe because it had been so long for me, after taking all those months out of the game. Maybe because the friends-with-benefits thing was uncharted territory. Or maybe because it was her.

"Oh-kay."

"I feel . . . fuck," I said, curling my hands into fists. "Anxious. Yeah, god. It's horrible. What is that about?"

"If it helps, I'm nervous too."

I paused. "You are? What on earth about?"

"Well, pregnancy changes your body, Eric." She fidgeted with the hem of her shirt. "My breasts aren't as firm as they used to be, for starters."

"Maybe, but they're still breasts. All breasts are great, Jean. Take it from a connoisseur."

"Right," she said.

"What else?"

"I've heard about some of the women you've slept with in the past. They sound like runway models, half of them." She shook her head. "And I am very much not a runway model. My belly is kind of a little weird and wobbly now. Not to mention my Frankenstein scar down below."

"I know Ada can be a handful at times, but saying a monster came out of you is a little harsh," I joked.

"Ha. I'm being serious."

188 | KYLIE SCOTT

"Okay, yes. Sorry. I get that." But seriously, like any of that mattered. The woman was nuts.

"Plus, I've obviously got some experience, but not as much as you. What if I suck in bed?"

"Huh," I said, realization dawning.

"What is 'huh'?"

"So this is normal for most people," I said, crossing my arms. "Worrying about your body and your performance and all that shit."

She thought about it for a moment. "Yes, pretty much. Performance anxiety, insecurity about bodily bits, fears of inadequacy in general, all of those sorts of things. I mean, you want to be enough for the person you're into. Hell, you want them to think that you're awesome in all the ways and worth the effort. You want to please them. And be pleased in return, of course."

"Jesus," I said, pacing once more. "It's fucking debilitating. How do you deal with it?"

"I can't talk for everyone, but I just try to put it aside and concentrate on the moment," she said. "I mean, at least it means you care. It's not all a sign of something bad."

I wasn't so sure about that. What if worrying about your performance actually impacted your performance? There was a serious issue here.

"I've known guys who basically ignore you in bed."

"Idiots."

"You're just reduced to being a vagina and a pair of breasts. Body parts for their entertainment," she said. "They're usually the kind of dicks who say they don't like the taste."

"Are you serious?"

"Nope."

"What useless sacks of shit."

"One sad sack I met wanted to debate whether the female orgasm is a myth or not," she said. "While we were in bed."

I hung my head. "Oh, man."

"Indeed." She half smiled. "But we were doing something before this discussion derailed us."

"Right. Yeah. Okay." I clapped my hands, rubbed them together. I just had to get my head back in the game. Get the mood back somehow. "How do you want to do this?"

"What if I give you something else to focus on?"

"Sounds good. What have you got?"

In response, she peeled off her top and tossed it aside. Then she immediately covered her belly with her arms, leaving her skinny jeans and siren-red bra on display.

"Okay, I did it," she said, speaking more to herself than to me.

"You certainly did."

"Your turn."

I kneeled in front of her, my gaze hooked by the promise of that bra. Trailing fingers softly back and forth along her arms, leaving gooseflesh in their wake. I licked my lips. So much soft, bare skin calling to me. I'd dearly love to make a feast of the woman.

Then she clicked her fingers in front of my face. "Eric, take off your shirt, please."

I ripped it off straight over my head, catching it on my ponytail for a second. Damn hair. Apparently the sight of me pleased her, because she stopped worrying about hiding her belly and started touching me instead. Fingers stroking over my shoulders and up my neck.

"God, you're gorgeous," she hummed, moving closer.

Jean slid off the couch and into me, forcing me back. It required some hasty work, but somehow by pushing aside Ada's jungle gym, blanket, and the coffee table, we found enough room to make out on the rug. With me on my back and Jean straddling my hips, the world was simply awesome. Christ, the sight of her red silk–covered tits and eager hands. Not that I was slacking off in the feeling her up category. She pressed her mouth to mine, her body to mine, and my mind was blown. The long line of her back and slender column of her neck. Her lips and tongue and everything.

Any earlier uneasiness, all of those bad thoughts, they were chased far away.

"Pants are the worst," she murmured, rocking against me.

Fuck, it felt amazing. "Absolutely."

"But we should probably take it slow."

"Whatever you want," I panted. "But what about the bra?"

Hands set beside my head, she eased back a bit. "I did say naked from the waist up."

"You did."

She exhaled softly. "Go for it."

"Yes!"

My experienced fingers got rid of that red bra in no time and then there she was. Perfect brown nipples. The woman was all sweet curves. She fit into my hands just right.

"I'm sorry you feel they let you down when it came to breast-feeding," I said. "But they are absolutely beautiful."

Smiling, she leaned down to kiss me again. If red silk had been fine against my chest, hard nipples and soft skin were even better. I couldn't even remember the last time I'd been this excited about just making out and reaching second base. Though I guess second base was really just copping a feel, while we were both half naked rolling around on the floor. So second base with a hint of stealing third maybe. We'd reversed positions, Jean under me, her legs wrapped around my hips. By the time we finally made it into a bed, we'd have dry-humping down to an art form.

"I can feel you," she whispered.

"This does not surprise me." I kissed a path up her neck, nibbling on her ear. "Pretty sure I'm about to break the damn fly on my pants."

She laughed, her hands running down my sides. But then she got serious. "Do you mind, taking it in stages?"

"No. I am perfectly happy right where I am."

"Good."

Our kisses got messier, longer, and deeper. My stubble scratched lightly across her soft skin. I wanted to explore every inch of her. Find out what made her sigh and what made her squirm and laugh. I'd happily worship her tits for hours. Kissing and licking them made her hips buck and there was every chance I'd die of the world's biggest hard-on. Because of course my dick ached to be inside of her. But this was all about what made Jean happy.

I could wait. I would wait.

God only knows how long we made out on the floor. Time did not exist. But Ada most certainly did and eventually she woke up wanting her late-night feeding.

"The books say you can start thinking about weaning her off the middle of the night feeding at four to six months."

"You're still reading the books?" asked Jean, hunting around. "Do you see my bra anywhere?"

"By the bear, and here's your top."

"Thanks."

"Yeah, I just . . . I'm interested in her development, you know?"

"I think it's sweet. You two are like buddies." She got her bra back on, a huge grin on her face. "That was some good clean adult fun, though."

"Maybe next time we can move onto having some good dirty adult fun," I suggested, pulling my shirt back on. "If you're ready."

"Oh, I think we're definitely ready for third base," she said as Ada increased the volume on her wailing. "Coming, baby."

"Pants are the worst." I gave her a quick kiss, then made for the door. "I better get home, hit the shower."

She made a little noise in her throat. "I know exactly what you're going to do in that shower. You disgust me. I wish I could watch."

"Another time." I grinned. "Good night, my friend."

"'Night."

CHAPTER FOURTEEN

Later in the week, we hadn't yet made it to third base. Mostly due to Ada deciding to be an overachiever and start teething early. Maybe she was making up for not smiling on time. I'd told her the books said she had another couple of months to go before she hit that stage, but the baby didn't listen to science and reason. So two nights ago, I'd done an emergency run to Walgreens to fetch teething gel and a teething-ring thing. With Nell getting more pregnant by the day, it was easier for me to run errands for Jean and I didn't mind. Hell, I loved being the person she asked for help. Being the person she relied on, someone she trusted, felt damn good. And it was way easier for me to go grab stuff than for her to load up the baby and the car at some crazy hour.

I got all the way to Thursday night, and third base was nowhere in sight. To be honest, I'd actually have settled happily for another romp around second. But I hadn't even seen either of them since yesterday morning. Still, maybe Ada's new teething gel would see an improvement. That would be a relief for all our sakes. I tried not to get my hopes up about it and just focus on the work in front of me.

"There you go," I said, sliding a French martini across the bar to Taka.

"Thanks." He nodded and went off to serve it to whatever customer.

It'd been a good night so far. Vaughan and I kept busy behind the bar due to a decent amount of people coming in for dinner and drinks. Nell had picked out an interesting mix of female artists for the music, making for a great atmosphere. Aretha Franklin, Björk, Sia, and more.

To my knowledge, she hadn't yet found out about Jean and me getting more intimate. Not that it was any of her business. But if she did know, the woman would be on the warpath. There'd probably have been knives thrown my way, the odd roasting pan—who knows how many weapons she could find in a commercial kitchen. I really didn't want to find out. Let sleeping dragon-ladies lie.

It was close to eight when Jean came in with the baby and an older couple. A man and a woman in their fifties at a guess. Ada was in one of those infant car seats that you can pop out and carry around. Weird, Jean hadn't made any mention of dropping by. Also, I had a bad feeling about who the people with her might be. Taka seated them at a corner table away from the main lights and some of the louder parties. A good call. Overstimulation could freak Ada out sometimes. And apparently worrying about Ada and Jean both could freak me out sometimes. A sudden sweat pricked at my shirt.

Shit. Were those really her parents come to visit from Florida?

When I caught Jean's eye, she gave me a tight-looking smile and a wave. Her (probable) mother spotted the movement, head snapping around as she sought me out with her eyes. Not a happy face, though it was a familiar one. Mother and daughter looked a lot alike.

The woman said something and Jean answered, still with that strained smile in place. Whatever she'd said had Jean's dad frowning at me too. Great. I tried standing taller, shoulders back, and head up. Jesus, I'd even worn a neat white button-down shirt with black suspenders today. You'd have thought rockin' style would make up for the long hair and tattoos with the older set. Apparently not.

"Trouble incoming?" asked Vaughan. Trust the musician to be the fastest at reading the crowd.

"Don't know. But it doesn't look good."

The ginger sighed. "Parents-in-law are the worst. It's just the way it is. Lydia's are next to fucking useless. Some people shouldn't be allowed to have kids."

"Jean and I are just friends."

He gave me a long look. "Dude, swear to God, you're going to get sick of spinning that shit someday soon and I for one cannot wait to see what happens."

"Fuck off," I muttered.

Instead of waiting for table service, Jean slipped out of the booth. She lifted Ada out of the baby carrier and brought her over. Poor baby. Two angry pink spots still lit her cheeks as she gummed at the teething ring.

"She still doesn't look happy," I said, reaching out to pat her soft little head.

"No." Jean gave me a glum look. "I thought she might like to see her best buddy, Eric."

"Man, I wanted to be best buddy," complained Vaughan. "Poor cutie. No smiles today, huh?"

Jean kissed Ada's cheek. "Not today, unfortunately."

"Being a baby is rough sometimes."

"That it is."

Taka came up to the bar and Vaughan got busy filling his order.

"Can I have a cuddle?" I asked, slipping out of the bar.

"You sure can." Jean carefully handed the baby over. For a

second, Ada startled, then seemed to recognize me and chilled. Well, as much as she was of a mind to chill.

"Hey, sweetheart." I cradled her in one arm, helping her to keep the teething ring up to her mouth with the other. "That tooth still giving you grief?"

"That one's cut. I think she's got another coming through." Jean wiped Ada's chin with a rag. With teething, the dribble had gone into overdrive.

"What's the rush, baby girl?"

Jean just looked at her baby and smiled. She'd gone to some effort for her folks. Hair in a bun, makeup, and the sweater dress and tights combo she'd worn to the Christmas party. God, she looked good enough to eat. But then, she always did.

"You look gorgeous," I said. "Got some friends with you tonight, I see."

"Yes. I, ah . . ."

"Your folks?"

She nodded. "Honestly, I wasn't sure they'd come. But they said they wanted to meet her and here they are."

"Mm."

"They're staying at the resort on the lake."

"That gives you all some space."

Ada chose that moment to remove the teething ring long enough to babble something. I helped her put it back in her mouth.

"Wise words, little girl," I said. "In fact, I was just about to say the same thing."

A hint of a grin appeared around the sides of the ring.

"For him, you smile. I've had nothing but tears and tantrums for days." Jean quietly laughed. "If her first word is 'Eric' I'm going to kill you. Just a warning."

"Fair enough," I said.

While I tried not to notice, Jean's mom most definitely had a look on her face like she expected me to drop the baby at any moment. Sheesh. Her body language was all rigid and her eyes were popping out of her head. Like I hadn't racked up hours of baby holding by now. Where the hell had she been when Jean needed help?

All right, so it might take me a while to drop my resentment toward the woman and her husband. Just staying out of their way while they visited sounded like a wise plan.

"How's the visit going?" I asked in a nice, calm, and pleasant tone. "When did they arrive?"

Jean smoothed back her hair, one hand on her hip. "Yesterday. I think it's going okay. There's still a lot of tension. They love Miss Ada, however."

"How could they not?"

"I swear, if Mom takes any more photos her cell's memory will explode."

"Hey," said Nell, barging in. "So your folks came. Hand her over, Eric."

I frowned, but did as told. Happily, Ada immediately burst into tears at being parted from me. If that didn't deserve a victory lap of the bar then I didn't know what did. Nell clicked her tongue and started cooing supposedly comforting nonsense at the outraged infant. None of it worked.

"Yes, they actually came," said Jean, rubbing Ada's back as she lay slumped over Nell's shoulder.

The baby's cries petered out and Nell said, "There we go."

Note: Ada only stopped crying because I stood behind Nell making funny faces. The baby and I were tight. Not bothering to point this out showed great restraint and maturity on my part.

"How are you doing?" asked Nell. "You were so nervous about their arrival."

Jean had told Nell about the impending visit, but not me.

Weird. Though I guess we had been busy lately covering our bases and dealing with teething.

"They're being really great about her." Jean's tense smile returned, her pretty face lined. "Even apologized again about the inheritance and everything."

"How do you feel about that?" I asked.

Nell turned, shooting me a strange look.

I just ignored it.

"Honestly, I don't know," said Jean. "So much happened, I think it's going to take some time to get over it all. But they are her grandparents. Speaking of which, I better get back . . ."

Nell handed over the precious cargo, fingers lingering against Ada's chubby little cheek. "Bye-bye, Ada."

"I'll introduce you to my parents later," promised Jean.

"Great." Nell waved, wandering back into the kitchen.

"We're not too busy, you want me to look after her while you eat?" I asked.

"We should be okay, thanks."

No mention of introducing me to her folks, but whatever. Like in the last thirty years of my life I'd ever wanted to meet a girl's parents. God, what a joke. I'd faked death at least once just to avoid it. Long story.

"Want me to stop by after work?" I asked.

"Mom and Dad are heading back to their room after dinner, so . . . I'll see how we're doing?" Her smile relaxed into something far more beautiful and it was all for me. "But that would be nice, Eric."

It had turned into a habit of ours now. If everyone was sleeping peacefully, or attempting to, Jean left a towel hanging over the doorknob so I'd know not to knock. Andre had laughed his ass off at our oh-so-discreet signal. Just because some unenlightened people used a towel on the door to signify screwing was taking place didn't mean it couldn't be used for sleeping babies as well. The man had a seriously small and dirty mind. Though, to be fair, there was at least a somewhat filthy subtext to the towel signal.

"I'll see you later," she said.

"Right."

And I wanted to kiss her on the forehead, give her shoulder a squeeze. Touch her in same small way out in public where everyone could see. So they'd know we were something to each other. But I didn't. Jean headed back to the table and her waiting parents while I went back to work. After work, however, well, that just might be a different matter entirely.

Later that night, she opened her apartment door with my name on her lips. A whisper like a secret. Guess it was a secret, mostly. What we got up to after hours. Or basically any hours we could steal when Ada was asleep and I wasn't working. I'd always scoffed at the idea of people with kids making appointments to get it on. As if sex was a job to get done, tick it off a list. Sex as something to fit in around the household routine and all that shit. But now I got it. Big-time.

"Hey," I whispered back hoarsely because oh boy.

The woman had on some silky gray robe with a matching slip underneath. It was sexy as fuck. The lingerie, the heat in Jean's eyes, and the general quiet of the place told me Ada was down for the night. Or, please God, at least for a couple of hours. Third base was officially in the cards. And maybe, just maybe, the glorious possibility of fourth. My heart beat double-time in my chest.

After looking around to check that the hallway was empty, she grabbed the front of my jacket, dragging me into her apartment with a quiet "Get in here."

"Yes, ma'am." I half smiled, shaking my head.

"What?" she asked, the door softly closing behind us.

"You, checking for witnesses."

Her nose crinkled in question.

"All of the people living here at least suspect what we're up to. If they don't already know what we're up to," I said. "Are you ashamed of me or something?"

"What? No, of course not," she told my shirt.

I tipped her chin up a little. "Tell me again, looking me in the eyes this time."

"You're the one in fear of castration if Nell finds out," she said. "I'm just making sure nothing potentially interferes with my new favorite hobby." She met my gaze squarely. "Now, can we save the talk for after the kissing . . . please?"

There was every chance I might be one of the great idiots of our time when it came to this woman. But I just couldn't resist those lips. Same went for her impatience, her greed when it came to this. I tried to kiss her sweetly and lightly, to ease into things. Heaven help me, the plan lasted last all of about half a second. The press of her mouth on mine and I was lost. Hands wound around my neck, her body against mine. My palms slid down her spine, going straight for her ass yet again. Because apparently I continued to be incapable of smooth moves when it came to her. Our tongues tangled, one or both of us moaning as she climbed me like a tree. From there, we kind of stumbled into the bedroom.

"You bought more candles," I said, but the words came out garbled. Apparently, the ability to kiss and talk at the same time took more skill than I possessed.

"You demanded at least three."

"Mm."

I set her down on the mattress, her hands pushing my jacket off my shoulders. "Everything off."

"Okay."

We disconnected long enough for me to ditch everything but my boxer briefs. Boots and socks hit the floor, while the jacket, shirt, undershirt, and pants got tossed onto a chair in the corner. Nowhere near any of the dozen or so candles because we did not need the fire department interrupting our together time. Meanwhile, Jean slipped out of the robe, but kept the rest on.

"What about you?" I asked, eyeing the slinky shift. "I like your taste in lingerie, but I like it when we're skin-to-skin too."

She didn't answer.

Fine. Lingerie it was. I crawled back onto the bed and on top of her. It was my brand-new happy place. Though I'm pretty sure being under or beside her would result in the exact same feeling.

But this time her head stayed back, not arching up hungrily for my lips. "Everything okay?"

Her chest rose as she took a deep breath. "I think I'm having a moment."

"About?"

"Watching you at work tonight." She gathered up my hair, holding it back from my face. Fingertips slid along my jawline while a line appeared between her brows. "I'd forgotten the effect you have on people."

"The effect I have on people?"

"You're the whole package . . . funny, charming, handsome," she said. "Not only can you string a full sentence together, but you're also gainfully employed and without a criminal record. I've been on dating apps. Believe me, that combination is rarer than you think."

I smiled warily. "Thank you. But what does that have to do with you not wanting to get naked?"

Neck arched, she kissed me slowly. Her tongue slid into my mouth, completely derailing the damn conversation. Without thought, I let some of my weight rest against her, pressing her body into the mattress. Jean eased her legs out from underneath me, her wiggling and me shifting until I lay between her thighs.

Forget happy place. This position made me fucking delirious.

"Sweetheart," I mumbled eventually, my face buried in her neck. Christ, she was so sensitive there. One of my hands slid a strap off her shoulder, acting completely separate from what little remained of my brain. Not that I didn't approve of the move. "Jean. Baby. We were talking."

"No," she moaned.

I swear the sound traveled straight to my dick. There wasn't a single inch of me not strung out and tense with need. "But—"

"I was just having a moment of insecurity. It's nothing."

"Doesn't sound like nothing."

"Later, Eric."

If only my mouth hadn't found a bare nipple right about then, I might have been able to resist and figure out the source of worry in her eyes. Or just generally try and make sense of the conversation. Even worse than her breast, though, was when I slid my hand up her leg, getting higher and higher . . . nothing but bare skin.

"You're not wearing any panties," I said, fingers curled around her hip.

"Is that bad?"

"No no no. It's so damn good, I can't even . . ."

Fuck. The lingerie dragged down off her shoulders and hiked up past her hips. I'd figure out what it was about later. Right now, only touching her, making her come, mattered. Honestly, I worked best with only one or two priorities. The way she squirmed when I dragged my tongue across her nipple was exquisite. Only barely surpassed by the hot damp feel of her naked pussy against my boxer briefs. Everything low in my gut drew tight while my balls grew hot and heavy.

Taking it slow might kill me. But it would be a hell of a way to go.

"I don't want to take it slow either," she murmured.

So apparently I'd said that last thought out loud. "Huh?"

"Let's skip third base," she said.

I slid my knuckles along the seam of her sex. Because not feeling her there immediately was not an option. Her body tensed, her mouth popping open. "Yeah. More."

"What, here?" I slid my fingers up and down those hot wet lips, making her writhe. Hands clutched at my shoulders and she nodded. Never in my life had I felt something so good. "But third base would be me tasting this sweet pussy."

The noise she made. Holy hell.

I teased the tight little nub of her clit with my thumb, my heartbeat taking up residency in my dick. She was so slick and perfect. Every reaction, each move she made, fed my need. Maybe all of those years of practice had been about this one moment. The superhuman ability required to please Jean without losing my load. It made a kind of sense. Not that I'd share the thought with her right now. Or possibly anytime in the future.

"Are you sure you don't want my mouth here?" I asked, pressing a finger into her opening, making her moan even louder.

Thank God Joe had been thorough with the soundproofing. None of the neighbors needed to hear Jean like this. Let alone if we woke the baby. Ada wouldn't be the only one crying. All of those excited little panting noises, moans, and groans were just for me. Once she was good with one finger, writhing against my hand, I gave her another. With my fingers hooked, I gently rubbed, working her inside and out.

"Or you could come just like this on my hand. Wouldn't that be good?"

"Eric." More moaning.

"You know, I could listen to you say my name like that all day." I nipped at her breast. "Makes me harder than a fucking rock."

She waved a hand at one of the bedside tables. "Condoms in the top drawer."

"But, Jean, oral is important."

"Next time," she breathed.

"Are you sure you don't want to stick to the plan?"

Fingers fisted in my hair, pulling it loose and tugging me up to meet her face. "Stop messing around. I mean it."

"You're so bossy in bed." I grinned, staying right where I was. My fingers were in no rush to leave their warm, wet place. "It's sort of surprising how much. I mean, I know you're a bit of a control freak and you like shit being organized. But this really goes beyond that. The minute we're messing around, you turn into like a little sex general. Pushing me against walls, tearing at my clothing, telling me what to do. It's hot as fuck, sweetheart. Keep it up."

Her face screwed up, breasts rising and falling at a furious pace on account of how hard she was breathing. "Eric!"

"Condom. Got it."

First I sucked my fingers clean because sweet treats shouldn't be wasted. Then I reached for the drawer. Christ, she'd really bought quite the selection of prophylactics. I bet they were even alphabetized. Whatever, the closest ones would do. Off with the underwear and on with the protection and we were good to go.

I dragged the wide head of my cock through the swollen lips of her sex. Just enjoying the sensation and torturing the both of us a little more. No matter how badly I wanted to rush this and get inside her. The black of her eyes was so huge, swallowing the surrounding color. And she had her lips open, a faint sheen of sweat on her skin.

Months of going without, wanting only her, had only made this mean more. Even if we were just friends who had sex. Even if it didn't mean anything. Doubts might have crept in then, concerns about losing my touch, forgetting how to do this. But no way would I let anything mess this moment up, including my own stupid head.

Slowly, gradually, I pushed in. Any lingering blood in the upper regions of my body rushed straight to my cock at the feel of her body opening for me. The hot clasp of her vagina around my dick. I should write the woman bad poetry. Hell, I probably would.

"You feel so good," I said, voice low.

Her mouth trembled so I kissed her. Soft lingering kisses, taking my time filling her. It'd been a while for both of us and the last thing I wanted to do was hurt her somehow. Not her body, her heart, or her mind. We might have rushed up to this stage, but now was the time to take it easy. When my body finally rested against her, she slowly exhaled.

"Okay?" I asked.

She nodded. "Just give me a moment."

I pressed my lips to her cheek, her nose, her chin. It wasn't easy, resisting the urge to move. Though I could manage. Right up until when she wiggled beneath me, her inner muscles clutching at my cock.

"Goddammit." I hid my face in her neck, trying not to grind into her and only losing the battle a little.

"Move now."

"Thank fuck for that."

I slid out nice and easy, plunging back in a bit harder. Then the next time a touch faster, building things up gradually. She made a good loud noise, digging her heels into my ass and her nails into my back. Hard nipples scratched at my chest, my balls slapping against her gorgeous ass. Her hips raised to meet every thrust, her body writhing beneath me. Everything fucking per-fect. I'd never thought much about exactly what was involved in making love. But sex with Jean felt about as good as anything could get.

Electricity spiked up and down my spine and I couldn't hold out much longer. With a hand beneath her ass, I gathered her body closer. All the better an angle to stimulate her clit and generally pray she'd come. All of her body tensed, eyelids squeezing shut, locking out the world. As everything inside of her focused, her pussy clutched at my cock, milking me dry. No way I could resist.

We both came, bodies trembling, skin dripping sweat.

My sight darkened, my mind blasted into outer space. Quite possibly, come shot out of me at something close to light speed. But since I had no way of measuring it, we'll never know. Pretty damn sure though that I died there for a minute. Still, even in death, it would be rude to just collapse on top of the woman.

I struggled off of her before collapsing facedown. Shit. What an experience. There was every chance I'd never need sex ever again. Until next time she opened her door with my name a whis-per on her lips.

Jean curled up against me and I rolled onto my side, drawing her in closer.

"Are you okay?" she asked.

I grunted.

Silence.

The musky scent of sex filled the room. But this wasn't just any sex. This was sex care of Jean and me. If only someone could bottle it or make a car air freshener out of it or something so I could smell it whenever I wanted. Slightly wrong and perverted, but I'd be willing to pay. Such great memories and hopefully there'd be many more to come.

"What are you thinking about?" she asked.

"Nothing," I blurted out. "Just, you know. Post-come float. My mind is far away."

"Okay." She shifted a little, the mattress moving. "Was it all right . . . the sex?"

I raised up on one elbow. "Are you kidding me?"

The expression on her face said no. Unbelievable.

"How should I put this?" I sighed. "Your vagina is officially my new new happy place."

She burst out laughing. "New new?"

"You don't take my feelings seriously at all, do you?"

"No, I do. Sorry," she said. "Please explain."

"Well, first hanging out with you was my happy place." I grabbed a pillow and shoved it beneath my head. "Then it was making out with you. But now, it's very much your vagina."

"Sure it's not just vaginas in general?"

"No," I said adamantly. "It's specifically what's between your legs. No one else's legs will do."

"That might just be the strangest compliment I've ever received."

"Not that I don't dig the whole package. But it's sincerely and affectionately meant."

Chewing on the side of her thumb, she rested her head on my bicep. "Thank you, Eric."

"For what?"

I felt more than saw her shrug. "I don't know. For just being you."

"I'm me all the time," I said. "It's something of a specialty of mine. But you're very welcome."

Then she yawned, jaw cracking.

"Actually," I said, thinking it over. "Not sure that's exactly true. Maybe I'm more me with you, if that makes sense."

For a moment, she said nothing. "It makes sense. In a lot of ways, I think maybe I'm more me with you too. You just take me as I am. I don't have to try to be more or pretend or anything. I can just relax and exist, you know?"

"Yes. I've got to go deal with the condom." I slipped out of bed, heading for the bathroom.

By the time I returned to the bedroom, Jean was fast asleep. Not a big surprise, what with Ada having extra trouble settling the last few days. Quietly, I got dressed enough to be mostly decent for the wander over to my own apartment before turning out the light. I was just about to pick up my boots when a certain little baby girl started making snuffling noises followed by a few small cries. I gave her a minute to decide if she was really going to wake up or just go back to sleep. But no, the cries got louder and more exuberant.

"Is that Ada?" Jean mumbled sleepily. And she'd had night after night of this followed by awesome sex with me. The woman was worn out and needed her rest.

"It's okay, sweetheart," I said. "I'll get her."

"You got her?"

"Yeah. Go back to sleep." Carefully, I closed Jean's bedroom door. I'd have patted myself on the back for being the best friend with benefits ever, but I had a baby to look after.

And that's how I wound up answering the door to Jean's parents the next morning half naked.

CHAPTER FIFTEEN

Jean's mom's mouth just kind of hung open. Meanwhile, her dad's lips disappeared into a very thin white line.

"Hi," I said, settling Ada a little higher on my shoulder. Bare because the baby had puked on my undershirt after her morning feeding a few hours ago. True, my hair was tangled to shit and I didn't exactly look my best. But at least I had pants on. "Was, um, Jean expecting you?"

Apparently this was the wrong thing to say because they both looked even crankier. Neither of them deigned to reply.

I stepped back from the door. "Ah, please. Come in. Jean's just sleeping so I was looking after the baby. I'm her neighbor, Eric Collins."

"Yes, she mentioned you at dinner last night," said her mom. "Do you look after Ada often?"

"Sometimes."

"You know how to look after a baby?"

"I learned. Ada's a great teacher."

"Thought Jean was only friends with Nell," said the dad, finally speaking. Though given the tone he used, I really wished he hadn't.

"Your daughter's a smart, kind, sweet woman," I said, getting a little cranky myself. "She's had friends here since the day she arrived. There are plenty of people *here* who care about her."

"You've heard something about our family dramas obviously," said the woman, smoothing back her neat head of thick dark hair. Easy to see where Jean had gotten her good looks from. Fine lines bracketed the woman's mouth and eased out from beside her eyes. But age hadn't diminished her one bit. Pity about the shit attitude. "It's easy to judge from the outside."

"Very easy," I agreed. "For instance, you're assuming all sorts of crap about your daughter because of me being here."

The dad grunted.

Fuck, I knew that noise. My own father made it all the damn time. Especially when he was seeing something he didn't like and hearing things that didn't suit him. Old bastard. The older couple stood in the living room, still giving me weird looks. Whatever. Without a doubt, they'd be reflecting on how much I was like the dick who'd knocked up Jean and disappeared. So I didn't look like a doctor or a lawyer or someone who wore a suit five days a week to work in a corner office. Tattoos and long hair didn't make you a bad person. All of this shit was on the inside.

"Where is our daughter?" the dad finally asked, looking around the apartment. As if she might be hiding in a corner and spring out at any moment to surprise them and save them from this awkward-as-fuck encounter.

I wished.

"She's sleeping," I said. "That's why I'm looking after Ada. With her teething, Jean hasn't gotten much rest the last couple of nights. So I crashed on the couch and took care of the baby so she could get some sleep."

"Oh."

The mom sighed. "We warned her having a baby on her own would be hard work."

"Jean's a great parent and she deals just fine." I kept my face nice and blank. These people, they hurt my head. "But everyone can do with a little help now and then. No one should have to go through life on their own. That's what family and friends are for, isn't it? Supporting each other, being there for each other even if you don't exactly agree with all of their life choices?"

Hint, hint.

Dad's frown increased by about a billion. Over guilt or me, who knew? Meanwhile, the mom seemed to be putting a whole lot of effort not to let her gaze drop to my bare chest.

"Ada threw up on my shirt," I told her.

"Oh." Again.

They actually seemed a bit startled by this new information. Judgey asshats. And even if I might in fact be having sex with their daughter, information like that definitely fell under the heading of none of their goddamn business.

I physically resisted the frown lines threatening to crease my brow. No sense making this more uncomfortable for Jean than it already looked like it was becoming. On my shoulder, Ada babbled happily while sucking on a fist. I don't know how she could be so happy with life on so little sleep, but at least she wasn't crying or puking anymore.

"I'll go see if Jean's awake," I said, walking, not running away from her parents.

All those years of avoiding meeting a girl's folks. I'd been so right. A shame I'd fallen headfirst into the situation here and now, but the rules for what I was willing to do for Jean were distinctly different than for just about every other woman I'd ever been involved with. It was a fact. No point denying it. Eventually, I'd probably have to give her the whole, "Hey, let's attempt being a couple" speech. Hopefully, she'd be more receptive to it than Karen had.

A guy could only hope.

Gently, I knocked on Jean's bedroom door before opening it to peek inside. Shit. Even first thing in the morning, the woman looked like my dirtiest dreams come true. Sometime during the night, she'd kicked off the blankets and the negligee had ridden up her thigh. I slipped into her room, closing the door behind me. Let her folks think what they liked. Honestly, the damage was probably already done.

"Jean?"

"Mm?" Slowly, she stirred. "What's the time?"

"Almost nine. And, ah, your parents are here."

"My parents?"

"Yeah."

At that, she bolted upright in bed, eyes wide. "But, Eric, you're only half dressed. In my apartment. First thing in the morning."

"Yeah, took me forever to get Ada back to sleep, and then she kept waking up," I said. "I just grabbed a cushion off the couch and crashed in her room so I could get to her before she woke you."

Jean's eyes went all soft. "You slept on the floor in her nursery?"

"You were exhausted, sweetheart. You needed sleep."

"Wow." She scratched at her head. "My parents are here and you're here and you've all met each other. Okay."

I gave her a minute. Clearly, she needed it. For her, this was probably the equivalent of Nell finding out about us. Only I'd long since accepted that that would happen and pain would follow. Jean was still navigating the ins and outs of having her parents meet me. Obviously.

She slumped. "God, they probably think I'm back to my old wild girl ways and we're having sex parties every time Ada goes down for a nap."

"I told them I slept on the couch and that I got baby puke on my shirt," I said. "Both of which are true. Mostly. Definitely the puke part."

At this news, the worry seemed to seep straight out of her. A hint of a smile lit her face. "You slept on the floor and got puked on."

"Being best buds with Ada has its perks, don't get me wrong." I bussed the baby's head. "But it definitely has its downsides too. Not that I mind."

"You're too good to us. I don't deserve a friend like you. But . . ." Her gaze darted to the bedroom door. The solid wood was obviously not up to the job of blocking her parents' judgey eyes.

"But what?"

She just shook her head.

"You don't need their approval, sweetheart."

"Logically, I know that. I guess it's just habit," she said. "I was so close to my grandma. She meant everything to me. To think Ada might miss out on having that sort of connection sucks."

"It's not your fault or really your choice, though. Is it?"

"No, I guess not." Jean gave me a smile that didn't work for shit. "They seem to be trying."

No comment there from me.

"Anyway, thank you for letting me sleep. I owe you big-time. We'll discuss this later." She bounded off the bed and started pulling on clothing. "Has she had her morning bottle?"

"A few hours ago."

"Did you get any sleep at all?"

"A little," I said. "You know, she's very demanding, made me sing Janis to her for hours. Babies are hard work."

Jean snorted. "Tell me about it."

"How'd you sleep?"

"Amazing."

"Good."

She took Ada from me, settling the baby against her own shoulder before leaning in real close. "Morning-breath warning."

"Lay it on me," I said without hesitation.

Her closed lips pressed firmly against mine. "You're the best."

"I know."

"And so humble." She laughed. "How did my parents react to you being here?"

"I think they're a little weirded out."

"Hmm. We're not much of a secret, you and me, are we?"

"I don't know about that," I said. "Nell still hasn't attacked me with a chainsaw or anything, so we can't be doing too badly. How long are your parents here for anyway?"

"Only a few days."

"Oh, hey. Before I forget, a friend's having a get-together Monday if you're up for it." I tried to sound casual, but I really, really wanted her to go with me. It promised to be pretty special. Plus the weekend was coming up and it was going to be a busy one at work. Since both Vaughan and Pat were occupied elsewhere, there wouldn't be much time for sneaking in visits to my two favorite girls. Doubtless, Nell would be inviting her to the party as well. Hopefully, however, I'd gotten there first. "Should be fun. What do you say?"

"Will it be baby friendly?"

"Of course." I gave Ada's little back a rub. "I think there'll be other kids there."

"Then I'd love to."

My heart stuttered at the mention of *that* word. The L thing on her lips had power for some reason. No biggie. It was stupid really. I'd maybe give my reaction some thought later. Or try never to think about it ever again so long as I lived. I wasn't sure which just yet.

"Okay," I said. "You distract your parents while I make a run for the front door."

"They're not that bad. Or were they?"

"Be ready with that distraction," I said. "I'm trusting you to have my back here."

She laughed again. Prettiest sound in the world. Right up there with her moans.

"I better go grab a few hours' sleep before work," I said. "Also, we need to make a date for adult playtime again soon."

"Yes, we very much do," she said. "Thank you again for looking after her all night so I could sleep."

"Anytime. Ready?"

I opened the door with a grin while she giggled. But all of that shit quickly stopped the minute her parents' gaze hit us. There was so much worry in their eyes. Disapproval, maybe? Then I remembered, they'd been the ones to drive away their only child. If Jean and Ada were halfway across the country from them, they'd been the cause. All the time I'd spent hanging out with Ada had given me a small taste of what it must mean to be responsible for a child, to get all wound up worrying about their future. So I could appreciate their reservations. Didn't mean you could go trying to make the decisions for your kid indefinitely, however.

Something seemed to change in her mom's demeanor, though. The woman stepped forward, holding out her hand. If anything, she seemed a bit flustered. "We didn't think to introduce ourselves to you, Eric. I'm Leah and this is my husband, Will."

"Nice to meet you." I shook Jean's mom's hand, then her dad's. He seemed hesitant at first, but then gave me a grim smile. Maybe they weren't so bad. It'd probably been a bit of a surprise to find me answering their daughter's door half dressed. But surely the baby on my shoulder clued them in to the fact that it wasn't all sex games and swinging from a chandelier. I was there to help their daughter, not harm her.

"Hi, Mom," said Jean. "Dad."

Immediately, a wide grin cracked her dad's face. "Sorry to drop in unannounced, honey."

Jean gave them both a kiss, handing over Ada for some cuddling from her grandmother.

"We thought we might take you to breakfast?" asked her mom with a smile. "How's my gorgeous granddaughter?"

Ada whimpered, then changed her mind and gave a rebel yell. After this came a small, brief smile.

"I better go," I said.

"Or you could join us for breakfast too?" asked Leah hesitantly.

"That's real kind of you, but I have work later. Need to get some sleep first."

"Another time."

"Definitely, that'd be great." Maybe. We'd see. Had to give the woman points for trying, though. Then Jean gave me a smile. One of those we've-got-a-secret-and-it's-really-damn-good kind of smiles. I fucking loved those. Or liked. Just really strongly liked them. Also, she probably shouldn't be doing that in front of her parents. Heh. Whatever.

"Nice to meet you, Eric," said Leah.

"You too." I gave both her and her husband a nod, grabbed my things, and got gone.

Great sex. Amazing, as Jean had said. But what a hell of a morning.

Also, I needed some sleep.

"Yeah, but who is your favorite in the band? It's me, right? It's okay to be honest. I deal well with adulation."

Jean opened her mouth, then closed it again with a small

frown, looking kind of overwhelmed. It seemed to be a common feeling when it came to this sort of situation. The guys, the mansion, the whole damn thing would be kind of huge if you hadn't seen it all before.

"Leave her alone, man," I said, holding Ada on my lap.

"Shh," said Mal, the owner of the insanely large log cabin–style mansion. "This is important. Don't interfere. I want her honest, unbiased, me-centric opinion."

Sitting over on the floor, playing blocks with his daughters, Jimmy Ferris shook his head. How the dark-haired bastard always managed to look like he'd just stepped off the cover of *GQ* magazine, I had no idea. If only I had his money to burn on suits and shit. That would be cool. Instead, bills, savings, and real-life shit came first. Sadly.

"Ever since he got less screen time than me in the Stage Dive documentary he's been like this," said Jimmy. "So insecure it's pathetic."

"That is not true," said Mal, pushing his long blond hair back from his face. "Take it back, Jimbo."

"This is the problem with rock stars," I said quietly to Jean. "Delicate yet enormous egos. I'm surprised their skulls don't explode from the pressure. Man, you're in a world-famous band. Have a little dignity."

"I'm dignified. See if I let you stay in my beach house again." Mal sniffed. "Hey, Zeny. You love Uncle Mal best, right?"

One of the dark-headed little girls had left the game of blocks to give the drummer a cuddle. Mostly, I think it was pity. Mal wrapped her up in his arms, lifting her off her feet for a moment. Except her sister, Stephanie, took that moment to come up behind Zeny and clumsily tickle her. Next came much screaming, making Ada start in surprise. The two girls then ran off down a hallway. Who exactly was chasing who was kind of hard to tell.

"And I thought you were loud," I told Ada.

Jimmy barked out a laugh. "You haven't heard anything yet. Their lungs get bigger and it's like . . . Jesus, I don't even know how to describe it. Some days we'd give anything for a mute button. Even for just a few minutes' peace. When they go to bed and everything's quiet, it's heaven. But when they're going hammer and tongs, it's like a rock band with too many drummers."

"Hey, what?" protested Mal, apparently trying to work out if he was meant to be offended. "Too many drummers? How is such a thing even possible?"

"At least they're big enough to understand some things now. We can occasionally reason with them." Lena rose from another grouping of couches, a glass of wine in her hand.

"You mean kids or drummers?" chimed in Jimmy.

"The toddler years are hard," Lena continued, ignoring him. "All of those tantrums over god only knows what. Speaking of which, I'd better go find the girls before they break something."

"Thanks, babe," said Jimmy.

Lena blew him a kiss.

Beside me on the probably billion-dollar leather couch, Jean still had a lot of white showing in her eyes. Guess we should have given her more warning. Only Nell thought it would be funny to just spring meeting the guys on her. To be fair, it kind of was. Jean had done little but stutter and stare for the first while. Apart from when she thumped me in the arm for not warning her. But it was a friendly thump, a loving one almost. I could tell.

"I still can't believe you went to school with Stage Dive," she said. "I mean, I'd heard they came from Coeur d'Alene, but still . . ."

"It was only forty-three more seconds of screen time," bitched Mal.

"Let it go," said David from over by the massive fireplace.

"Easy for you to say. You got way more close-ups than me."

Anne came up behind her husband, placing her hands on his shoulders and proceeding to massage. "Mal, we talked about this."

"I know, I know."

"Let's just enjoy our time with our friends, okay?"

He sighed unhappily. "Fine. It was a stupid documentary anyway."

"Hear it's up for some awards," said Ben with a smile. "Isn't that great?"

Anne swore quietly under her breath.

There were a bunch of couches and armchairs set up around the space. Floor-to-ceiling windows looked over the lake and a roaring fireplace. It was all pretty damn spectacular and the turnout had been good. All of the Stage Dive crew including their significant others. Nell and Pat, Andre, and Vaughan and Lydia. Taka, Rosie, and Boyd and Co. were running the Dive Bar in our absence. It might take a few more years for me to get used to having kids running around during our rare get-togethers, however. Each time, seeing everyone getting a little older, a bit more mature.

"Besides," Mal chirped up, "every minute of my screen time is worth ten minutes of anyone else's."

Except for Mal, the idiot, of course.

"Well, I agree every minute of your screen time *feels* like about ten minutes," Jimmy shot back.

And maybe Jimmy. Though beneath his needling of Mal, he seemed a lot more relaxed in his own skin since he and Lena had gotten together. Speaking of which, still no sign of her or the twins. Beside the bass player, Ben, sat a young boy playing games on a tablet. The kid was totally engrossed. Couldn't help but wonder what Ada would be like in a few years, running around yelling her head off like a wild child or sitting quietly lost in her own little world? It'd be amazing to watch her grow. Not that she didn't have her own personality from the start. But to see her get bigger, to hear her first words, and see her first steps maybe.

"Didn't think I'd ever see you going all gaga about a baby." Mal smirked and took a sip of his beer.

I shrugged. "Just happened. Hey, Ada?"

She kicked her feet in reply, little hands clinging to my fingers.

"I think it's lovely," said Anne, giving Mal a pat on the head.

"I've changed diapers. I've dealt with babies." Mal grimaced. "Between Jimmy and Ben setting their sperm free, we've got enough kids running around."

Anne sighed. "Quit bitching about it. We're having one after the next tour is over and that's that."

"Fine. If only to prove our progeny would be even better looking than the rest." He leaned his head back, drawing Anne down for a kiss. "We might need to have a couple of them. You know how competitive the rest of the guys are. We'll need to keep up."

"Sounds good," said Anne, rubbing her cheek against his.

"In the meantime, lots of practice, pumpkin. Every day, morning and night."

"Got it."

"Hours' worth of practice," he continued. "We need to attack this like we're training for the Olympics. The sex Olympics. We'll even video some, watch it for quality-control purposes. Give ourselves ratings. I'll always score a ten, though. Actually, probably eleven."

"Jesus," I muttered. "Can you two lovebirds go talk about your weird sex life in private?"

Anne laughed.

"No," said Mal. "But thank you for asking."

I did a quick check for any kids, then covered Ada's eyes and flipped him the bird.

"I know," said the blond drumming idiot. "Let's discuss your sex life instead. It'll keep things even. Eric's letting you down in all ways, right, Jean?"

Jean just blinked.

I looked to heaven for help. Because despite what Mal might think, he wasn't in fact God. No help, however, was forthcoming.

"It's okay, you're among friends," he continued. "Eric's a complete disappointment to you, isn't he? You find yourself falling asleep mid-action, things like that?"

"Enough," said Anne, taking the beer off Mal and having a swig herself. "Stop talking now."

"But I want Jean to feel supported."

Lips tight, Anne shook her head.

"Plus, we probably need to find out now if people ever actually manage to have sex again after a baby," said Mal, looking around the room. "You'll notice neither Jimmy and Lena nor Ben and Lizzy have gotten pregnant again. What if after a baby everything just stops working? We need to find this sort of shi . . . um, stuff out."

"You just moved here last year, Jean?" asked Anne, ignoring her husband.

"Yes." Jean latched onto the change of subject. "I love Coeur d'Alene. It's such a pretty place."

"It is. I always enjoy spending time here."

"You're way off track there." Nell waddled over to join our group. "They're not together. No sex life to talk about."

Head cocked, Mal narrowed his eyes.

"It's the truth." Nell shrugged.

I kept my gaze on the baby. Beside me, Jean fussed, hands fiddling with a rip in her jeans. Next she raised Ada's bib, wiping away a particularly spectacular line of drool.

Mal cleared his throat loudly, and the hairs on the back of my neck leapt to attention. "Nell, my dear, how is it you're not sensing the chemistry between these two fine folk?"

"Shut it," I said, voice low so as not to spook the baby. "None of this is any of your business and you're embarrassing Jean. She's never even met you before and you're acting like an ass."

The easy smile fell from Mal's face. "Sorry, Jean. Didn't mean to make you feel awkward. Just Eric."

"We've all known each other a long time," said Nell, hand on her lower back. "The gossiping can get a bit out of hand. Not that there's any gossip here to talk about."

Mal muttered something.

I swear to God, I could have killed him.

"What did you say?" asked Nell.

Pat came up behind her. His big tattooed hands cupped her belly. Thank fuck, someone with some sense had arrived. Now if he'd just pretend to faint or something to take all of this attention away from me and Jean. That would be great. Or he could cart Nell off to one of the rooms for some very careful sex or something. I didn't care. So long as this topic of conversation got buried.

"What's going on?" he asked in his gravelly voice.

The frown on Nell's face was epic. No amount of Botox could get those lines out. "Mal's just stirring things up, same as always. He's trying to insinuate something's going on between these two. Like Jean doesn't have better taste."

And honestly, I'd kind of had enough. Of people sticking their noses into our business and of Nell thinking she was in charge. And apparently, I wasn't the only one.

"Nell, I love you. You're like the sister I never had," said Jean, back straight and chin jutting out. "You have been nothing but kind and supportive to Ada and me. And I thank you for it. But you need to give Eric a break."

Nell actually seemed taken aback for once, her brows high.

"Also, what goes on between him and me is private." Jean exhaled. "That goes for everyone."

Holy shit.

Apparently the keeping it on the down low rule had changed. On my lap, Ada started fussing. Probably picking up on the tension or something. I lifted her up, holding her against my chest where she continued to grizzle and grumble. Fair enough. The whole conversation made me want to do a little of the same myself.

"Hold up," said Nell, outrage in her voice. "Something is going on between you and him? Are you serious?"

Holy shit.

Jean said nothing.

I sat very, very still.

Nell, of course, was only getting started. "But I warned you about what he's—"

"Babe," said Pat, gently trying to turn her to face him. "Let it go."

"No, but—"

He bent down, whispering in her ear, saying all sorts of things. Stuff about Jean being an adult and making her own decisions. How Nell had no business trying to keep Jean and me apart if we wanted to be together. And lastly, that Nell needed to forgive me and move on. All of the shit I would have liked to say, only anything I had to say, Nell didn't want to hear. Apparently, she didn't want to hear it from her husband either, because she stormed off down the hallway. Much like the twins had earlier only with less screaming. Pat followed quietly behind.

And all the while, I rubbed Ada's back, trying to soothe us

both. Honest to God, it felt like we were back in fucking high school. Everyone involved in everyone else's business.

"Wow," said Mal. "That was intense."

Anne ignored his comment, pasting a determined smile on her face. "Jean, would you mind helping me bring out the food?"

"Sure," said Jean, getting to her feet. "Just let me heat up a bottle for Ada first. Eric, are you okay to give it to her?"

"Yeah." I nodded.

"I'll come too," offered Evelyn, dragging David behind her. Not that the guitarist seemed to mind. They were always holding hands as if they'd been surgically attached. Something that previously would have weirded me out. The constant touching and carrying on of couples. But now with Jean, I actually wouldn't mind some of the same. Without everyone else breathing down our necks, of course.

The twins chose this moment to zoom back into the room, their mom following at a slightly more sedate pace. Lena looked puffed just the same, cheeks pink and breathing fast as if the two small girls had led her on one hell of a chase. She collapsed onto a couch, giving us all a smile. "Nothing broken. Or at least, I don't think they broke anything." Then she frowned. "What did I miss?"

Every eye seemed to focus on me.

"Nothing," I said.

Silence. From everyone except Mal, of course.

"Apparently Eric and Jean are doing the nasty. Not a surprise, right? The way those two look at each other . . . I mean, there are children in the room. Now we just need to find someone pretty to mess with Andre's bachelor status," said Mal. Because, as I might have mentioned previously, he was an idiot. "Look at you, man. You silver fox, you."

Andre just smiled. "I'm not holding a baby like Eric. Start with me and I can and will come over there and hurt you."

Still sitting on the floor, Jimmy hid his laughter behind a cough. He didn't even bother to do it particularly well. Think I liked him even more for it.

"I'll help," offered Ben.

Mouth turned down, Mal sank into the corner of the sofa. "That's just rude is what that is."

CHAPTER SIXTEEN

"Sorry. That wasn't exactly what I had in mind when I asked if you'd like to come with."

Jean looked up from where she was sorting out all of Ada's stuff on her kitchen table. The empty baby bottles were taken apart and set beside the sink, ready for washing. Next came a couple of dribble rags and a bib, followed by the bagged dirty nappies. "It's fine. I had a good time."

Apparently these days I was too polite to call shit. But my brows rose just the same.

"No, really," she said. "I did."

"All right. What can I do to help?"

"Grab a seat and keep me company." She filled the sink with hot soapy water and got busy cleaning the bottles, plastic nipples, and all those bits. Then they got placed in the microwave sterilizer thing.

Like I'd sit while she still worked. I bustled around trying to find something to do. "Chuck these in the laundry bag in the bathroom?" I asked, picking up the rags and bib.

"Thanks."

Ada had conked out in the car on the drive home. She'd stirred when we lifted her out of the baby seat, but happily drifted off again back in her crib. All of the noise, people, and excitement had been a lot for a little girl. After the revelation, Jean had taken her over to Nell for a cuddle and they'd talked for a while. Hopefully their friendship was okay. It would survive. Nell just had a tendency to believe she knew best when it came to the people she cared about. But Jean could make her own choices.

And thank fuck she'd chosen me, even publicly, in front of everybody.

Hard to tell if she wanted to talk about it all or not. It'd been one hell of a day. I was still catching up with the changes. What it all meant. If everyone knowing something was going on between Jean and me meant anything at all. To say nothing of the small fact about Nell knowing something was going on between us— and what wrath she might currently be plotting against me. God, trying to figure it out made my head hurt.

While she popped the sterilizer into the microwave, I got rid of the bagged dirty diapers and then went and washed my hands. She finished up wiping down the counters and emptying the sink.

"You want those put somewhere?" I asked, nodding at the baby bags.

"Just in the corner over there, thanks."

We worked in silence, sorting everything out. It was nice, peaceful, after all of the drama at Mal's place. Jean's apartment was pretty organized these days. Each week a little bit of her former control was being reclaimed, corner by corner, bench by bench, room by room. By now, everything was neat and tidy and in its place most of the time. We had that in common. Both of us liked our surroundings nice. How long it would last once Ada started crawling, we'd have to wait and see.

"Are you hungry?" she asked.

I shook my head. "You?"

"No, not really. There was a lot of food."

"Yeah, they have a habit of going overboard."

She bit at the edge of her thumbnail. A definite nervous tell.

"Want to tell me what's on your mind?"

Back set to the kitchen counter, she groaned. "I guess I'm still a bit embarrassed that all of that came out while we were there. Not that I mind people knowing. It just seemed such a stupid thing to come out, given—" She broke off and shook her head. "I mean, god, talk about making a scene. What must they think of me? Stage Dive, for heaven's sake. I used to have their posters up on my wall. And you hardly ever get to catch up with your friends and I ruined it."

"Hey, if Mal and Nell hadn't stuck their noses in where they weren't needed, none of that would have happened."

"Mm."

"Also, if Mal didn't like you, no way would he have been stirring shit like that," I said. "Playing matchmaker with us. Or whatever the hell he thought he was doing."

The whites of her eyes seemed huge. "That's what he does to people he likes?"

"You don't even want to know how he is with people he hates." I laughed quietly. "He pretty much harasses them into an early grave."

"Yikes."

"I'm sorry if it caused any friction between you and Nell. It's not fair for you to get judged on the basis of her opinion of me. That's all on me. Not you."

"Eric." Jean put her hands sternly to her hips. "You're my best friend. And that's what I told Nell. End of story." My heart gave a sudden squeeze in pleasure at her words. Jean sighed and shook her head. "Besides, I've got enough other things going on in my life to care less about her tick of approval."

I frowned. "Other things?"

She blinked, and then smiled. "Right," she agreed, moving over to me. "Other things." She linked her arms around my neck and leaned in. "If the whole world has to know that we are friends with benefits, then I want my benefits." My hands went to her hips, and her neck arched, granting me better access to it. Warm skin and the scent of my woman. "That's nice. Don't stop."

Hands slipping beneath her top, I couldn't help but smile. "Jean, between you and me, there's no chance I'll stop until you tell me to. Not today, not tomorrow, not even the day after."

"I'm going to hold you to that."

Her fingers dug into my shoulders. And whatever the hell we were, right then, it didn't feel the least bit fucking casual. Not after her standing up for me with Nell. And pressing her body into me now.

I really did need to work on the girlfriend speech and deliver it sometime soon. Just to make sure things were sorted between us.

My attention turned to her mouth, kissing her senseless. My tongue slipping between her lips and making itself right at home, tracing her teeth before rubbing against her tongue. She moaned and I swallowed the sound, burying it deep within me. Kissing this woman easily topped my list of favorite things to do.

"Now, about third base," I whispered, dealing with the button and zip on her jeans, sliding them down over her hips.

"What about it?"

"Nice red panties." I knelt before her, slipping off her shoes, socks, and all the rest. Steadily but surely getting her naked from the waist down.

She had such a pretty pussy. The tuft of curly dark hair and pink lips. As much as I liked talking dirty to the woman, words failed me. Sure as hell, there were far better uses for my mouth right then. I peppered her thighs and belly with kisses, pushing aside her hand when she tried to cover the scar from Ada's birth.

The small noise of distress from her throat faded fast when I kissed her mound and her musky scent made my mouth water.

"Hands on the counter," I ordered.

Once she'd complied, I slipped her leg over my shoulder, opening her up to me. Good access was everything when it came to doing this right. With one hand wrapped around her thigh and the other teasing her labia, I got busy eating her. Long licks of her sweet lips before teasing her clit with the tip of my tongue. The woman was gratifyingly wet in no time at all. I opened her up with my fingers, all the better to get at her. No part of her pussy missing out on my attentions. Her moans got louder as the muscles in her legs quivered.

"Shh. Jean, you've got to be quiet or you'll wake up Ada."

"Oh, god," she muttered. "You're really good at this."

"I know." I grinned. "Now it's up to you to keep me in practice. You realize that, right?"

"Stop talking." Her hand slid into my hair, pulling just a little. My sex general. So demanding.

I fucked her entrance with my tongue, pressing the wet pad of my thumb against her asshole just for fun. Her breath stuttered, body shivering, and yes, she liked it. She liked it a lot. Hips pressed to my mouth, every muscle in her seemed to be drawn taut. I could have happily kept eating her for hours. But there'd be other occasions. It was time to finish her off. With my thumb embedded in her ass, I zeroed in on her clit, sucking and licking. Giving it all of my focus. Strangled little sounds came from the back of her throat, her pelvis rocking against my lips, tongue, and teeth.

So beautiful; the woman rode my mouth like she was made for it.

On a choked sob, she came. Her body trembled, knees shaking, while I held her firm. All in all, a perfect outcome. She'd even managed to stay relatively quiet. I made a mental note to high-five Jean for her efforts later. While keeping the volume down during sex had never been a concern for me before, it'd fast become a priority. Kind of made me wonder what things might be like at some future date when we could be loud. More out of control.

Sweet baby Jesus, it would be fun.

"Your turn," said Jean, still breathing heavily.

"I'm way ahead of you." I wiped off my mouth with my hand, then whisked her top off. Same went for the bra. Going, going, gone. Ah, breasts. So great. "You know, Jean, these counters are the perfect height."

"Are they now?"

"Absolutely," I said. "But um, let's test them to be sure."

She undid my button-down shirt, pushing it off over my arms. Then for some unknown reason she started putting it on herself.

"But I just did such a good job getting you naked."

"I'll leave the buttons undone."

"Hang on a sec," I said, putting my hand beneath her chin. "Sweetheart, is this about you worrying about your belly? Noticed you tried to cover the scar. You don't need to do that, you know?"

She kind of half shrugged, then paused. "I like the shirt because it smells like you too."

"Look, it's really hard for me to form words while my dick's this hard. But . . ."

Her gaze dropped to my pants. "That is impressive."

"You get that I think you're fucking perfect, right?" Damn, her eyes were so pretty. Her tits were even prettier, but I did my best to focus.

"I'm not," she said. "Appreciate you saying that, though."

Crazy woman. I took her mouth in a slow kiss while she fumbled with my belt buckle and the rest. Happily, I'd thought to slip a condom into my back pocket just in case. Shows she wasn't the only person who could be organized. When it came to getting sex with Jean, I'd be happy to itemize and micromanage with the best of them. I ripped open the wrapper, right on time actually. My boxer briefs were shoved down and delicate hands started petting and stroking my already hard dick.

"You're a bit wider than normal," she said, staring at me.

"Am I?"

"Mm. I like it." She leaned in to give me a kiss. "You know, I think about this sometimes. You and me . . . naked."

"I think about your pussy constantly."

She laughed. Such a nice sound.

I widened my stance a bit so she could cup my balls. Oh man, was she good with her hands. Lots of massaging and rolling my balls between her fingers. All surefire fucking winners in the feel-good department. The muscles in my ass tensed and I thrust into her hands, unable and unwilling to stop myself.

"Jean."

"Want me to go down on you?"

"Let's save that for later." I eased her eager hands off of me, rolling on the condom. "Right now, we've got a date with this countertop."

Damn the shirt she had on. It would be sad, but I just might have to throw out every one I owned if the woman was going to start insisting on wearing them during sex. Still, the way its open front fluttered around her breasts was the stuff of dreams. Wet ones, obviously. Letting her nipples play some wildly tantalizing game of hide-and-seek, one moment hidden, the next peeking out at me.

Hands on her waist, I lifted her up and she shuffled her butt along the edge, getting into position. Then her legs were around me and I was pushing into her and I'm pretty sure I saw God. Fucking Jean definitely rated right up there with heaven. I was so hard and she so soft. Her pussy hot and wet as she took me in deep. With her hands on the counter behind her and her head back, the shirt front fell fully open and the maddening game of hide-and-seek was over. Because when I started thrusting into her, there was the most awesome view of her gorgeous tits bouncing.

Also, I'd been right about the counter. Absolutely spot-on perfect fucking height. I needed to buy my brother the builder a bottle of something special as a thank-you gift. Not that he could have possibly known at the time. But still.

"Eric, harder," she said and I did.

Every time I pulled out her hot sweet cunt clutched at me. Then when I thrust back in, the woman made the most amazing groaning sound. It hit me straight in the balls. I swore up a storm. Dammit. Normally being too quick was not a problem. I prided myself on being able to keep going all night. But all that easy control seemed to go out the window with Jean. I cast around in desperation for some distraction to keep things under control. Needless to say, it wasn't easy. What I needed was a topic of thought boring enough to quench my excitement a little, important enough that I could actually focus on it despite the ecstatic sensations screaming at me from every nerve ending, but not so stressful or off-putting that my performance would actually suffer. Like I said, not an easy task. I seized upon the latest budget numbers for the bar. Sales had been up for the top-shelf cocktails, and some high-end restocking would have to be done.

Jean groaned again, louder this time. The nipples on her bouncing breasts had gone dark and hard. Crap. All sanity-inducing thoughts of budgets and booze vaporized in an instant. "Not sure this is going to last long."

My reputation was in ashes.

"Next time, I promise," I panted. "Much longer."

"Mmhmm. Don't hold back."

Only she was so close, there was sweat on her skin and a flush on her chest. Her legs gripped me tight, but her body gripped me tighter. Skin slapped against skin as I worked us up. But so soon after her last orgasm, she needed a little more help. I wet my other thumb, sliding it in the slick juices covering the lips of her sex. Jean's clit just might be every bit as pretty as her nipples, all small, round, and hard. I dug my fingers into her hips, hard enough to leave marks. All the better to keep her in place for the good hard fucking we both wanted.

Honestly, I never knew kitchens could be this useful.

My whole body felt electric. Toes curled and muscles tensed. Just a little longer. Her mouth opened and she gasped, coming around me. And all of the pressure in my balls and gut burst free. I slammed my dick into her, once, twice, and it was all over. I'd never come so hard in my life.

World? Gone. Body? Gone too.

It was like there was just me and Jean. Our essences floating around the cosmos or something. Don't get me wrong, never in my life had I been the least bit fucking spiritual. But sex with Jean seemed to take me to a whole other level. Heaven. Nirvana. Call it what you like.

I came to with my face pressed against her bare belly. At some point, I must have pulled out of her. It was all a blur.

She sighed happily. "That was . . ."

I lifted my head, meeting her still slightly dazed eyes. "What was it, sweetheart?"

"Definitely eleven."

"Yeah?"

"Oh yeah."

My turn to sigh. All was well. All was positively eleven.

"She said my name!" I grinned, beyond fucking delighted. "Did you all hear that?"

Jean had brought her folks back to the Dive Bar the next day. The lunch rush had finished and I was about to have my break and grab something to eat. I had moseyed on over to them all when Ada squealed my name.

Jean frowned. "She said 'ew.' Your name isn't 'ew.'" Her parents also looked pretty skeptical.

"It was an *e* sound, for Eric," I demanded, undeterred. They were all just jealous. "Obviously, she's trying to say my name."

Jean held Ada's little fist. "Mom-mom-mom-mom."

"Stop trying to brainwash the child," I said. "She knows who she loves best."

"You're full of it." Jean smacked me on the ass of my jeans, making me laugh. We were so on for PDAs. Awesome.

"E for Eric," I said. "That's right, Ada. What a clever baby you are. Total infant genius."

"You wouldn't say smelly old Eric's name first, would you?" Jean kissed her chubby cheek. "Of course not. You're Momma's girl."

All of the carrying on made Ada smile.

"We're off to the airport soon," said Leah.

"Heading home?" I asked, trying to avoid Ada's little fist. The baby was in a feisty mood.

"That's right," said Will. "It's been a good trip."

"Cold time of the year to look around." I nodded. "But the snow is beautiful."

Jean slid out of the booth, giving my forearm a squeeze. "Eric, I'll just visit the bathroom while you've got her."

"Sure thing."

She smiled, her hand trailing across my back, keeping contact until she finally stepped out of reach. The temptation to pull her back at the last was strong. But shenanigans in front of her folks might be a bad idea. Like, a definitely bad idea.

Last night, I hadn't wound up going home. I'd meant to, but Jean had asked me to stay. Happy to report she wasn't too bad of a cover hog though the woman did have a bad habit of pressing her cold feet against my skin. Also, I'd have slept like a baby if only the baby hadn't woken up for a bottle at two in the morning. I normally wasn't too big on sleepovers. Once the fun stuff was finished, why bother?

But the usual rules didn't work with Jean. They never had.

"Won't you join us?" asked Leah.

"Ah, thanks." I perched on the edge of the seat. Just in case an emergency exit was needed. "So . . ."

"Jean's told us quite a lot about you since we met," said Leah.

"She has?"

Ada let out a wail then attacked my shirt, attempting to sink her baby teeth in. Fortunately, she was easily enough diverted with the trusty old teething ring. I'd been slightly covered in baby spit, but whatever. Biting and whacking things really seemed to be the kid's specialties. Sure as hell, they made her happy.

Will crossed his arms over his lean chest. "It's lucky she has friends like you and Nell to help her."

I gave a halfhearted smile, not sure where this was heading.

"But raising a child is a lot of work," said Leah. "It's lovely to see how well you get along with Ada."

I kept my mouth shut.

"I'm not sure exactly what your relationship is with my

daughter, but she's coming to depend on you quite a lot." Leah straightened the coaster her drink sat on. Wine spritzer. About what I would have guessed for her. "We just don't want to see her get hurt again."

Then they both just stared at me.

"Wait a minute," I said. "Are you asking what my intentions are toward your daughter?"

Neither of them spoke for a moment.

"No, no," soothed Jean's mother. "From what I understand your relationship is in its early stages and maybe that's for the best."

For all the talking Jean and I did, I wasn't even sure myself exactly where things were heading. The last damn thing I'd be doing was discussing it with someone else. Pretty sure I'd rather be waterboarded than be sitting here having this awkward chat with her folks.

"What we're trying to say, here," said Will with a sigh, "is that we want Jean back in Florida."

"And Ada," said Leah.

"Of course." Will shrugged. "We want them both back home."

"You asked her to leave, to move back there?" My head emptied. Panic hit me hard. "Christ, I . . . you know, Jean hasn't even mentioned any of this to me. I'm not discussing it with you when I haven't even talked to her about it first."

Her mom raised her hand. "We were hoping you could . . ."

"What? Talk her into it?" I asked, scowling. "Are you kidding me? You want me to talk her into leaving her home? Leaving me?"

"Family is important, Eric. I'm sure you understand that."

I shook my head, bewildered. "It was family that made her want to leave in the first place."

"We've made mistakes," said Leah. "We accept that. But Ada is . . . she's wonderful. I'm sure you know that. We want to be a part of our daughter and granddaughter's life. We want to be there for them."

"Pretty damn sure that going around behind Jean's back talking to me like this isn't the way to earn back her trust."

"We're not going behind her back. It was more that we thought . . ." She broke off, and her eyes flitted briefly to her husband. "Well, I thought that you seemed like a very decent young man, who cared about doing what's right for Jean and Ada in the long term. Because you might be enjoying being part of their life now, but do you really think that's going to last? There's a lot of years between now and when Ada leaves for college," she said. "They need constants in their life, people who can stick with them for the long haul. Babies are cute, but do you really want to be dealing with toddler tantrums?"

I said nothing.

"We just want what's best for them, Eric." Leah gave me a patient look, making me even more pissed off.

I rose, holding Ada carefully against my chest. "Excuse me."

Their faces fell and I did not give a single shit. Time to get out of here. So I turned my back on them and headed for the front desk where Lydia and oh shit . . . Nell. Awesome. This day was the worst. It had gone from the triumph of me being Ada's first word to the ninth layer of hell in about four minutes.

"What's wrong?" asked the ginger monster, holding her hands out for Ada.

I gave her the baby, but not much of an answer. "Nothing."

"Then why do you look like someone just peed in your favorite bottle of single malt?" asked Lydia, blond head cocked.

"God," I said. "What a horrible thought. Where the hell do you come up with this stuff?"

Ada babbled at Nell. Guess it was important girl talk, because I didn't understand a word of it. And I could feel Leah's and Will's gazes burning holes into my back. If I never spoke another word to those people, life would be great. All of their talk about babies growing up and tantrums and shit. Of course I realized Jean and Ada needed people who wouldn't let them down and weren't going anywhere. Like I had plans to hit the road or something and do a runner. But did I really need to decide right here and now if I was starting a college fund for Ada?

Fucking ridiculous.

My experience with actual relationships with women might be minimal. I was, however, pretty sure you didn't just meet someone and start planning your lives together on the same day. This sort of shit took time, getting to know one another, figuring out if you could even live together. I'd spent a total of one whole night in Jean's bed, the other having been spent on the floor. We had time to figure things out. Surely. The last thing either of us needed was her parents pushing their own agenda yet again.

Still, the words stung. As if doing my best for Jean and Ada would mean getting out of their lives. My stomach clenched with anger at the insinuation. Not sure if I was angry because it was false, or because of the possibility it might be true. "You know, I get that eventually you're old enough to figure out that your folks aren't infallible. They're just people too, they make mistakes," I said. "But some parents just don't seem to learn."

Nell and Lydia frowned in unison, but before they could fashion their frowns into awkward questions, Jean appeared at my side.

"Hey," she said, but her smile dimmed at the look on my face. "Eric, you okay?"

"I'm fine, sweetheart," I murmured, kissing the side of her head.

"You don't look fine. You look angry," she said. "What's going on?"

"Did you have a nice lunch?" I asked, trying to steer the conversation elsewhere. Anywhere. Just the thought of her leaving set me into a spin. I could hardly get my head around the possibility. Her apartment empty. She and Ada living their lives away from me, and on the other side of the country. It was all impossible, stupid nonsense. I slipped my hand around the back of her neck, rubbing the tense muscles there. Touching her because I needed the connection.

And why the hell not? Everyone knew stuff was happening between us. If I wanted to whisper sweet nothings and kiss her in public, then I damn well would. The original agreement might have been friends who fucked, but things had developed since then. Or at least, I thought they had. And it wasn't like Jean was complaining about the open affection.

"Shit," she mumbled, a guilty look immediately going to Ada. "My parents asked you to talk to me about Florida, didn't they?"

I nodded, but my heart sank in my chest at her words. She had known about this. And she hadn't told me.

"They've been pushing for me to move back since we started talking again."

And I'd had no idea. Just like that, the panic surged again, my heart hammering. Maybe I should get checked out by a doctor. "You never said anything."

There were so many things she could have said right then. Like that she had told them the idea was nonsense. That she had a life here. But Jean just sort of shrugged.

"And I'm going to go clear that table," said Lydia, disappearing.

"Damn," muttered Jean. "I'm sorry they tried to drag you into this. They can be a little overwhelming when they get an idea in their heads sometimes."

"Just a little," I muttered. "But is moving back something you've been seriously thinking about?"

"They want you to move back home?" asked Nell, eyes wide.

"Her *home* is here," I said, reaching for the baby. The fact that Nell handed Ada over without a fuss just went to show her surprise. "They want her to move away."

Jean sighed, saying nothing. Her expression was impossible to read. She was pissed off that her parents had broached it with me, but beneath that I couldn't gauge her thinking.

On a rational level, I could get my head around the idea that she might want to move back to Florida. I mean, she'd spent her whole life there. Obviously it was what she knew best and was probably comfortable with. But she'd gone to a hell of a lot of trouble to start over in Coeur d'Alene. Just the thought of her leaving gave me heart palpitations, made me break out in a cold sweat. The thought of losing her and Ada both. Fuck. We'd barely gotten started and it might all be over. To go back to the way things were, being alone, not having Jean in my life, not seeing Ada every day.

"I should get to the, um, kitchen." Nell's words were slow. Maybe it went against the grain for her to realize that Jean and I had stuff to talk about without her. "To do the, um, thing." Forehead furrowed, she gave Jean and me a somewhat confused look before disappearing back into the kitchen. Seemed she and Jean still had some making up to do after the party at Mal's. But while Nell might not like the state of play between her friend and me, my care factor remained low to nonexistent. Jesus. Relationships were complicated enough without bringing friends and families into it all. Most days, I was too busy trying to figure out what I could do to help Jean to have time to worry about everyone else's delicate little feelings. Especially when it came to shit that was honestly none of their concern.

But now that Jean and I were sort of alone . . .

"How do you feel about moving back to Florida?" I asked. "That's the question."

Her hesitation felt like a fist to the gut. "I don't know. Even after everything, I do miss them. People make mistakes, right?"

"Sure. But I thought you were happy here?"

She said nothing.

"Jean, sweetheart?"

Beautiful eyes looked my way. "Eric . . . let's talk about it later. I need to get Mom and Dad to the airport."

"Right."

She took Ada.

"Dive safe, okay?"

"Will do." A fleeting smile curved her lips, there and gone in an instant.

It didn't help the sudden horrible feeling she might be slipping away from me.

When I went to talk to her that night, everything was silent. A towel hanging over the doorknob signaled all lines of communication were closed. I had the worst fucking feeling she was avoiding me.

CHAPTER SEVENTEEN

The moment Jean opened the door, I sprang into action. "Mom, this is Jean. Jean, this my mom, Audrey. She wanted to meet Ada. Now's a good time, right?"

"Hi." Jean put a hand to her bed hair, trying to smooth the tangled nest out. "Ah . . ."

After shooting me a perplexed look, Mom attempted a smile. "Nice to meet you!"

I didn't drag Mom down the hallway because how rude. But I did steer her inside the apartment and straight over to where Ada was lying on her blanket, whaling on the plastic turtle as per usual.

"See, Mom?" I asked. "Here she is. Isn't she gorgeous?"

"She's beautiful."

"Sit down there beside her," I directed. "You two should spend some time together. I bet you'll get along great."

Mom's gaze went from me to Jean and back again. "Honey . . ."

"This is cool with you, right, Jean?"

The woman opened her mouth to answer, but it took a while for the words to start flowing. "Of, um, course. How lovely to meet you, Audrey."

"I'll get some coffee going," I said, wandering over to the kitchen. "You having sugar or not today, sweetheart?"

Jean just gave me a weird look. Guess she was still waking up.

"Some days she doesn't have it, 'cause she worries about the weight she put on when she was pregnant," I told Mom, shaking my head. "Crazy, right? She looks great. Doesn't she look great?"

"You look wonderful, dear." Mom held the tip of her tongue between her teeth. Something she often did when she was thinking. "Eric, you said Jean knew we were visiting this morning."

"I did?" I asked, sorting out the coffeepot.

"You did."

"Right, I meant to say that I was going to check, but that last night she had this towel signal out so—"

"Its fine," said Jean, her smile steadier now. More awake.

God, she was gorgeous. I couldn't resist stealing a quick kiss off of her.

"Morning-breath alert," she mumbled.

"I don't care." I grinned. "You know what those hedgehog pajamas do to me."

Mom cleared her throat. "Jean, I'm terribly sorry about this. And Eric, honey, it's really not right to descend on people at eight in the morning without warning them first. I thought I raised you a little better than that."

"But you've been dying to hang out with the baby."

"Even so," said Mom, kneeling beside Ada's play mat. "I hope you don't mind, Jean, if I quickly say hello to her?"

"You're very welcome to stay for coffee, Audrey," said Jean. "It's lovely to meet you."

"See?" I said, not that I'm sure anyone was listening to me right then. "Everything's fine."

Jean grabbed my arm. "Let's make coffee, Eric."

"Sure thing."

"What's going on?" she asked in a lower voice while Mom got chatting with Ada. It was a mostly one-sided conversation, but Mom didn't seem to mind.

"Well," I said. "I was reading in the baby book last night about how important multigenerational influences can be for creating a stable and secure environment for children to grow in. You seemed worried about your parents living so far away and everything. Them not being able to have the kind of close relationship you had with your grandma. So I thought . . . we need to get Ada and Mom together."

"You thought all of that, huh?"

"I did." I smiled. "You should see what Mom's like every time I go over there. It's always, 'Show me pictures of the baby.' I'm pretty sure she doesn't give a damn about me at all anymore. Ever since Ada was born, it's all about her. Honestly, I feel a little neglected."

Jean relaxed, the line between her brows fading. "I think it's lovely she wanted to meet her. But eight in the morning?"

"Too early?"

"Just a little," she said. "And you couldn't give me any warning?"

"You had the towel on the door last night so I didn't want to disturb you."

"Okay." She sighed. "Let me go brush my teeth and put on some clothes. We're not finished talking about this."

"About what?"

"You rush over here first thing with your mom the day after you find out about my parents wanting me to move back to Florida?" Jean crossed her arms. "I'm meant to think there's no connection there? Seriously?"

I mimicked the movement. "It's not what your parents want that keeps me up half the night with worry, sweetheart. It's trying to figure out what you want."

It was like someone slowly let the air out of her. Her jaw dropped a little, followed by her shoulders. Then she was pressed up against me, holding me tight. And saying something into my shirt, if I wasn't mistaken.

"What was that?" I asked.

Over on the living room floor, Mom did a great job of pretending to ignore us. Ada started fussing and she picked her up, singing her some old song. Not Janis. I'd have to tell her later that Janis was Ada's jam.

"Jean?"

"I said . . ." She leaned her chin on my chest, looking up at me with wet eyes. "It was meant to be casual."

"Yeah, I know." I shrugged. "But shit happens."

The woman snorted. "Shit happens?"

With my arms wrapped around her, I rested my forehead against hers. "Is this why you jumped me on the kitchen counter the night before last? When I was asking you about the other things in your life, and you said you wanted friends with benefits? Because you were already thinking about Florida, and you wanted to keep it casual?"

Her eyelids shut tight. "Maybe," she admitted. "It was so frustrating that us being together came out at the party, when at the same time I'm wrestling with maybe going back home. So part of me just wanted it to be physical and fun. It would make everything so much easier."

"Look at me. It's okay."

"You're not angry or anything?"

"How hypocritical would that be?" I said. "I've spent my life keeping it casual to keep things easy."

"Hmm." She opened her eyes. "That didn't actually answer my question."

"The question is, is casual still what you want?"

She pressed her ear against my chest, listening to my heartbeat or something. I don't know.

"Because this isn't casual for me, Jean. I want you to know that."

"Ada and I are going on a diaper changing adventure," announced Mom in a singsong voice. Way more cheerful than the topic warranted, honestly.

"Nursery's on the right and everything's in there," I said. "Thanks, Mom."

"Off we go then!"

Glad poop got her so excited. Christ knows, I was more than happy to avoid it if possible.

"Your mom must think I'm so weird," said Jean in a quiet voice.

"No, mostly I think she's upset at me for dragging her out of bed to come visiting so early without even warning you. It was a major crime against manners," I said, resting my head against her hair.

"Mm."

"Bet she gives me like a box of broccoli for Christmas. Maybe a couple of potatoes thrown in for fun."

Jean snickered. "I think I like your mother a lot."

"Great." I took a deep breath. "We casual or not, sweetheart? What's your answer?"

"When other women flirt with you in the bar, I get violent urges," she said, choosing her words with care. "And if I don't see you for a day or two, I miss you. Badly. It's about more than just how good the sex is with you or how you help me with Ada and everything else. I miss talking to you, being with you."

"Same goes for me."

"But, Eric, I don't have an answer about Florida," she said. "I wish I did. There's positives and negatives to living in both places, you know? Mom and Dad shouldn't have talked to you about it. That was wrong. But they were so great with Ada while they were here. She really enjoyed being with them too, and I do have some friends back there."

"All right."

Her sigh seemed bone deep and weary. "On the other hand, I love this apartment and you and Nell and all of your friends have been so great to us. But I'm worried that Mom and Dad were right about how raising a child is always difficult, just in different ways as they get older."

I kept my mouth shut, letting her get it all out.

"I also think I was pretty naive, because winter here has been a lot more challenging than I expected. Beautiful, but a little hard in some ways too. Having to stay inside so much and all of the heavy coats and everything," she said. "Pretty sure long-term I'd be fine in either place, but I just don't know where Ada would have the best life."

"You're right, there's a lot to consider. But there's no rush to make a decision, right?" I asked. "You can take your time, see how you feel about everything."

"Yeah." Her grip on me tightened as a happy voice drifted down the hallway. "Eric, is your mom singing a song about . . . baby poop?"

"Yes, she is."

"Wow. I think I love her."

Jean trailed kisses over my stubbly chin, down my neck, and onto my chest while I lay flat on my back on her bed. An excellent place to be. When the baby slept, the adults played. If that meant midday sex shenanigans, then so be it. Fine with me. I still wasn't sure where Jean's head was at, and whether sex with me was just what she liked to do to avoid making any big decisions. But I was beginning to think maybe the thing that mattered was where my head was at. And I had some increasingly firm thoughts about that. So I just relaxed back into the mattress and enjoyed her attentions.

"Can't believe you made your poor mom show up here at the crack of dawn," she murmured.

"Let's not talk about my mom while we're naked."

Amusement lit in her eyes. "Hmm."

"Please?"

"All right." Her hand wrapped around my aching dick, giving it a pump, making my head spin. Ever so slowly she worked her way down my torso.

"You're going to be the death of me."

The grin she gave me was an even mix of evil and delighted. Wicked woman.

Basically, being in bed with Jean was like every Christmas, birthday, and any other happy event all rolled into one. I shoved another pillow beneath my head, all the better to watch her do her thing. Currently, that involved lightly nibbling high on my hip bone. I shifted restlessly, sucking in a breath, and her fingers tightened, playing with me.

"You're ticklish," she said.

"Am not."

"Liar. But I'll revisit the issue later."

I just watched her.

"I have other plans right now."

Thank fuck for that. So being tickled wasn't my favorite thing in the world. Pretty sure, however, having Jean's gorgeous lips wrapped around my dick would be. It was on the edge of my tongue to blurt out that I loved her or other such craziness (not saying it wasn't necessarily true—just that spitting it out right at that point in time would be insane). To tell her all my secrets, though she probably knew most of them already. But luckily, she used her tongue first, swiping it across the head of my cock.

She smacked her lips at the bead of pre-cum and honest to god purred. "Salty."

"I love . . . being with you." Oh, shit. Good save. "Yeah. This is . . . this is really nice."

"Nice?" Her brows quirked. "I'll give you nice."

And she did.

The woman sucked my cock like she owned it. Let's face facts, she probably did. Eager tongue and just a trace of teeth. Her lips working me up and up. Holy hell, I'd never been so hard in my life. Clever fingers rolled my balls, pausing to tug a little now and then. Next, the pads of her fingers massaged my perineum, slipping back to tease over my asshole occasionally. At some stage, I gave up trying to watch and just let my eyes roll back into my head. So much sensation.

"Jean. Sweetheart," I said, voice hard and gritty.

"Nice enough, Eric?"

"Fuck me, yes."

Her tongue traced lines along the veins in my dick before teasing around the ridge around the head. Then she took me deep, dragging her lips up the length of me before giving me her tongue again. The muscles in my thighs and stomach were rock hard. Come boiled in my ball sack, just like my blood. Then, when I was almost there, she whipped out a condom and got me sheathed. Threw a leg over me, and took me deep into her hot wet cunt.

I tried to say something appreciative. But nothing came out.

Over the last thirty years, I'd been to bed with a lot of women. But nothing came close to Jean. The way she rode me hard, digging her knees into the mattress beside me, giving me everything. Fingernails dug into my pecs, her gaze boring into mine. She whispered my name, rising and falling onto me again and again. My hands grabbed her hips, guiding her, not that she needed it. Jean had it all under control, including me.

Happily, sucking me seemed to have gotten her good and hot. Because the chances of me holding out for long were nil to none. My sexual prowess was shot to shit. Just when her body started tensing around me, her back bowed, pushing out her spectacular tits, and I came. My body emptied, every emotion and sensation going into overload. Electricity filled my body, the current short-circuiting my head. I went into free fall and so did she, collapsing against my chest.

When I came to, the perfect, familiar scent of our sex and sweat filled the room. I dragged up a blanket, covering her before she could start to cool. My arms went around her, holding on tight.

"Nice." She panted, her breathing slowly evening out. "I missed you last night."

Huh. And she'd left the towel on the door. I stared at the ceiling, trying to figure it all out and not really getting far. Brief seemed best. "Missed you too."

"We went to sleep early for a change, but when I woke up later . . ." Her lips pressed against my chest. Then out of seemingly nowhere, she said, "What if you had a key? Would that be weird?"

"You want to give me a key to your place?"

She shrugged. "It would make things easier."

"Yeah, it would. If you want me sleeping here."

"You might as well."

"Well that sounds inviting," I said with a smile.

"Eric, you know what I mean." She shifted. "I like you being here."

"And you want me here every night or what?"

After a second's hesitation, she nodded. "I feel better when you're here. And it'll make finding the time for the sex stuff easier, right?"

"Right," I drawled.

"It's not a big deal," she said, a touch defensively.

I said nothing.

"I'll, um, grab you one of the spares before you go."

From across the hall, Ada let loose one of her "I'm awake" war cries. Effectively cutting off any further discussion about our apparently new living situation. Never in the history of time had I accepted a key from a woman. A few had suggested it, but I'd always declined. It was another step on the commitment ladder and I generally liked keeping my feet on the ground.

"And so it begins," said Jean, climbing off of me to check her cell on the bedside table. "Good timing, Mom wanted to Skype us and read Ada a book she picked up from the library."

"Let me guess, *To Kill a Mockingbird*? Oh, no, Shakespeare." I smiled. "That'd be the one. I got it, right?"

"Absolutely." She grinned back at me over her shoulder. "Figure we'll start her off with something light like *Macbeth* and work our way up from there."

"I really hated that class in high school. Give Ada my condolences," I said. "I better go get ready for work."

"We'll see you later?"

I nodded. "You know, I never accepted a key off a woman before."

Another shrug. I don't know if I was getting better at reading her or she was getting shit at keeping her guard up. But I could tell this mattered to her. Big-time. Her movements were jerky as she pulled on her clothes and she avoided my eyes the entire time.

"Things change," she said. About the key or me, I couldn't say.

"They sure do. You ever given a man your key before?"

Lines appeared on her forehead. "It's seriously not a big deal."

"You feel better when I'm here and you want me here *every* night, but it's not a big deal." I rose off the bed, stretching some before reaching for my pants. "Sweetheart, it's a big fucking deal. We'll basically be living together."

Silence.

"And I want that. I do. I just want to be sure that's what you want," I said. "Because trust me, it's a big deal."

"Yes." She tugged her hair back into a ponytail with way more force than needed. "It's what I want."

"Okay. Just making sure we're on the same page." I wandered over to her side of the bed, caging her against the wall.

"What?"

"You're giving me the key to the place," I said, taking her hands and peering into her deep blue eyes. "*The place you're thinking of moving out of.*"

Her brow furrowed, and she bit her lip. "I know," she said in a little voice. "I don't mean to be jerking you around, I swear I don't." Wide blue eyes looked up at me, anguish behind them. "It's just complicated."

"No." I shook my head. "It's simple." My mouth moved to hers, my voice a whisper. "Where you go, I go."

At first, I kissed her gently, sweetly, encouraging her to relax and open up for me. Then I took it deeper, sliding my tongue into her mouth. It was the same every time. The crazy amount of heat and feeling. We didn't stop until her arms were wound around my neck, my hands gripping her hips tightly. I never wanted to let go.

She lay her head against my shoulder, getting as close as she could. "This scares me. You scare me."

"Sweetheart, I'm pretty much wrapped around your finger."

The woman snorted. "You know what I mean."

"I know." I kissed the top of her head. "But we'll work it out. Okay?"

"Okay."

Ada screamed in outrage at being kept waiting and Jean took the opportunity to bolt after throwing one last worried glance my way. For some reason, I couldn't stop smiling.

"You're serious about this?"

I nodded over my drink. "Serious as I can be."

"Huh."

My brother sat on the bar stool next to me at the Coeur d'Alene Lakeside Restaurant and Bar a couple of days later. We were basically there to spy. Not to check out the competition, but to assess what kind of joint the resort people who wanted to buy the Dive Bar ran. Honestly, I was a long way from impressed.

"It looks good," said Joe, sipping his beer from the tap.

"About half an inch more froth than needed."

"Yeah."

I stared at my margarita resentfully. "They used a piece of lemon instead of lime to garnish. The fruit's old and discolored."

"How's it taste?"

"Pretty hard to fuck up a margarita," I grumped.

Sure, flames blazed in the big-ass stone fireplace. Very impressive. And the floor-to-ceiling windows looking out over the lake were reasonably spectacular. Top-end tables and fancy chairs, some plush cushioned couches in the corner. Local artwork beautifully framed hung on the walls. On the other hand, the young idiot behind the bar was snoozing instead of keeping an eye on customers. I raised up on the stool a little to check out the situation back there. Ice needed topping up and a good wipe down of the area wouldn't go astray.

Lazy fuck.

Then there was the bar itself. The bottles across the top shelf looked like they came right out of a catalogue. Some vacuous idiot's laundry list of what a top-shelf selection should look like. My eyes narrowed. Most of the bottles were unused. Display purposes only. No personality in it at all. It was the worst thing in the world: a bar made by people who didn't actually like to drink.

Dammit. I should like the place. Everything would be easier if I could just like the place.

Joe nudged me, pointing to a couple of waiters chatting by the front desk while a woman at a table in the restaurant section waved her hand, trying to get their attention. Because providing a little customer service was so difficult. God knows who was in charge or exactly what they were doing with their life. Not working, apparently.

I took a handful of the complimentary nuts and popped them one by one into my mouth.

"What do you think?" asked Joe.

"Hand me that menu?" He did as asked and I flipped through the bar menu. "Way overpriced for what they're stocking on the shelves."

A grunt. "You know you were never going to be happy with the place."

"The staff don't like it here," I said. "None of them give a shit."

"Maybe we came on an off day."

My turn to grunt. "They have no pride in their work. It's depressing."

"Just think about all the money they're willing to pay you and smile. Everyone will find other jobs. It's not the end of the world." Joe scratched at his beard. "Still can't believe you're seriously thinking of going."

"Shit happens."

"That's fucking beautiful, man." He laughed.

"She's the one," I growled. "What do you want me to say?"

He just smiled.

Which only irritated me more. "Just because your social life revolves around me, you sad fuck."

"Ah, brother." He sighed. "I take it back. Go to Florida, I don't give a shit, you dick rash."

"Charming." I grinned. "Order a manhattan, would you?"

"Hey," Joe shouted at the snoozing bartender. "Manhattan, thanks."

The kid jerked to attention, face startled. Maybe even a little pissed at the disturbance. "Right. On it."

"If he worked for me, I'd kick his ass into next week." I pushed the margarita aside, then said loudly, "I'll have a paloma."

The kid's eyes tightened, but he nodded.

"He's going to need to look that one up," I said, keeping my voice low.

"You bastard," laughed Joe. "I've never even had anyone order that. What is it?"

"Basically tequila and grapefruit juice."

"Sounds disgusting."

"Some people like them. It takes all kinds." I slumped sulkily on the stool, eating some more nuts. "Hate the thought of someone else in charge of my bar."

"I know, brother. I know." He gripped my shoulder, giving it a squeeze. "But you can open another bar."

"Won't know the scene as well. Won't know the right people to hire."

"You'll figure it out, you know you will." He exhaled. "What's really bothering you?"

I just frowned.

"Having second thoughts?"

"No," I said. "Jean and Ada, they're it for me. I'm there whenever I'm not working or hitting the gym with you. They're my life now, man, and it's good. It's really good. I can talk to her about anything, you know?"

"Are you sure this is what she wants, though, you guys selling the Dive Bar?"

"Honestly, we haven't gone into specifics. I've kind of avoided it because I didn't want to put any more pressure on her. She just wants stability and the best life for Ada," I said. "She never expected to be a mom this early and I know she worries a lot about messing things up. God knows her own parents aren't the best example. Though they're making an effort with Ada."

"Mm."

"But you can't fault Jean for being a good mother and putting her kid first," I continued. "Whether she decides what's best is here or down South, I guess we'll see."

"Fair enough." He slapped me on the back hard enough to nearly knock me off my seat. Bastard. "No shit. I'm going to miss you if you go, man."

"Are you going to cry?"

"Shut up."

"'Cause I think I'll cry if you do. Really. It will be beautiful."

He ignored me.

We both watched the idiot behind the bar screw up a few more cocktails in silence for a while. Jesus, he was incompetent. My fingers itched to hop over the bar and take charge. Teach him what was up or fire him, one or the other.

"It'll all work out," I said, willing it to be so. "Think she'll make a decision soon, though. Then we'll know what's going on. Yeah."

Joe just nodded.

Fuck, I hope Jean made her mind up soon. The suspense was driving me crazy.

"You going to tell Lydia and Nell about this visit?" asked Joe.

"Yeah, I think I should be honest with them. After all we've done to put the Dive Bar together. They deserve to know."

"Bet you won't tell your girlfriend, though." He picked up a couple of nuts, chucking them in the air and catching them with his mouth. "You don't want to put any pressure on her."

I scowled. "What's your problem?"

"I don't know." He shrugged. "Just seems like, if everything's so great between you two, don't you think you should let her know where you're at?"

I said nothing.

"When there's shit to be decided between Alex and I, we hash it out together."

"You're forgetting, I'm not Ada's biological father," I said. "Legally, I'm not Ada's anything. I can't make that decision for them."

Joe just raised his brows.

"What does that mean?"

"Worried that if you don't talk to her about all of this, lay it on the line, one day you might regret it," he said. "That's all. And she won't have a fucking clue because you never talked to her about it. For all she knows, you're happy to pick up and move tomorrow, right?"

"She's got enough on her plate as it is. I don't want to stress her out."

"What, you think she's going to kick you out or something for having an opinion?"

"No."

He didn't even pause. "Because I've seen the way the woman looks at you. Even from the first day she turned up in town, you two have been stupid about each other in your own sweet ways."

I swore, but actually it was kind of nice to hear that. Still, talk about sticking your nose in where it wasn't wanted . . . "I've got it under control."

"No, you don't. She's a grown-ass woman, Eric. Start treating her like one. Talk to her, tell her about this place and what you're thinking," he said, his voice serious, even stern. "I know you're crazy about each other. But you have to communicate. You're not sheltering her from shit. Not really."

"Okay, okay. I'll think about it. Jesus."

"Good."

Unfortunately, it didn't feel good at all.

CHAPTER EIGHTEEN

"Eh!"

"How's my best girl?" I crooned, taking Ada off Jean about two seconds after she'd walked into the Dive Bar. It was the night after Joe's and my ill-fated trip to the resort, and I'd been basking in being back in a proper bar again. Basking? Hell, I was glowing. The poor schmuck who'd wandered up to the bar and innocently asked if he could have a paloma hadn't known what hit him. In the history of the world, no one had ever mixed tequila and grapefruit into such an art form.

"Thought we'd come have dinner down here and sneak in a visit," said Jean.

"You're always welcome here." I stole a kiss off her. "It's been a slow night. The storm's keeping people home. How's your day been?"

Jean fluffed up her hair. "Busy. You're now the official owner of half of the cupboard."

"First you buy me a toothbrush and now you've made room in the cupboard?"

Pink tinged her cheeks. "I want it to feel like home for you too. I know there's no immediate plans to get rid of your apartment, but . . ."

"It'll be easier."

She smiled. "Yes. It will be."

"Sweet." I patted Ada's diaper-clad butt. "Kind of sounds like we're settling into that apartment together, though. Is that a sign?"

"You mean about Florida?" She leaned her forehead against my shoulder. "I know I'm dragging it out and just need to make a decision. God, I'm sorry. I feel like such a flake. Every time I think I know what the right thing to do is, I get panicky and change my mind."

"Eh. Eh." Ada smacked me on the nose, demanding my attention.

"Yes, Ada?"

She gave me a dribble-filled grin.

"Clever and gorgeous." I smooched on her chubby little cheek until she giggled. "Yes, you are."

"Thank you," yelled Joe from behind the bar because he thought he was funny.

"Shush up."

At that, my brother laughed. Vaughan, sitting at the bar, joined in. Chuckleheads.

"Give me the baby," demanded Nell, appearing at my side and forcibly removing the child from my arms. Though I didn't really fight hard, on account of the fact the woman was huge. I'd told her to go home and get off her feet hours ago, but she wouldn't listen.

Before I knew it, Rosie was there too, crowding me out while they gushed all over the baby. It was hard to blame them. Ada had hit a stage where she would stare right at you for about four seconds, and then her whole face would light up in this radiant smile, as if you were just the best thing ever.

"Come on," I said, taking Jean's hand to lead her to a table over by the bar just in case I was needed. "What do you feel like eating, sweetheart? You hungry?"

"How's things, Jean?" asked Joe.

"Good." Jean smiled. "How are you and Alex doing?"

"Great, yeah." The bearded wonder kept polishing glasses. "We've been talking about lots of things lately. Lots."

Jean just blinked. "Um, great."

Bastard.

"Communication is the bedrock upon which any kind of solid relationship is built," joined in Rosie for some goddamn reason. I really did regret ever seeking wisdom from any of them. "Don't you agree, Eric?"

"Absolutely," I grated out. "Sounds like you've all been talking a lot. Really building those relationships."

"Well, we're a family." Nell came closer, rocking Ada in her arms.

"Are we?" I asked, raising a brow.

"Yes," she said. "Even when we disagree almost to the point of violence sometimes."

"Or quite frequently," I corrected. "Can you guys not do this?"

"Not only does it affect us all, but I'm not convinced it's what you want."

"So you read minds now? Seriously, Nell?" I grabbed the edge of the table, trying to stay calm. "It's her choice. You all need to stay out of it."

Nell's chin went up, ginger hair fiery beneath the lights. Guess she might have been on her way home, because her chef's cap was missing. "And because she's my friend, I respect her enough to tell her everything."

Beside me, Jean stirred, leaning closer. "All right you guys, what's going on?"

"Do you love him?" asked Nell, gaze zeroing in on Jean.

She just stared.

"Because he loves you." Nell shifted Ada to her hip, trying to make allowances for the size of her belly. "I honestly never thought I'd live to see the day he put anyone ahead of his own interests. Don't get upset, I'm not out to insult him. It's just the way he's always been . . . until you."

Jean tipped her head. "Where are you going with this?"

"Do you love him?"

"It's all right, you don't have to answer that," I said.

"He helped build this place with his hands," said Nell, forging on. Goddammit. "And I'll be the first to admit he's been slack sometimes, being late, going off early. But not anymore, not for a while now. Even when he was driving me nuts, he always put everything into each drink he made. It's like he thinks he's a cocktail wizard or something. I don't know. But slinging drinks is his gift and that over there is *his* bar."

"Okay," said Jean, her voice quiet.

"I'm asking you to think about staying here and not moving to Florida."

"Shit," I muttered.

"I know you'll miss your folks sometimes. Despite all of the crap they pulled, they're still your parents. It's a given," said Nell. "But let us be your family. We won't let you or Ada down, I promise. We're not temporary and we're not fair weather, we'll be there for you both."

"We will," said Joe. "Just give us a chance to prove it."

"You're all ganging up on her." I rose to my feet, shoving my chair in. "This is not fair."

My brother, Vaughan, Nell, Rosie, and Taka stood around us, forming a circle. I don't know if they'd organized it beforehand, but it was not cool. They were like an out-of-control mob of loving idiots.

"No, Eric," Jean said, reaching out to take my hand. "It's all right. I needed to hear this. I want to."

"The idiot thinks you're some fragile princess or something that he needs to protect. And that he doesn't want to pressure you by letting you know that some part of him will die if we sell his bar to a bunch of soulless suits. But I know you're not that fragile." Nell smiled gently. "You're tough. You wouldn't have moved here alone in the first place if you weren't. I know there have been some downsides, but you've been happy here too. Thank about staying, Jean. Please. Maybe we're selfish, but we don't want to lose either of you."

Slowly, I gave her fingers a squeeze, watching her face carefully. Her gaze moved from me to take in every member of the circle of people I might just be about to kill if they'd upset her. God knows what she was thinking.

"I don't think you're a fragile princess," I grumbled. "But I do love you."

"I love you too."

Fuck, my heart. It was hammering. I rubbed at my chest with the palm of my hand, trying to get it to settle down.

She smiled. "I should have told you that already. It's just, I've been too scared to commit to anything: you, being here . . ."

I said nothing, just waiting.

"Mostly, I was scared something would happen and I'd lose you," she said. "That being here with you wouldn't work out somehow, like how things didn't work out back home."

I drew her up onto her feet, holding her close. "You're not going to lose me. Whatever you decide."

A tear spilled down her cheek and I swore again.

"I'm okay," she said, then pointed over near where Joe stood. "But, Eric, they're right. This *is* your bar. Florida isn't home anymore, not really. All of my best memories are here."

"What are you saying?"

Jean's shoulders rose as she sucked in a deep breath. "Let's stay. I want to stay."

"Are you sure?"

She nodded, more tears spilling over. Her beautiful blue eyes were red-rimmed.

"Stop crying," I said, swiping gently at her cheeks. "You're killing me, sweetheart."

"I'm happy."

"Then why are you crying?"

"I don't know."

Grinning, I wrapped her back up in my arms. And the idiots all around us, the family, they actually broke out into cheers. Someone suggested champagne, but Joe had the good sense to start pouring beers. Various people slapped me on the back, giving Jean's arm a friendly squeeze. And maybe I kind of appreciated their help after all.

"I should have talked to you," I said, resting my head against her hair.

Jean sniffed. "We got there in the end, with a little help."

"Eh," screeched Ada. Always knowing exactly what to say.

EPILOGUE

"You're sure this is how you want to do it?" asked Nell, her new baby Samuel held tight in her arms.

"Yes," I said. "Definitely. Damn the cliché. It feels right."

"Okay." Her red brows drew together, and she shot a look at Jean. Blissfully unaware, Jean was still seated happily at the long center table, talking to Joe. "Do you think she suspects?"

"The woman does not have a clue."

Nell kept rocking Samuel in her arms, a kind of contented look on her face whenever she looked at the little guy. It was sweet. "You're going to have to make a speech, you know."

"What?" Shit. "I'll make it up as I go along."

"Sure you don't want to go romantic and do it when you two are alone?" she asked.

Trust Nell to inspire me with a vote of confidence. "No. This is right."

It was a slow night at the Dive Bar, perfect for what I had planned. We'd called everyone in for a group dinner. Officially, the reason was that Nell, Lydia, and I had formally rejected the resort's final offer to sell the bar. After we rebuffed their initial approach, they had come back with an inflated figure, and a formal offer of purchase. But once Jean had settled on staying in town, there was just no reason to seriously consider the possibility. Deep down, we all belonged to the place. It was ours, like a second home.

Outside, the weather was warm, typical summer in Coeur d'Alene. Jean's nose was still pink from our expedition to the beach yesterday. Ada loved the water, despite the screaming fits bath time sometimes seemed to bring on. Go figure. She was a complicated little girl. I think she just liked to let loose with the yelling occasionally, make her voice heard. Perhaps, many years from now, she'd be the lead singer of a rock band and all of this practice would come in handy. That would be cool.

"What if she swallows it?" asked Nell, the concerned look back again.

I scoffed. "She's not a toddler. It's a decent size rock, she's not going to swallow it."

"Alright."

"You're freaking me out with all the questions, Nell," I grumped. "Stop it."

"I was just—"

"You've been reading too many baby books. It is not a choking hazard," I said. "It's an offer of marriage."

"Sheesh. Fine, Uncle Eric. We know when we're not wanted," Nell griped to Samuel. "Don't we baby?" She wandered back over to the table. Pat moved in beside her and gently stroked Samuel's little hand. They made a nice family. A good one. And that's what everything was about, really. Family.

Suddenly, I knew exactly what I was going to say. Champagne bottles started popping over at the table, Lydia giving me a knowing glance. So some people knew why we'd all gotten together tonight. Not enough to risk spoiling the surprise.

"I'd like to make a toast," I said loudly enough to make all of the chuckleheads quiet down. My family. With the exception of mom and dad, who were in Hawaii. Again. And good on them.

"What's up?" asked Rosie, curious.

I handed the special glass of champagne to Jean, keeping another for myself. Her blue eyes were shining, a smile hovering about her lips. Fuck she was pretty. And all mine. I intended to keep it that way. Ada sat on her lap, trying to make a dive for anything within reach so she could stick it in her mouth. Napkins, cutlery, you name it. Keeping shit out of grasping range was our new mission in life, and would be for quite a few years to come.

Ah, parenthood. It was the best.

"To my girls, Jean and Ada," I said, glass held high. "You've filled my life with joy."

"Thought we did that," mumbled Joe. I ignored him.

"Before you two, I wasn't really sure where I belonged, what I was doing. I was just cruising, you know," I said. "Going with the flow, taking the easy road."

"Diapers are not easy," Pat said with a pained expression.

Nell nudged him to be quiet. Christ, was she crying? Already?

I just shook my head. "If a bit of poo scares you, you've got no chance surviving what's ahead. Just saying."

Pat laughed.

"Anyway, back to the toast." I raised my glass a little higher. "I wanted to ask you a question in front of all of our family and friends tonight. So, Jean and Ada, my wonderful beautiful precious girls. You've filled my heart and my life, and I can't imagine being without you both."

Jean's smile was huge, eyes glossy. Then, with an arm tucked around Ada's waist, she raised the glass of champagne to her lips. Her head tilted back, just a tiny amount, but my gut squeezed in sudden alarm.

"Fuck, don't drink it!" I shouted in a panic. "There's a ring."

Her eyes widened to the size of plates. "My throat was dry. Wait. What?"

Even Ada looked up at me, mouth trembling at the loud noise.

I took a deep breath and smiled. "Sorry, sweetheart. Didn't mean to freak. But there's an engagement ring in your glass. Maybe don't down it, in case it chokes you, okay?"

So Nell had been right. Dammit. I hated when that happened.

"A ring?" Jean looked into the champagne, brows drawn tight. "Oh my God."

"Will you marry me?"

Ada yelled out something no doubt highly important yet completely undecipherable. A couple of other people were expressing their surprise and delight. But only my girls mattered.

"Marry you?" Jean repeated, still looking mighty stunned. "Really?"

"Yes," I said, swallowing hard. "I was trying to propose to you."

"Wow."

"Why don't I take Ada?" asked Lydia with a smile.

"Thank you."

The minute our girl was out of her lap, Jean had her fingers in the champagne flute, fishing for the diamond. Surprise, elation, more surprise, it all crossed her expressive face. Also, a whole lot of determination. The woman obviously wanted that ring.

"Are you going to give me an answer?" I asked, not too concerned. Okay, honestly, I was still nervous as all hell.

"Hmm? Got it." She held the ring up, triumphant. "Look at it, it's gorgeous! I love it."

"Is that a yes? Jean?"

Finally, she stopped, ring already on her finger and gaze full of emotion. "Of course I'll marry you."

Christ, the smile on my face. It was huge. "You will?"

She jumped out of the chair, throwing her arms around me. "Yes, yes, yes."

"Okay. Good." A wave of relief washed over me. "Whew."

"I love you, Eric."

"Love you too, sweetheart."

My brother Joe stood, holding his glass aloft. "To Jean and Eric."

"And Ada," added Nell.

"Too Jean, Eric, and Ada. Congratulations, guys."

There was cheering, clapping, and more bottles popping. Even Ada seemed caught up in it all, doing her cute little baby laugh. Samuel woke up with a cry, but Nell soon settled him with hugs and kisses. I had my girls, I had my family, I had my bar.

Everything was good.

LUST...
ON THE ROCKS

Read the entire DIVE BAR series

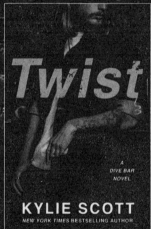

"**WHIRLWIND ROMANCES** with plenty of **SEX** and **LAUGH-OUT-LOUD HUMOR.**"

—*BOOKLIST* (STARRED REVIEW)

KylieScott.com

"Pure rocker perfection."

—NATASHA IS A BOOK JUNKIE

Read the entire
STAGE DIVE SERIES

"Nobody writes inked-up, sexy-as-sin rockers like Kylie Scott!"

—EMMA CHASE

KylieScott.com